W9-AYN-842

Praise for *Forgery:*

"Sabina Murray writes with such a rich palette that the tale she tells is both delicate and cunning; both ominous and sexy; satiric yet profoundly tender, too. She renders perfectly the chiaroscuro of Greece, of its culture as well as its landscape, and brings together a disarming cast of characters from whom I was very sorry to part. *Forgery* is the genuine article: a novel well worth reading."

—Julia Glass, author of *Three Junes* and *The Whole World Over*

"Stylish . . . Fascinating . . . With assurance and style, Murray plumbs issues of identity and provenance. She plays with notions of deceit and of rebellion on levels ranging from personal to political."

—Barbara Lloyd McMichael, *The Seattle Times*

"A haunting, sexy, and very smart novel."   —Joanne Sasvari, Canada.com

"Complex, intelligent, and rewarding."   —Luisa A. Igloria, *The Virginian-Pilot*

"Slick and stylish, *Forgery* is the story of one man clinging desperately to the vestiges of a life that no longer matters, looking for hope and redemption in a way he is not prepared for. Whether or not he finds it becomes moot; it's not the sort of answer a man can find. The journey is what's important and with this intelligent exploration of coping, the author has turned in a brilliant, convincing performance."   —Bill Webb, *I Love a Mystery Newsletter*

"Contagiously suspenseful . . . A miniaturist portrait of how grief looks, smells, tastes, and in the end, conceals itself beneath the surface of things."

—Jennifer Gerson, *Elle*

"This novel is itself happily on the light and shiny side — people are gorgeous, jokes are quick, drinks flow freely and the plot moves trippingly along. And what, it asks, is wrong with that?"   —*Austin American-Stateman*

FORGERY

Also by Sabina Murray

Slow Burn
The Caprices
A Carnivore's Inquiry

Sabina Murray

FORGERY

Grove Press
New York

Copyright © 2007 by Sabina Murray

All rights reserved. No part of this book may be reproduced in
any form or by any electronic or mechanical means, or the
facilitation thereof, including information storage and retrieval
systems, without permission in writing from the publisher, except
by a reviewer, who may quote brief passages in a review. Any members
of educational institutions wishing to photocopy part or all of the work for
classroom use, or publishers who would like to obtain permission
to include the work in an anthology, should send their inquiries to
Grove/Atlantic, Inc., 841 Broadway, New York, NY 10003.

Published simultaneously in Canada
Printed in the United States of America

Library of Congress Cataloging-in-Publication Data
Murray, Sabina.
Forgery / Sabina Murray.
p. cm.
ISBN-10: 0-8021-4368-7
ISBN-13: 978-0-8021-4368-6
1. Art—Collectors and collecting—Fiction.   2. Americans—Greece—Fiction.
3. Greece—History—1950–1967—Fiction.   I. Title.
PS3563.U78F67 2007
813'.54—dc22   2006052645

Grove Press
an imprint of Grove/Atlantic, Inc.
841 Broadway
New York, NY 10003

Distributed by Publishers Group West

www.groveatlantic.com

08 09 10 11 12   10 9 8 7 6 5 4 3 2 1

For my father,
a citizen of neither Athens nor Greece.

Beholding beauty with the eye of the mind, he will be enabled to bring forth not images of beauty but realities (for he has hold not of an image but of a reality), and bringing forth and nourishing true virtue, to become the friend of God and be immortal, if mortal man may.

—Socrates, *Symposium*

If men cease to believe that they will one day become gods then they will surely become worms.

—Henry Miller, *The Colossus of Maroussi*

1

I will never be the sort of person to make a major contribution to mankind. That has never been my goal. I am not a creator, but a man of taste, and my story, like the story of civilization, begins with art. Who were we before art?

I think of our prehistoric cousins desiring to make a fire. The ape says, "I am cold, and my meal, less pulse, is exactly the same as before I ran it down." And perhaps this is the first instance of civilized humanity: a distinct encounter with dissatisfaction. Then the sparks ignite, and the ape casts his kill upon the flames—a willful transformation—and the ape comes out the other side of this experience warm, dining on . . . what did they have then, woolly mammoths? Other apes? I'm not sure but, having cooked it, he's eating it, and the fire is leaping into his face, and his mate is sharing the feast, and the ape can finally say, "This is good." Because before that, there was no good. There was just the absence of food against the presence of food. No choice really, that, just hunger and certain death or satiety and survival. As a man, the ape can compare food to food. The creation of man is tied to the development of taste.

So here I have carried the ape to man. It all begins with art. Art is what gives man his soul. Man is man because he has an appreciation of what is useless. Recognition beyond death? Only man wants such a thing. The need to transform the blank walls of a cave into a narrative tapestry. The need to fashion the female form from the earth. The need to approach the inanimate bulk of solid marble and find himself within it: idealized, beautiful, immortal. Without art, we have no hope of discovering our divinity, our oneness with God. Am I a believer? Someone to be avoided at cocktail parties? Not really. I tried to believe in God and, because of this, refused to follow the question all the way to its logical conclusion. I ended up someone who didn't want my questions answered, because of course there is no God, no heaven of cerulean skies and caftaned deities, but I live in the realm just short of this knowledge. I stop short and stay in the creation of trees, the creation of man, and then man creating back at his God—like an angry child—this canvas, this statue, create, create, create, because we are of God and cannot help ourselves. We are a circuit: us making the divine, and the divine making man. I will not pursue this question to its limit—its betrayal, its refutation—because I lost someone I loved and I need to believe in something. Maybe in science, a sort of art, and transference of energy. After all, where did he go?

How could I be left with nothing, left with—well, myself, an apartment, a street, shoes walking on it, rain that pounded through the most miserable of Aprils and into May. And into June. That rain that seemed to reach around the world and leave no one unmolested, bringing all of us creatures together in its grip, rain that gave voice to the gloom of space—space, space, and more space—within me, that hissed outside the window, that sang its timpani on the Dumpsters and trash cans of my neighborhood, that sent the homeless into dark corners tented beneath their soggy blankets: rain that only whiskey could improve. Whiskey turned its blue to a sort of glowing and acceptable amber.

And then one day I was packing my bag and, ticket in hand, was headed for the airport. Uncle William had said I needed a change of scenery. I was to travel to Greece, where it never rained in the summer, or only rarely. Once, he said, the sky had gone from brilliant blue to black, as if Zeus himself had carelessly stepped in front of the sun, and then a cloud tore open and a flood of raindrops the size of plums had clattered onto the marble of the alleyway, where the restaurant's tables were set up. And everything washed away, and everyone was wet and laughing.

"It wasn't raining like this, ever," he said.

I said, "I don't think it's just the rain."

He said, "Try to convince yourself that it is.'

And I asked, "Why?"

And he said, "Because that we can fix."

2

I arrived in Athens on a Tuesday, a day unloved by Greeks, the day on which the Turks, back in 1453, had sacked Byzantium. Lucky for the Greeks, on this particular Tuesday, it was only me and they had nothing to fear. I felt more easy prey than predator. There was no one to meet me at the baggage claim and, although I know the intelligent thing to do would have been to wait there, I felt a need to keep moving. My first thought on exiting the terminal was that somewhere near, something had died and that the smell of rotted flesh hanging in the air, sweet and sickly, was, strange to admit, not unlovely.

The street that fronted the airport was flooded with traffic, tourist and otherwise. The sky was an even primary blue, not a cloud in sight. I idly watched a woman from the plane slip her bra strap up her arm. She had complained the whole trip over, New York to London, London to Athens. At first I'd sympathized with her husband, but this had turned to resentment when he hadn't shut her up. She led the way, the husband followed her, a mountain of luggage followed him, and pushing it along was a desiccated porter with a luxurious mustache.

"Can you believe the heat?" the woman said.

She was complaining again, as if this would suddenly make it cooler.

At first look, Greece was disappointing. There were a lot of Greeks milling around, but without some fantastic backdrop—the temple, cliffs, and sea of Sounion, for example—it wasn't that impressive. I felt bad for the Greeks. It was 1963, and although they'd managed to weather the last two thousand years, they had the bad form to let it show. Something in my Western education had encouraged me to view Greece as a beloved anachronism, a culture that, thus preserved, entered the modern age in England, and the space age in America, as the great baton of civilization got shuttled around. Greece should have been something I could go back and visit—Ancient Civilization Land—as if it were a pavilion at the World's Fair. But the architecture was all recent postwar-boom concrete and the music was the belch of misfiring engines and pragmatism. The people had been through a lot, and it showed in their shabby clothes.

My Uncle William's friend, Kostas Nikolaides, was supposed to pick me up. But he wasn't there, or he wasn't recognizing me, and I, certainly, had little hope of recognizing him. Uncle William hadn't seen Kostas Nikolaides in twenty years, at which point Kostas had been losing his hair. Uncle William thought he'd be completely bald by now, but his eyes would give him away. "He has blue eyes, not normal blue but blue like the Greeks have blue eyes." I had never known any blue-eyed Greeks. "Blue like the Aegean," said Uncle William, in an uncharacteristically poetic moment. "And he's loud."

Uncle William had originally traveled to Greece to see the sights. The Second World War had cut short his travel. In the mayhem following the Italian invasion, he had managed to escape, first to Alexandria and then—on board a British transport plane—to London. Over the years the escape aspect of the story—as well as the number of women who had hidden him, in a variety of surprising and predictable places—had increased exponentially. At any rate, the adventure was genuine. By the time he reached Boston, he had lost or sold all his belongings—clothes, silver brushes, books. Only two things survived: his love for everything Hellenic and a small Minoan statuette, a woman with her arms snapped off but with a beguiling expression and a stiff skirt that hung down like a cowbell. This was the foundation, the inspiration, on which Uncle William had built his formidable art collection. Uncle William called her *the goddess* and, despite the fact that I was of the opinion that the statue was at best overly restored—a composite of

ancient pieces—and at worst a brazen fake, the goddess was responsible for sending me now to Greece. I was grateful to her and disin-
clined to expose her to too much scrutiny.

I wondered if my plane had arrived early. Perhaps Kostas was
back at the luggage carousel, but my suitcase had been waiting for
me when I got through immigration, and going outside had seemed
like the right thing to do. My ears were blocked. I yawned and waggled
my jaw and some sound was restored. I looked at my watch, still set
to the time in New York. Athens was plus six hours. And what was
the time of my plane's arrival anyway? I entertained myself by trying
to decipher the signs on the buildings across the street. I'd only taken
Ancient Greek and that had been in high school. It was fairly amazing that I remembered as much as I did. I realized that my lips were
moving as I read.

Down the street a taxi pulled up. I began wondering if I should
take a taxi. Then I began wondering where I would take it. I wondered if I'd end up in a hotel, then carried the scenario through
to its extreme conclusion: I would spend a week in Athens, never
managing to find Kostas, and after that I'd return to New York,
having accomplished nothing. A man got out of the taxi; I considered flagging it down and decided against it. Then I heard someone calling my name from the opposite direction, and there was
Kostas, pushing through the people and suitcases, and he was at my
side.

"Rupert Brigg. Rupert!" he said. "I am Kostas Nikolaides." Kostas
mopped his head, which, as predicted, was completely bald, making
the shock of his blue eyes all the more brilliant. I set down my suitcase and he kissed me on both cheeks. "You are like your uncle, better looking, definitely, but with that same chin with the hole in it.
How do you shave that?"

"With care," I replied.

"Ah, there he is!" A black Mercedes pulled up. It was polished
to a brilliant sheen, but I recognized it as an early-fifties model, maybe
ten years old. "My son Nikos is driving. How was your flight?"

"Fine," I said.

Nikos got out of the car and extended his hand. "I am Nikos." He took my suitcase and put it in the trunk.

"Sit in front," said Kostas. "I am fat, but don't mind sitting in the back."

I got into the car. Nikos, with a lot of honking, accelerated wildly to get away from the curb and then hit the brakes so we could do the five miles an hour that the traffic allowed.

"Were you waiting long?" he asked.

"Not long at all," I said. "Thanks for picking me up."

"Your uncle has told me that you won't stay in my house," said Kostas.

"I didn't want to be a burden. And my uncle says you're quite the host. He made it seem as if I'd never get anything done." I imagined myself doing something—sitting at a desk—but even in my fantasy the action was vague and suspiciously pointless.

Kostas shook his head. "I rented you a tourist place, which he said you wanted. But I said, 'When Rupert gets here, he will not want to be by himself.'"

Nikos said something to his father, something lilting and full of humor. He smiled, as if we shared a secret.

"Nikos picked out the room. It is right by Omónia Square with all the young travelers. Nikos likes to go walking with these crazy Americans, Swedes, girls walking all over Greece alone. They put on these boots, like Communists."

"They have their virtues," said Nikos.

The car picked up a little speed, but a half hour later we found ourselves stalled in a mass of vehicles. A gray billowing smoke obscured everything. I saw an old woman in a black scarf right in front of the car, then the smoke hid her and she was gone. Kostas covered his face with his handkerchief and I felt my eyes tearing up. I smelled burning rubber. The car crawled forward and I saw a flaming truck surrounded by people.

"As if it was not hot enough," said Nikos.

Kostas laughed and leaned forward, placing his hand on my shoulder. "And what are your first impressions of Athens?"

"Very nice," I replied.

The car began to move again, faster now, and a false breeze moved the air within it.

"How is your uncle?" asked Kostas.

"Enjoying his retirement. He's looking forward to traveling."

"But he sends you."

"And his regrets," I said. "Uncle William is planning a visit, but he was told to wait until after the November elections."

"Elections?" said Nikos, and laughed. "Papandreou will win."

"How can you be sure?" I asked.

"Because America wills it."

"My son is a cynic," said Kostas.

"Your son has his eyes open," said Nikos. "And you know this is true. But as usual, what is good for business, in your mind, is good for Greece."

"Would you give Greece to the Communists?"

There was some anger building here, but not much, since the conversation seemed to be an old one and the resolution not far off.

"Nikos here has no political affiliation. He can afford to be this way. He is young. But if I said that the Communists would take away his car, he would develop an affiliation. If I said that the Communists would create such mayhem that all the Swedish girls would not visit, he would have an opinion."

"Will you vote?" I asked.

"Yes," said Nikos. "At least twice."

And this made Kostas laugh.

The car ride took close to an hour, although nothing like the flaming truck was encountered again. We talked about the weather, hotter than usual for June, and Kostas pointed out buildings that had housed various relatives and restaurants at different times but now held nothing of interest except for these memories. Nikos worked for his father, but it was unclear exactly what he did. Something with the export end of things. Something that involved filling out forms and government agencies. I nodded and asked questions and understood nothing. Nikos asked me the square footage of my apartment in New York, how many bathrooms it had, whether or not I employed a servant, and what the rent was. I asked him if he'd had his suit made or if it was off the rack, whether it was all wool or a synthetic blend, and what he'd paid for it.

"Is this what you young people talk about?" asked Kostas.

And this made me laugh because I was thirty years old and Kostas was right to be critical.

"We're almost there," said Nikos.

The buildings were now older, more graceful, and shoved up against one another, the narrow roads barely passable. I saw a small chapel rise out of a sidewalk, a balcony filled with caged birds, boys in shorts shouting at each other. I was still feeling the occasional rise and dip of the airplane. I lit a cigarette and was in a peaceful mindless state, hypnotized by some new argument between Kostas and Nikos, a music of disagreement, when Nikos cut the engine.

"We are here," he said.

"My hotel?"

Kostas threw up his hands. "Don't you eat?"

"This is our house." said Nikos. "You want a shower. I know how the American thinks." Here Nikos tapped his head with his forefinger. "But I don't agree. You need a drink. We have ouzo—and wine, of course," he said, pushing the door open, "but I got some beer. For you."

"That's very considerate," I said.

Nikos said something to his father, who nodded and went in. I could hear him yelling and the voice of a woman responding.

"I want to show you something," said Nikos. "Just the end of the block."

I followed. At the end of the street a view presented itself, a river of air through the banks of the houses. I followed the space. There was a rise, a cliff of stone, and I realized what I was looking at. The Acropolis stood in the distance, silent, stately, decayed.

"Well?" said Nikos.

"It's the Acropolis."

"This is the best way to see it, from a distance. Like everyone, you will want to go walking around, but when you get close it's not that great. You see one column. You don't see the mountain. And it's hot as hell. All the good sculpture gone, in England or wherever."

"Why go there at all?"

"Athens is a terrible place," said Nikos. "You know we are from Constantinople."

"Yes. Uncle William told me that."

"You can't live in the past," said Nikos. Nikos rested his hand on my shoulder and steered me back down the street. "You like old things. You are an archaeologist."

"Not exactly," I said. "My background is in art history."

Nikos seemed surprised. "A professor?"

"No. I worked at an auction house, and now I suppose I am an art dealer, an art supplier, but I haven't dealt anything yet. Or supplied it," I said.

"Soon enough," said Nikos. "My father is a businessman. He will not be able to talk about other things for long. We will go have lunch. He will say things about the Turks, the Communists, but always he is counting the money in his head."

I was momentarily dizzy.

"Are you all right, Rupert?"

"Yes," I said. "Yes. But this is incredible. Here I am on a street in Athens with"—I gestured dramatically over my shoulder—"the Acropolis at my back."

Nikos smiled. "I have the Acropolis at my back every day. Every Greek has the Acropolis at his back. What I want to know"—he raised his eyebrows—"is what is at the front."

"You are a philosopher," I said.

Nikos laughed. "I have been called many things, but never that." We began to walk. "My father already has tomorrow planned."

"And what is on the agenda?"

"First, we have to register you with the police. That will take forever. Do you have photos?"

"Passport pictures?"

Nikos nodded.

"Yes."

"How many?"

"I have at least four."

"That's good for registering with the police, but you should get more taken before you leave Athens. You might need them in the islands."

A table was set on the rooftop terrace. There was no view of the Acropolis from here because the terrace faced the wrong way, backed up against another taller building. Kostas sat, impatient and hungry. Two beers sweated on the table, but Kostas was drinking coffee. There was a bowl of stew, an eggplant dish, and a salad. I wasn't hungry, but the stew was very good. The beer was going straight to my head.

"They say the spring is the best time to visit Athens," said Kostas. "We are not so overrun with travelers then, and the air is good."

"It is also hot in New York now," I said. "Many people have houses on the beach and spend their weekends there. The city is emptied of women and children." I didn't actually believe this. I wasn't even sure why I was saying it, but I had to say something. "Uncle William," I said, fixing Kostas with what I hoped was a sincerely engaged look, "tells me that you are something of an amateur musician."

Nikos laughed. "He sings, but many Greeks sing."

"Your uncle is something of an amateur Greek," said Kostas.

"Yes, I suppose he is."

"I met him because he kept coming into my store but never buying anything. He kept looking at the vases and sighing."

"Sighing?"

Kostas laughed. "I asked him what he was looking for. And he told me how much he wished he were in Greece. He wanted to know if there was a place where he could get some good Greek food. I said there was. He had dinner at my apartment that night."

"Why haven't you been back to New York?" I asked.

"My brother lives there now, as you know. Every year I say I will visit. This year I am still saying it."

"I want to go to New York," said Nikos.

"There are many things to see," I responded in a moronic way.
I applied myself to the food.

"You like the rabbit," said Kostas.

"It's very good. What do you call this?"

"*Stifado*."

"Is that rabbit?"

"No," said Kostas disparagingly. "It means with onions."

"Where does the rabbit come from?"

"Same as in America. Out of a hole in the ground."

I wasn't sure if Kostas was teasing me or if I was just affected by
the heat. Finally Kostas pushed away his plate and yelled something
into the house. A woman dressed in Western clothes came out.

"My wife," said Kostas. "Elena. This is Rupert."

I stood up from my seat and shook her hand politely. The woman
was smiling through some haze of disagreement. She seemed suspicious of my presence and unsure of why she was attending.

"Pleased to meet you," she said.

"Pleasure is mine," I replied.

"Please," she said, gesturing for me to sit. The woman seemed
capable of charm but unwilling to use it. "How do you find Athens?"
she asked, expecting the worst.

"I find it very pleasant," I replied, my mind suddenly swimming
with images of burnt out trucks, rabbits peering from holes, the Acropolis.

She smiled politely and went to sit in a chair, not at the table
but at the edge of the terrace by the railing. Nikos raised his eyebrows
at me pointedly. He got up and went to sit beside her. I could hear
Nikos's consoling Greek, cajoling, entreating.

"She was a great beauty," said Kostas, "but her temper makes it
less appealing. And she speaks no English."

"But she does," I protested.

"You heard it all!"

The woman looked over, insulted, wounded. "*Káteleveno*," she said.

"She says she understands," said Kostas, and then, without explanation, his expression softened. He said something to her and she
nodded, stood, and came back to the table.

She smiled then, beauty and charm restored. "Kostas and I are always angry and looking for the reason. We are back-to-front people. I see you soon."

I stood again and she left, letting the door slam loudly behind her. Nikos smiled broadly.

"I thought your mother didn't speak English," I said.

"She doesn't," said Nikos. "She asked me how to say that about the back-to-front people."

"Is that a saying in Greek?" I asked.

"No," said Kostas. "No. No. Enough of this speaking like crazy people. Rupert is here for the art and I will talk to him about this now."

"No Turks?" asked Nikos, smiling. "No Cyprus?"

"He talks like an idiot," said Kostas, "but he is actually very smart. With a good head for business, my son. I wanted him to study in America, but his mother could not bear the idea of his leaving. Why do we listen to her?"

A sparrow landed on the table and cocked its head a few times, as if in sympathy, and then took off.

"Tomorrow, first the police. You will tell them you are a tourist. I have letters for you to give to them, one from me, one from my cousin in the Ministry of Education. There will be no problems."

"There are always problems," said Nikos.

"Nothing we can't fix," said Kostas. "I must warn you not to talk with anyone of why you are here. You are a tourist snapping pictures. Your uncle has told me that he would like the classical pieces, and this is not easy. I have other things to give that are dug up here and there, coins, jewelry, icons. All beautiful. The hills of Epirus are full of the stuff, and in the Peloponnese, but he says he wants the classical. Big. Marble. For that you will have to leave Athens. But one week here first. There are people for you to meet."

"There are things to see," said Nikos.

Kostas shrugged. "There is the bank, where you should set up an account." He thumbed at the edge of the table. "Why am I like this? All the small things, but we are here to fulfill your uncle's dream."

"Very kind of you to help him," I said.

Kostas's eyebrows shot up intelligently, looking for irony in what I'd said.

"Americans live in pieces," he said. "The business piece, the friendship piece. Why not put them together? Is there shame in that? I know what Americans say about the Greeks. Do not trust them. They are always looking for a way to profit. And I am profiting, but who else can help your uncle find these things? We met over business, and after we became friends."

"That's absolutely true," I said. "Besides, my uncle doesn't like people doing favors for him. The fact that you're somehow benefiting from this situation is, I'm sure, a source of comfort."

"He's a proud man!" said Kostas, and laughed out loud.

"We are all in agreement," I said.

Nikos smiled at the harmony, at his father. "Let Rupert shower and shave," he said.

"*Endáxi*," said Kostas. "Do you speak any Greek?"

"Some words sound familiar. I speak decent German and my Italian's better than that." I thought for a moment. "I have read Plato and some Socrates."

"Plato," said Nikos, "will not help you here."

The Mercedes had mysteriously disappeared from the front of the house, but Nikos readied a Vespa, which sputtered and then purred.

Kostas stood on the doorstep, rocking on his heels. "Tomorrow I will see you," he said. "One more thing. My wife asked why you are not married. I did not tell her that you are divorced. It would upset her. She asked me if you were a homosexual." Kostas paused. "It is one reason to get divorced."

"I am not a homosexual," I replied. The thought amused me.

Nikos yelled something from the Vespa.

"My son thinks I have no manners. And he's right. But how can I keep talking to you if I am thinking this?" And Kostas laughed.

I straddled the Vespa and balanced my suitcase on my knees. This was precarious but I felt precarious, somehow off balance—

ignorant and unknown—so there was some comfort in this danger.
Soon Nikos and I were rumbling through the tunnel of air toward
the Acropolis, through the streets deadened by the afternoon heat.
After a twenty-minute ride, which seemed possibly shorter on foot,
we pulled up in front of a modern building on Nikis Street. All the
buildings in Athens seemed either ancient or modern, nothing in
between, and this building was agressively ugly, all plate glass and
unadorned concrete. Nikos had booked the apartment for a week.
If I needed to stay longer, he could easily extend the lease.

"Elevator," said Nikos. "Stairs."

The hotel was dark but seemed clean. A concierge with a bob-
bing head materialized at Nikos's elbow and rapidly explained something. He had a key in his hand. Nikos nodded, suddenly profoundly
bored. He fixed me with a sympathetic look.

"Stairs," he said.

The concierge took my suitcase, although he was half my size
and, I thought, less capable of carrying it. I had some drachma, but I
hadn't yet figured out what it was worth. I hoped Nikos would take
care of the tip. When the concierge unlocked the door, it was Nikos
who first stepped inside. I followed him in.

"This looks fine," I said. "I appreciate the offer to stay in your
house. I hope I haven't offended your father."

"Him? He offends everyone."

"People like that are often very sensitive."

Nikos nodded and picked up the telephone receiver. I heard a
scratchy dial tone. "You need your freedom. You are a young man.
How is it that you are divorced?"

I never had a good answer. My marriage was so irrelevant
to my life now that the divorce actually seemed unreal. "Something," I said vaguely, "in American culture. All our marriages fall
apart."

"You are too young to be divorced."

"I am thirty."

"How long were you married?"

"Four years."

"I am twenty-six." Nikos went to the window and peered out. He gestured for me to join him. On the sidewalk was a pair of young blond women, arms linked, in sandals and short skirts. He looked at me then, as if he'd asked me a question, but I wasn't sure how to respond.

The concierge, waiting patiently at the door, said something to Nikos, and Nikos responded with some feigned anger, not really convincing to anyone.

"What was that about?" I asked.

"He's bringing more towels. There are never enough towels."

Nikos went into the bathroom and held up the two small towels as proof. "Now it is five. Take a nap and I will get you for dinner at ten."

The concierge appeared at the door with a small stack of towels and placed them on the bed. He was a very proud man, proud of his towels, his shiny suit, his too-large shoes bent up at the toes.

"I am Yorgos," he stated. "You need anything, we help you. If you need to clean your suit, my brother does the dry cleaning here. Very good. No holes, and the suit is not getting small."

I nodded but was losing my ability to speak. Nikos said something to Yorgos and looked at me. "He will call you to wake up at nine."

"Thank you very much, Nikos."

We shook hands and Nikos thumped me affectionately on the shoulder. "You need to have a good time."

When Nikos was gone, I had a moment to appreciate what had happened over the last couple of hours. I had walked off a plane. I had made the acquaintance of Kostas Nikolaides and his son, Nikos. I had seen the Acropolis and enjoyed a Greek meal. I had listened to the groundwork laid out before my visit. I had left my past behind; now, parted from my history, I was not sure what was left.

The time for afternoon naps was over and the street was filling with noise. I took off my jacket and shirt, kicked off my shoes, and appraised my new home. The furniture was spare and modern, a sign of the new affluence brought by tourists like me. The bed was relatively new and, although the mattress was on the thin side, seemed adequate. I unpacked a few things from my suitcase, placing my two new books about coins and the latest catalog of the Boston Museum of Fine Arts on the desk. I took out my extra suit, which was new, and hung it up in the closet.

And now what? I said to myself. As if in response, a door slammed in the hallway. A woman laughed loudly and the door opened, then slammed again.

Intriguing as the laughter was, it was easy to convince myself that it did not concern me. I sat down on the bed, bounced a couple of times on the squeaky springs, and was just about to stretch out for a nap when there was a knock at the door. I got up, ready but unwilling to believe that someone actually wanted me. The knock was repeated. I waited a moment and turned the knob. The door swung inward. There was a man in bare feet and suit pants, T-shirt, with his back to me. He had flaming red hair. He turned quickly.

"There you are," he said. He was American. "Do you have a cigarette?"

"Yes, I do," I replied.

The man extended his hand. "I'm Steve Kelly," he said. "Do you have anything to drink?"

"No," I said. And then, by way of explanation, "I just got here."

"Well, I'll fix that."

Steve Kelly padded down the hallway to his room and returned with a bottle of whiskey. I didn't think I needed a drink, but realized it wasn't my decision. Kelly came back and I stepped aside to let him in.

"Just like my room, only everything's on the other side. It's almost a mirror image." Kelly went into the bathroom and brought back the single glass. He poured a couple of shots into it and offered it to me. "Cheers!" We both drank, he from the bottle.

"I'm Rupert Brigg," I said.

"Rupert!" said Steve. "There's a name. What do you do with a name like that?"

"I'm a tourist," I said.

"A tourist?" Kelly said. "I'm a journalist."

"Is there much to write about?"

"A lot," said Kelly, smiling. He went over to the window and helped himself to one of my cigarettes. "Not that much makes it into print." He gave me a knowing nod.

There was an awkward moment while we studied each other. "How long are you here?" asked Kelly.

"Athens? One week, and then I'm going to see the islands."

"Which islands?"

"First Aspros."

"Aspros? It's in the Cyclades, isn't it?"

"Yes."

"Not much tourism there."

"I hear the hiking is good."

Kelly looked down at my empty shoes, leather-soled wingtips, which were side by side next to the bed. "Okay," he said. He sat down on the bed, but I remained standing. "Can I offer you one of your cigarettes?"

"I'd appreciate it." I took a cigarette and sat in a chair at the small table. "What do you recommend in Athens?"

"There's the National Archaeological Museum, and you can get all your souvenirs in the Pláka, which is just over there." Kelly gestured out the window. "And there are some interesting clubs, places where you can hear music. Do you have plans for tonight?"

"I actually do," I said. "A friend of mine is meeting me for dinner."

"Male or female?"

"Male."

"Another tourist?"

"No, he's Greek." I smiled my best charming smile.

"And how does a tourist know a Greek?"

"My uncle traveled in Greece back in the early forties. He has friends, and I am meeting them all, and they have friends on Aspros, who have agreed to let me stay with them." I felt like I was giving him my life's story. I stopped talking.

Steve noticed but didn't seem bothered. It probably happened to him all the time. "Don't mind me," he said. "I'm a journalist. Always looking for the story."

I said, "I'm sure you'll be disappointed."

"Somehow," said Kelly, getting up, "I doubt that." He tapped a couple of my cigarettes out of the pack and put them in the pocket of his T-shirt. "You need to sleep." He went to the door, tipping another shot into my glass on the way. "Don't let Yorgos talk you into letting his brother clean your suit, not unless you're planning to lose weight."

"Thanks for the tip."

"I'll check in tomorrow," he said. "Maybe we can have a drink."

"I'd like that," I replied.

I watched Kelly retreat down the hall and closed the door. The air in the room was still. I turned on the fan, which shuddered at the start and then began a clattering chug, like a steam engine in a Western. I peered out the window. On the street below a man pushed a cart loaded with oranges. A woman stopped him, and I listened to their bargaining back and forth. Somewhere, a church bell was ringing. A cloud of sparrows landed on the balcony across the way, and a cat sprang out, scattering them into the sky. I drank some more of the whiskey.

"Shower," I said out loud. This habit of stating things loudly and with purpose had come to me in the last couple of years, years spent learning how to spend time in quiet rooms. The shower was of the handheld variety, and after a few air-expelling gasps the water trickled out. It was lukewarm and there was barely enough of it to get my shampoo into a lather. I made use of five of the six small towels. I put on a clean pair of undershorts and lay down on the bed, but I couldn't fall asleep. I was dizzy, somehow too exhausted to sleep, dozing but still conscious. I pictured Uncle William standing by the mantel in his Upper East Side apartment, holding the goddess, whispering to her, and then, looking across the ocean, fixing his eyes on me. There was whispering through the walls, the sound of my wife crying, her being soothed by a man whose voice I didn't recognize. Then someone was covering me with a blanket, pulling it over my head.

3

There was a loud knock at the door, and in this room, wherever it was, I heard the voice of the concierge call out, "Mr. Brigg. It is nine o'clock."

"Yes, I am awake," I called back. And then, "Yorgos?"

"Yes?"

"Can you bring me some coffee?"

"I will bring it!"

"And some hot water, for shaving."

"I will bring it!"

I shaved, using hot water from a clay pitcher. The pitcher was a replica, from one of the tourist stands no doubt, a milk jug with a black image of Hercules and the Nemean lion worked onto it. As was my habit, I had a cigarette in my mouth and shaved around it, moving the cigarette around with my teeth. I parted my hair and combed it neatly. My eyes were still a mess, bloodshot and puffy. I put on my suit, forgoing a tie. This was, after all, a European holiday and an open collar was fine. I'd seen it in the French movies, mostly set in places like Rome. I played with my collar, unsure of what it was supposed to do. This new casual attitude left me on shaky ground, which was a novelty, since I'd always had a reputation for being perfectly presentable: stylish, even. Cutting edge. I put on my jacket and swung my arms around a few times, trying to work the stiffness out so it would match my new relaxed attitude. There was still some of Kelly's whiskey in the glass, and I had the last of it while watching the street for Nikos.

At ten, a woman, Greek, appeared in front of the hotel and Steve Kelly walked out to meet her. There was an awkward pause where the two seemed to be evaluating each other; then Steve offered his arm and the woman gripped it. I watched them walking down the street together, and then Nikos pulled up on the Vespa. He hopped off, lit a cigarette, and looked around. Nikos was tall and thin, very handsome, with his father's blue eyes and considerably more hair. He was wearing a dark jacket and matching dark pants, light material a bit on the shiny side.

I called down to him. "Nikos!"

Nikos looked up and waved.

"I'll be right down. I'd have you come up for a drink first, but I don't have anything."

"We'll take care of that," said Nikos, nodding with conviction.

The elevator was still out of order, so I took the stairs. I thought I was in a hurry, I'm not sure why, and when I finally exited the building I was out of breath. Nikos seemed to find this amusing.

"The elevator," I said.

"Yes," said Nikos. He offered his hand and I shook it. "Are you hungry?"

"I don't know," I said. "Maybe."

"You want to hear bouzoukis?"

"Do I?"

"People dancing around and breaking plates?" Nikos had a twinkle in his eye.

"Well, I've heard of that. And also read in one of my books that they charge you extra."

"You want to see the real Athens?"

"I do?" I lit a cigarette and looked out on the street. "The fake Athens would be fine. What do you for fun?"

"Me? Everything I do is fun."

"I read about that in the tour books too." I didn't really trust it, and Nikos saw that and laughed out loud.

"You like Greek food?"

"I like the rabbit. I don't need it again."

"Let's walk," said Nikos. He rolled the Vespa onto the sidewalk and parked it. Nikos gestured to the street and we crossed together. "How is the room?"

"Well, you saw it. There's a very friendly American guy down the hall. Steve Kelly."

"Steve Kelly. He is a journalist."

"Yes. That's what he said. But I wondered."

"Why?"

"He seemed a little too friendly."

"He is interested in what you are doing?"

"Yes."

"I am interested in what you are doing," said Nikos. "You were with an auction house? That seems like a very good job. And now you are here. . . ."

"I needed a change," I said. Nikos had stopped walking. We were in front of an elegant bar.

"An aperitif?" said Nikos. I followed him inside. I had the feeling that I would follow him anywhere. The bar was paneled floor to ceiling, with heavy light fixtures and dim mirrors. The effect was fin de siècle. There were mostly men but a few well-dressed women, Greeks and others. I could hear a woman's voice, English accent, protesting the price of a tablecloth. We went to stand by the bar.

"I am having a Scotch," said Nikos.

"Do they have bourbon?"

"Of course," said Nikos, nodding slantwise. "So, the auction house?"

"My ex-wife's father owned it."

"That is how you got the job?"

"No," I said. I fixed Nikos with an admonishing gaze. "That is how I met my wife."

"No wife, no job?"

"It was my choice. How about you, Nikos, why aren't you married?"

"I've been engaged for two years," he said.

"But not married?"

"The man has four daughters, and I am engaged to the young-
est. Her older sister is still waiting to have money for the dowry. . . .
This is boring and stupid. If you want the ancient Greek, look at
our marriage customs." Nikos laughed. "I could be waiting years for
this to work out."

"Doesn't stop you from looking around," I said.

"When I marry," said Nikos, raising his glass, "it will be forever."

I took the comment as he intended and raised my glass. We
drank.

"Another?" said Nikos.

"Of course," I said. "Next one's on me."

Nikos nodded appreciatively. "Do you know why there are so
many Western women touring here in pairs?"

"Because of the art?"

"Of course," said Nikos, "but also because Greeks do not yell at
the women. We don't hassle the tourists. We wait and are patient,
not like the Italians. The women feel safe here."

"Well, are they?"

"Are they what?"

"Safe."

Nikos pondered this. He looked around the bar. The English-
woman was casting furtive glances at the handsome Nikos. She was
a bit soft in the face and forearms and had the overall effect of an
overripe fruit. Nikos smiled at her, then leaned over to me. "That
one," he said, "is safe."

An hour later and three drinks the better, Nikos and I decided
it was time to leave.

"Hungry?" asked Nikos.

"Not exactly," I responded, "but not addled enough to not eat."

"Addled," said Nikos. "I like that word."

"Confused, befuddled."

"It is a bit more polite, a bit funny."

I nodded.

Nikos gestured into the street with his cigarette. "I have an idea,"
he said. "Instead of sitting in a nice place, we can get a gyros with

pita and walk around. We are young men. There's no reason to sit with a salad as if we are waiting for death."

This seemed like a very good idea, although I wasn't sure what a gyros was. I was enjoying following Nikos and was beginning to forget that I was a depressed man.

Nikos said there was only one gyros place to go to, so we went there. We sat on stools, eating, mugs of beer in front of us. We were quiet as we ate. I was thinking about Uncle William, how he and I had argued about this trip. I'd told him I would not have fun in Greece, that trying to have fun did not seem like fun at all, but here on the street all the couples were beautiful and somewhere, echoing but out of sight, some drunks—Scots? Australians?—had burst into song. A skinny cat took to scratching its neck against my shoe, which was no doubt mere convenience, but I felt wanted. I considered the possibility that I might be having fun.

"Is that your cat?" asked Nikos.

The cat looked up and fixed us with a worldly expression. Nikos tossed it a bit of meat.

"It is its own cat," I said. I gave it another bit of meat and it started purring. The cat was sitting between us on the ground but getting bold. It stretched to standing and seemed to have intentions of leaping onto the bar. I looked up to see what Nikos thought of this, but he was far more interested in viewing something across the street over my shoulder. I turned around. Two girls with a map stood a short distance away, dressed in skirts and sandals. There was something disheveled about them and they seemed to be operating through a fog of confusion. Nikos smiled at me and raised an eyebrow.

"Eat," he ordered.

"Do you think they're American?" I asked.

Nikos shook his head. "They're English."

"How do you know?"

"The shoes."

I stole a look at the girls' sandals, which were stout, sturdy, nunlike. "Not that I'm interested, but they're looking at us."

"They're going to come to us," said Nikos. I was about to question Nikos's apparent sixth sense when the two girls walked up with their map.

"Excuse me," said the taller one. She had dark hair, an Irish paleness to the skin, and green eyes. She was, as predicted, English. "I don't mean to bother you, but we're supposed to be meeting people at this restaurant and I don't know how to get there." Her companion, blond, mortified, more delicately pretty, stood back as if aware that girls in ugly shoes shouldn't talk to men in suits.

"You are not bothering us," said Nikos, suddenly serious. "And what is this restaurant?"

"It's called Bacchus. I think it's here." She pointed at the map, and Nikos nodded sympathetically. "But I don't know where I am, so it doesn't really help."

"And you are meeting friends there?"

"Yes. We're a bit late."

I caught the blond girl rolling her eyes.

"Bacchus is over there, at the foot of the Acropolis." Nikos gestured vaguely. He seemed deeply concerned. "Must you go there?"

"Why?" said the dark-haired girl.

The blond girl started looking quite scared and I smiled at her, trying not to laugh.

"The food. . . ." Nikos shrugged. "It's in the tour book so everyone goes there, but for that money you can do better."

"We're eating sandwiches," I said. I held up my gyros proudly. "Lamb with yogurt sauce. Very tasty."

"Maybe you would like to eat here," suggested Nikos, "and meet your friends later?"

"What do you think, Sue?" asked the dark-haired friend. Sue hesitated.

"My friend Nikos is in the export business," I said gravely, "and I am an art dealer from New York. Have a sandwich, then we'll walk you over to wherever your friends are."

Sue, fed up but apparently resigned, crawled onto the stool next to me. Nikos vacated his seat for her friend, whose name was Helen.

"That is a Greek name," said Nikos.

I smiled into my beer. Without looking, I knew that Helen had blushed appealingly. "The sandwich is good," I said to the more choleric Sue. "You can have a bite of mine, if you'd like to try it."

"Thanks," said Sue, "but what I really need is a beer."

I called to the waiter to bring her a drink.

"She's been like that in every city we've been to. It's a bloody nightmare. 'Let's go on holiday, Sue. See the sights.'" Sue rolled her eyes again and took a rather long drink.

"Susan," I said, exercising my maturity, since I guessed Sue to be around twenty, "it's just a sandwich."

Sue and Helen were from outside of London on a trip financed by their well-heeled parents. They were on an adventure, had packed light (this explained the ugly shoes), and were in search of the real Greece. Sue, the serious one, had brought along a volume of Byron's work and had pictured hikes through mountains and valleys dotted with goats and lyre-playing goatherds.

"We did see the Acropolis today," said Sue, "but Helen forgot her hat and was scared she'd get a burn, so we had to leave after half an hour." She drank more beer, finishing off the glass. "What's he saying to her anyway?"

Nikos and Helen were to my right. I listened in. "He is telling her the story of the Trojan war," I informed Sue, "fitting, since her name is Helen."

"Bloody hell," said Sue. "And she's listening? She had to translate it two years ago, third-year Greek with Ms. Warrior. I should know. I was in the class." Sue waved for the waiter to bring her another beer. "Is he all right, your friend?"

"An absolute gentleman," I replied, but I really didn't know.

After Helen had finished her sandwich and Sue her second beer, it was decided that there was no reason to escort the girls to Bacchus, because, no doubt, her friends had finished their meal and most likely moved on. Sue was not so prickly now. I had done quite well as the calm, honest friend. If she hadn't thought me handsome before, she thought so now. I looked younger than I was, maybe twenty-five, and after my last two beers I was finding Sue's edgy cleverness attractive, even though I was most often attracted to dark women with sharp cheekbones and withering gazes.

"Let me carry your bag for you," I said. "It looks quite heavy." And Sue handed me her canvas satchel, which wasn't heavy at all.

Nikos, who at this point was holding Helen's hand, looked over his shoulder and yelled, "Jazz?"

I looked at Susan, who shrugged. After all, what was Nikos asking? But I yelled back, "Why not?" which seemed like a good response.

The jazz club was down a dark and nearly deserted alley. A few shops selling vases and other trinkets were still open, the owners calling from the steps, but Nikos waved them off. Sue was now clutching my arm a little desperately, and I began to wonder how much she had had to drink.

"Come on, you two," yelled Helen. She seemed in her element, the dangerous friend. She and Nikos were poised at the top of a stairwell that led down to the club. On drawing closer, I could hear the metallic edge of light drum music, the whine of a saxophone.

"Well, here we are," I said to Sue. She giggled.

The club itself was crowded and smoky. Nikos clearly knew people and raised his hand when he entered, prompting a chorus of welcome. In rapid succession, I was introduced to a number of well-dressed Athenians, their girlfriends, and the proprietor, who brought drinks to the table. Whiskey, which I drank. I watched Sue drain her glass as if she'd forgotten it was to be sipped.

Nikos tapped me on the shoulder. "So, how do you like Athens?"

Nikos's arm was now wrapped around Helen's waist and he was rubbing up and down her side. "Not as much as you do," I replied. "But that's quite all right."

The next song was a Chet Baker cover, a bit sadder than the others, recognizable but not one I knew well. I lit a cigarette and looked over at Sue, who was smiling in a pleasant way. "Can I get you another drink?" I asked.

"What?" she called back. The club was noisy.

I leaned in and smiled. "Do you want another drink?"

"Yes, please," she said.

An hour later, with Sue collapsed warmly against my side, I felt the old sadness welling up. I'd been running away all evening, happy for the distraction, for the pretty English girls, for the urbane Nikos. I felt twenty-five again, as if the last five years had never happened and I was still somehow innocent. Sue's hair was soft against my chin. I watched Nikos dancing slowly with Helen, Nikos whose face seemed impossibly serious, and although this would have made me laugh an hour before, I now felt a weird nostalgia. Nostalgia, yes, and strangely enough a nostalgia for the present, for now—this night that was still unfolding around me. Sue tangled her hand into mine, and with my left I shook a cigarette out of the pack and lit it.

"Can I get you something?" I asked Sue.

"What?"

"A drink."

"Robert, I don't feel very well."

I moved her away from me and studied her face. "Let's hold off on the drink," I said.

Sue struggled to her feet. "Will you excuse me for a minute?"

"Let me escort you," I offered. She looked wobbly, deathly pale, and it occurred to me that during the past half hour of my reverie she could have been asleep. I got up, and walked Sue to the back of the club. I stood by the ladies' room, holding her up. Finally, a striking Greek woman—big cheekbones, withering glance—exited the bathroom. I felt Sue grow heavier in my arms. I watched the woman navigate the narrow hallway, her skirt pulled tight across her broad hips.

"The bathroom's free," I said. I opened the door, poured Sue inside, and closed it behind her.

After ten minutes of waiting in the hallway, I decided that something had to be done. I tapped on the door. "Sue," I said, "I'm going to check in with Nikos, and then I'll take you home."

"All right," came a weak voice.

I walked down the hallway, checking over my shoulder. The proprietor looked at me in a concerned way. "I'm taking her back to her hotel," I said. And then I added, "where I will leave her in peace."

On the dance floor, Nikos and Helen were still propped up against each other, swaying romantically, arhythmically. I tapped Nikos on the shoulder.

"Yes," said Nikos, as if he had just woken up

"I have to take Sue home. She's been in the bathroom for the last ten minutes."

"Too bad," said Nikos.

"Where can I get a cab around here?"

"At the end of the street, by the kiosk."

I nodded and was about to return to Sue when Nikos placed his hand on my shoulder. "Can I have the key to your hotel room?"

I looked at Nikos, feeling suddenly that I was back at Columbia and would be sleeping on someone's couch. I gave him the key. "You owe me," I said.

"We are friends," said Nikos dramatically. "We are constantly indebted to each other."

By the kiosk, waiting for the cab, Sue threw up on a tree. I wondered about this. I too would have chosen the tree rather than the sidewalk, but why? I held her shoulders.

"I'm so sorry," she said. She looked as if she were about to cry.

"Don't be," I said. "I shouldn't have given you so much to drink."

"I can usually handle it. It must be the heat."

"Yes," I agreed. "The heat. Do you think you can manage a cab?"

Sue nodded stoically. I remembered my handkerchief and gave it to her. "Something to remember me by, along with the hangover."

And Sue laughed.

Her hotel should have been a five-minute drive, but with the two stops and one false alarm, it took nearly half an hour. I tipped the driver extravagantly and steered Sue up the steps. The hotel was small and neat with a hand-shaped Venetian door knocker, mail-boxes, and a polished marble floor. The elevator was the size of a broom closet. "What room are you in?" I asked.

Suddenly a woman came running out from the back room. She was wearing an apron, apparent industry at this late hour, and when she saw me with Sue her eyes ignited.

"*Ochi! Ochi!*" she said.

I stopped obediently.

"No mans!"

"What?"

"No mans!"

I patted Sue lightly on the shoulder. "Sorry, Sue, no mans. You're on your own."

Sue nodded. She entered the elevator and pressed a button. She turned back to me, her face full of remorse, "I'm so—"

But the elevator whisked her into the heavens and out of harm's way. I faced the woman, raising my hands in surrender.

She was still muttering at me when I went into the street.

It was a nice night and I decided to walk home. Sue's hotel was not far from the National Gardens, and from there Hotel Nikis was just a short distance through Syntagma Square. The air was still and barely cooler than daytime, but walking felt good after the closeness of the club, and I knew I should proceed at a leisurely pace; although I did not know Nikos well, I thought it safe to assume that he was a man who took his time with all things pleasurable. The moon was nearly full and the palace lit up. A few honking taxis circled Syntagma. Businesses were finally closing. I wondered how late it was. Two small boys, one with a bicycle, played unattended by a fountain; near them a stray dog lay passed out, apparently napping.

"Hello, dog," I said.

In response to this, the dog wagged its tail.

I stopped at a shop where the owner was busily going around shutting off lights. I stood at the counter, feeling invisible, until the man finally noticed me.

"*Kalispéra*," the man said.

"Can I get some whiskey?" I asked.

"Whiskey." The man nodded and took a bottle off the shelf.

I took a handful of money out of my pocket. I didn't know what it was worth, so to be safe, I handed him a large bill. The man shook his head. He gave the bill back to me and went through my cash picking out a smaller bill and a couple of coins. He folded my hand around the remaining money.

"*Endaxi*," the man said.

"*Endaxi*," I replied.

It was with some displeasure that I noted Nikos's Vespa still parked on the sidewalk. The window to my room was closed. I was not sure how to proceed, but I found myself walking up the steps to my room. The hallway was dimly lit and mostly quiet, other than the staccato of a typewriter coming from Steve Kelly's room. I walked quietly down the hall and listened, feeling like a pervert, at my door. Nikos's voice was whispering sweetly in there and, although I was well within my rights to knock, I couldn't seem to find the energy to do it. I walked back up the hallway to Steve Kelly's room and knocked on the door. The typewriting stopped and I knocked again.

Someone yelled out in Greek. I was quiet, and more Greek words issued forth. It was Steve and I thought that his Greek might be very good.

"It's Rupert, from down the hall," I said.

"From down the hall?" he responded. He had been deep in thought.

"Not to be confused with that other Rupert."

I heard him laugh. "Come in," he said.

I swung open the door. Steve was in his undershorts at his typewriter.

"Do you want a drink?" I held up the bottle of whiskey. "I know my timing's awful, but there are extenuating circumstances."

Steve's eyes lit up. "And here all this time I thought it was you."

"It's my friend Nikos. I can wait downstairs. . . ."

"No, no. Don't be ridiculous. I'll stop and have a drink now. I do have a deadline tomorrow, but you're welcome to stay. You can nap in the armchair."

"Thanks very much."

"You must be exhausted."

"Yeah." I kicked off my shoes. "How long have I been here?"

"Not even a day."

"Oh my God," I laughed. "Funny thing is, I feel like I've been here forever, but that I'm getting younger."

Steve, who had fetched the glasses from the bathroom, poured me a whiskey. "Younger?"

"My friend is having sex in my room." I massaged my forehead. "I spent the evening buying drinks for a girl wearing sandals."

"What kind of sandals?"

"The kind that girls wear at school."

"I didn't realize that footwear was a function of time or age."

I took a long drink. "It is," I said. "Most definitely." Steve was now seated on the end of his bed. "What are you writing about?"

"The north. The Communists."

"Are they really a threat?"

Steve shrugged. "Their threat is really a threat. The right-wingers exploit them, and they are a bunch of lunatics. Then there's the Center Party, Papandreou's party, which is more moderate."

"How long have you been here?"

"Six months."

"And you speak Greek?"

"I think I do. Some of the locals might disagree." Steve sipped his drink. "I held off learning for a while. I originally came to cover the situation in Cyprus. I thought it would be over in a matter of weeks, but Cyprus is still Cyprus. And there are other things going on."

"Other things?"

"Like tourism," said Steve, and he smiled pointedly.

Rather than keep me up, Steve's typing lulled me to sleep. It was the Vespa, protesting on the sidewalk directly below Steve's window, that told me my room had been vacated. Steve was now asleep, sprawled on top of his bed, snoring. I went over to the window and saw Nikos disappearing into the night. I glanced over at the typewriter, but there was no paper in it. In fact, there was no paper on the table at all except for a virginal stack of white sheets.

4

I awoke to a knocking at my door. The room was bright and I was in my undershorts. The knocking continued.

"What are you doing?" I called out.

"I am knocking."

It was Nikos.

I struggled out of bed and opened the door. Nikos was standing there in a sport shirt and slacks, his hair neat, his face composed.

"There is something in you, Nikos," I said, in quick retreat, "that wants to separate me from my bed." I lay back down. "I feel like hell."

Nikos nodded sympathetically. "We have to go register with the police."

"Now?"

"You should shower."

"What time is it?"

"It is eleven."

"I misrepresented you," I said. "I told Sue you were a gentleman."

"It was Helen who wanted to leave the club," Nikos said. "Would I have been more of a gentleman if I had said no?"

"I suppose not." I got up and went into the bathroom. "Are you going to see her again?"

"I am taking Helen and Sue to Sounion to see the temple of Poseidon this afternoon. Would you like to join us?"

"I don't think so," I said. "Sue is very nice, but I'm a bit old for this."

I turned on the shower and the water trickled onto my head.

"She will be disappointed," called Nikos.

"Well, you'll tell her something," I called back. "Can you get Yorgos to send up some hot water and coffee?"

"Of course," said Nikos.

I sat on the back of the Vespa shaved, showered, and caffeinated. The building that housed the Police Department was not far from my hotel.

"Did you remember your passport?" asked Nikos.

I patted my jacket pocket.

"The pictures?"

"Yes."

We took the elevator to the fourth floor. A door opened to a large room filled with desks. A herd of confused foreigners clutching their passports stood idling in lines, sitting across from the clerks, begging for answers from various unsympathetic officials. I was not optimistic.

"Why do I have to register?" I said. "Does everyone register?"

"Not everyone," said Nikos. "It is a formality, but better that you register now than try later. What if you have to extend your visit?"

I shrugged. "What do I do?"

Nikos gestured with his head over to the receptionist who was arguing in French with a man who was responding in German. Nikos stood beside the German, elbows on the counter, and interrupted in Greek. The woman told him something and with her palms open, in apparent disgust, indicated the man across from her. Nikos nodded sympathetically.

"You need to go to the third floor and pay the clerk twelve drachmas," Nikos said, addressing the German. "He will stamp your form, and then you bring it back."

The German man took back his form, shot an angry look at Nikos, and stomped off.

"He could have said thank you," I said.

"Why?" replied Nikos, smiling. "There is nothing on the third floor. Only apartments."

I laughed.

"Give me your passport," said Nikos, "and fill this out." He reached over the counter and picked up a form, smiling at the woman, in her forties, big black beehive, who seemed all of a sudden pleasant. While I was filling out the form—passport number, address in Athens, intended length of stay—Nikos produced an envelope from his inside jacket pocket and gave it to the woman.

"What's that?" I asked.

"Letters."

I finished off the form while the beehive woman and Nikos lit up cigarettes and lapsed into some pleasant-sounding conversation. I couldn't understand a word of it, but the woman was laughing, charmed by Nikos, as everyone always was, even Nikos himself. "The form is complete," I said.

"Give me your pictures," said Nikos.

I handed them over.

"And now we are done," said Nikos.

"That's it?"

"We go get lunch, and then come back, and she says she will have everything ready for you to sign."

"How?"

Nikos shrugged. "She doesn't like Germans," he said.

Nikos and I took the stairs down. The German was on the third floor talking to an old woman in an apron, who was standing in the doorway of her apartment. He was brandishing his form in her face, apparently not noticing the knife that she held tightly in her right hand.

Nikos chose an open-air taverna by a church not far from the Pláka. Black-clad priests walked back and forth, their feet obscured by their long robes, which made them look as if they were skating. An older man in seersucker sat across from us with a young Greek, who was perhaps eighteen years old. And there was a Frenchwoman, who was arguing with her two overdressed children, insisting that they had liked the *pastitsio* the night before. I had left the ordering to Nikos again, and he'd gotten us some roasted chicken and an eggplant thing stewed in tomato.

Nikos tapped his cigarette on the table. He was not happy with me. " Why won't you go to Sounion?"

"I would like to see the temple, but today is not the day for that. There's something I want to check out in Athens." I pulled out my Fodor's and opened it to the marked page. "Look. What do you think of this Monastiráki shopping district for antiques?"

"They're all fakes."

"Studying the fakes is part of my work."

I took some more eggplant, which was putting out fires in my stomach. Nikos was done eating. He fixed me with a contemplative look.

"What?" I asked.

"You will not want to tell me." He lit his cigarette.

"What?"

Smoke floated around his face, and he had his legs crossed. "You are still in love with your ex-wife."

"No," I said. "I'm not. For a marriage that only lasted four years, it seemed quite long."

"What is her name?"

"Whose name?" I said, but this ingenuousness did not fool Nikos. "Why?"

He looked at me with mild surprise.

"Her name is Hester," I said.

"Why did you divorce? Did she do something?" He thought for moment. "Did you do something?"

"It's nothing like that at all," I said wearily. "The Greeks don't divorce, do they?"

"No, not really."

"So how could I explain it to you?"

After lunch, Nikos and I headed back to pick up my forms, which, as promised, were in order. He dropped me off somewhere in the

Monastiráki area. The Acropolis stood up against the sky like a
Hollywood backdrop.

"See the mosque?"

"Yes."

"Go there. After that you go to the left. It's Pandróssou. There
are also shoes for sale here."

"Okay."

"Don't buy anything," said Nikos. "And there are pickpockets,
so be careful."

I'm really not sure why I still wanted to go to Pandróssou. I suppose I felt that I should at least see what was being reproduced and
how the people were hoping to pass it off.

The first store I went into was full of reproductions on a par with
the jug that Yorgos sent up with my hot water for shaving. The man
was very eager for me to purchase something, which had the effect of
hurrying me back into the street. After that, I did my observations
from a distance over the haze of my cigarette. I picked up a sandal
from a display of leather goods, but was really interested in the neighboring store—clay knick knacks, bronze fragments—but something
in these items didn't seem quite right. I was beginning to feel profoundly self-conscious and absurd when a small sign posted in the
corner of a shop caught my eye. It said CLEARANCE CERTIFICATE
POTTERIES. I did not know what this meant, but the plainness of this
unassuming sign made me feel that it was pitched at someone in the
know. I set down my sandal, much to the disappointment—or perhaps
relief, it was much too small for me—of the attending shopkeeper and
made my way across the narrow alley.

The door swung open noiselessly and I entered. It was dark inside and cluttered with things, some swords and helmets from Turkey, icons, silverwork, maybe a couple of hundred years old, and a
glass case of coins. I was startled then by a man sitting completely
still on a chair in a shadowy corner. I had not noticed him at first—
then, for a half-second, mistook him for a statue—but I caught his
eyes following me. My heart missed a beat.

"*Evkaristó*," I said.

"That means *thank you*," said the man. "Why are you thanking me?"

I shrugged. "Because you have scared me but not killed me?"

The man laughed and stood up, and I was surprised at his height. He must have been six feet tall. "It is very dark in here," he said. "And bright outside. You like old things?"

I picked up an icon. It seemed genuinely old, the wood soft and worm-eaten in places. The painting—virgin and child—had a life to it, as if it were a photograph developing into detail only to immediately begin the return to nothing. I put it down.

"We have better ones in the back," he said. "Are you interested in icons?"

"I'm not sure what I'm interested in," I said.

"You are American," he said.

I nodded.

"I have many American clients. They come here year after year. I have a good reputation," he said, then raised his eyebrows as if a reputation were not worth that much.

"I'd be interested in any classical coins."

The man gestured for me to sit down at a wooden table. He pushed a pack of cigarettes and an ashtray towards me. "Help yourself," he said.

I nodded and when he returned with a case of coins, was happily smoking.

"Some of these are very old. Look." He opened up the case.

"May I?" I said, gesturing at the coins. He nodded. I picked up a small silver coin with a man's head on one side and, on the other, a drunken Silenus with folded legs, leaning on one muscled arm, drinking wine from a shallow bowl. "This is charming," I said.

"It is from Náxos, 460 B.C."

I nodded, impressed, but I had detected a tiny line around the perimeter of the coin. The coin was a good replica of the sort that filled the cases of eager collectors throughout the West. I set it down

and picked up a different coin, this one small and bronze but with a
striking crack, a split, that happened beneath the hammer a few thousand years earlier. "I like this one more," I said.

The man leaned back and laughed. "Bronze over silver. I feel
that I am in a fairy tale. What is the fairy tale?"

I shrugged. "*Merchant of Venice?*"

The man nodded in agreement. "What are you really looking for?"

"Classical stuff. Anything, but it has to be genuine. And I can
pay for it."

The man shook his head. "I had one piece that might have interested you, but it is already sold."

"What was it?"

"It was like this, a vase, for drinking." He made a shape the size
of a head. "There were figures. One handle missing, but the rest—
without a crack. And the color . . . red figures on black." He shook
his head.

"It was real?"

"Yes," the man said. "Sometimes we are lucky."

"Where did it come from?"

"The man who brought it said it came from the south—dug up
in the Peloponnesus maybe."

"You don't know?"

"They all lie. They are all scared, these amateur diggers. But I
saw this and it was real. The vase he showed me was small, but he
said there was another. I don't know what the English name is for
this, but in Greece it was used for mixing the water with the wine.
Big." He showed a space the size of a beach ball.

"A bell krater?"

"Maybe."

I took a pencil and did a quick sketch on the corner of something written over in Greek that looked to be a bill of lading. And
there was my picture, an amateur but recognizable bell krater with a
wide mouth, narrow pedestal base, and handles that poked out at the
sides like ears.

"And the smaller one was similar in shape?"

"Yes."

"And do you think there were more?"

"The man said there was more, but I do not think he had more. I think he probably worked as a digger and managed to hide the smaller piece, bring it to me. He was not educated, but he knew he had something."

I took out one of my old business cards from the auction house and wrote the name of my hotel on it. "If any more of this Peloponnesian pottery shows up, do let me know."

"Of course," he said, nodding. "Are you buying the bronze coin?"

I looked at him eye to eye. "If you show me a vase of the caliber that you have described, I will buy many coins."

I had a couple of ideas about the bell krater. I'd heard of a find while still in New York, a burial site, Greek but situated in the heel of Italy's boot. Italy was still rich with such things. And I had to think about where the bell krater might have come from because, in many ways, that was more my job than merely looking at the style, the materials, and making an educated decision as to whether or not the object was genuine. More important than this arbitrary assessment of authenticity was my ability to provide a past. I had to determine the provenance and the provenience, two seemingly similar words but so much more than that to the dealer in antiques. Provenience spoke to origin; provenance to history. For example, Abraham Lincoln's pencil was just a pencil from Illinois, approximately a hundred years old. Not that remarkable. The provenance of that pencil—if we could prove that it was Lincoln's—made the pencil desirable. And if that that same pencil had been used to draft the Gettysburg Address, it would of course be priceless. The pencil would no longer be a pencil, because who would write with it? But it was something you could hold in your hand, a concrete reminder of the significant, historical, and dead.

The value of an object is whatever it can fetch at auction. I knew this, and as I wandered through the shops of Pandróssou, pick-

ing up the various clay lamps and worn daggers, vases chipping
yesterday's paint into my hand, I could see how someone like Kostas,
with his gift for palaver, had been able to make himself quite an
empire, because provenience requires only some knowledge of re-
gional industry, and provenance a good imagination and a willing
customer.

I worked my way through a few of the other antique shops in a couple
of hours and found myself at the edge of the Pláka. It was nearing
that time of day when the heat becomes unbearable, but I started
wandering up a set of steps in the direction of the Acropolis. My shoes
were feeling a bit tight. I wondered how the marble steps would feel
beneath my feet. My wingtips, despite being correct, were not comfortable and they were slippery. The sun was bleaching everything.
The heat, rather than warming the air, was displacing it. I would not
make it to the Acropolis like this and was wondering whether to get
a drink, find a cab, or start walking back to the hotel when a familiar
voice called out to me.
   "Rupert!"
   I looked over at the terrace of a small café that had insinuated
itself into the rise of rock that marked the first ascent to the Acropolis. The tables were small and jammed together, festive with bright
blue-and-white checked tablecloths. A waterfall of bougainvillea
blanketed one wall and beneath this sat Steve Kelly. There was an
extremely striking woman seated across from him, most notable for
her ample bosom, who was stubbing out her cigarette. She rose and
when she saw me waved me over, pulling her chair out in invitation.
   "Hello, Steve," I said.
   "What are you up to, Rupert?"
   "Me? I think I'm about to pass out."
   "Well, come sit and have a drink. Alexandra is about to abandon me to the heat of the day and I'd rather not drink alone."
   "And I'd rather drink." I gave Alexandra my best handsome
smile and extended my hand, which she took. "Rupert Brigg."

She nodded and said nothing. Maybe she thought *Rupert Brigg* was an unusual American greeting, much like *howdy*. She kissed Steve goodbye on both cheeks and we watched, a little sadder, as she stepped carefully down to the alleyway and disappeared off to the right.

"She's charming," I said.

"Yes," said Steve. "Not much for conversation, though. What have you been up to?"

"Window shopping."

"I passed you on Pandróssou Street," he said, smiling. "You're a coin collector."

"Am I?"

"There was a book on your desk, something about coins. I noticed it when I was in your room."

"Of course."

Steve stuck a cigarette in his mouth, lit it with a match, and waved the match out in my face. "You're not very forthcoming."

"We numismatists are a private lot," I said.

"Numismatist," repeated Steve. "Sounds like someone who's into clouds or having sex with mummies."

"That's why we're so private."

A waiter came over and I ordered my drink.

"When are you heading out to Aspros?" he asked.

"I'm not sure."

"I need a vacation."

"From what?"

"Tell me something about coins."

I really didn't know very much about coins, but if I'd argued it, Steve, who was clearly suspicious of me, would have thought it meant something. "What would you find interesting?"

"Why coins over, say, women?" he asked.

"I am recently divorced."

"Why coins over, say, politics?"

"I am interested in politics."

"What in particular?"

"Whose in particular," I corrected.

"My politics?" He looked almost bored. "I'm a journalist. I don't have any. That's why they pay me."

My drink arrived and I took a sip. Steve Kelly looked like one of the people I'd gone to college with, who were ardent athletes but upon finding themselves graduated and purposeless, flocked to Wall Street for the easy money and requisite safe life. Steve Kelly resembled these people, but he wasn't one at all. I looked across his freckled nose and into his milky green eyes, and they glimmered at me in a way that seemed almost taunting. There was nothing handsome about him, but I knew women liked him and I was beginning to see why. He had a masculine confidence that appealed to women, that made them feel safe.

"How can you tell if they're fake?" asked Steve.

"Who?"

"Them. The coins."

"Oh." I looked thoughtfully at Steve. "Well, in the ancient world coins were struck, not cast. They have a flattened look, and there's often some sort of split on the edges. Forgeries, ones that are cast, will have a telltale line around the rim. Also, bubbles. Not obvious ones, but a slight roughness to the touch that would make me, for one, suspicious."

"What would you say if I told you I'd detected a faint line around your rim?"

"I'd say you'd passed up a good opportunity," I said, "and probably needed a second opinion."

Steve and I had another drink, but the day was reaching its deadest hour and we decided to head back to the hotel. By the time we began to negotiate the narrow walkways of the Pláka, all the storefronts were sealed against the heat except for a few establishments, door opened, but closed for business, where the employees and proprietors dozed off at desks and counters. Through one door, an upright bartender slept soundly with his face cradled in his hand, his elbow on the bar, as if he were enchanted.

Steve was from Indiana. His father was an Irishman and his mother from the Ukraine. In addition to Greek, Steve was fluent in Russian and French. He had originally wanted to be a writer of fiction and thought that journalism would be a good way to support his habit.

"Do you write fiction?" I asked.

"No," he said. "I keep thinking I might start, but I never do."

"You're still young."

"I'm twenty-eight."

"You look younger."

"I feel older."

We reached our hotel. Yorgos did not greet us, but I saw his feet in the crack of an open door that I knew led to the broom closet. He must have been asleep. I'd wondered what the chair was doing in there.

"And what will you do now?" asked Steve.

"I need a shower, and then a nap seems in order."

"I'll see you later, then."

And we parted.

I spent the next hour reading up on coins. In my time at the auction house, I had been an expert in decorative arts, furniture in particular. I was the hero of Hepplewhite, monarch of the macassar, captain of the late-eighteenth-century commode. I was reputed to distinguish a Sheraton from a Duncan Phyfe at a distance of fifty feet. Was this true? Perhaps. But what was more interesting was the desire that Max Grolsz, then my future father-in-law, had in creating this image. I remember Max introducing me to all his friends when I was merely apprenticed to him, saying, when I didn't know anything, "This boy knows his furniture!" But I would learn. His was a backward process. Max had hired someone who looked like he would age well—that was the furniture dealer in him—and then trained me superbly. I knew the value of things.

A part of me missed the auction house. And Max. There is a good deal of detective work that goes along with any involvement in antiques. Rarely did the object announce itself beyond question. Knowing what something was usually involved long encounters with what it wasn't. I'd enjoyed my communication with the in-animate, duplicitous pieces of furniture and the deranged, special-ized conversations that went along with working at Grolsz's. We had a language of finials, scrollwork, inlay. Wedgwood and Limoges. Lalique and Whitefriars. Sheffield and Windsor. Jugendstil and Biedermeier. All very important. And now, leafing through my book, coins seemed rather dry. Coins: flat, metal, round. Not fasci-nating at all. I felt like calling up Steve and telling him that I was not a numismatist at all but rather an expert in chairs—a possessor of a soul!

When the phone started ringing, I was so out of practice that at first I didn't know what to do. I picked up the receiver.

"*Milaté angliká?*" I said. Which meant, *Do you speak English?*

"*Né,*" replied the person. *Né* meant *yes.*

"I'm sorry, I don't speak Greek," I replied.

"Then why are you speaking it?" It was Kostas. "Are you learn-ing Greek?"

"I picked up a phrase book."

"And that is your phrase, *Milaté angliká?*"

"There are quite a few phrases in this book."

"You are hungry."

"Yes. No. I will be later."

"What are you doing now?"

"I'm reading."

"Do you think that's better than eating?" Kostas laughed. "We'll meet for dinner, not now, later, when you are hungry. Who eats now? Only American farmers. There's a restaurant. . . ."

I wrote down the address and the directions, confused and nervous, wishing that Nikos wasn't gallivanting around with his English girlfriends—wondering on which street the cabdriver would abandon me and how long it would take his cousins to show up and rob me—when Kostas said, "I will pick you up at nine-thirty."

I should have been relieved but I was momentarily annoyed at having had my adventure taken from me.

He hung up without saying goodbye.

Kostas was thoughtful in the car. I told him about the rumor of the bell krater and he listened, rubbing his chin.

"You say red with black?"

"I didn't see it myself, but that is what the man told me."

"And you think this is from Italy?"

"I have heard from reliable sources that certain items of classical pottery have been unearthed from burial sites in and around Puglia."

"Where is that?"

"In the heel of the boot."

"How do you know it's not fake?"

"I don't."

"Rupert, I am not always this suspicious, but I have learned from a certain man that I know, one who has great interest in this classical pottery, that there is a way of making that red pottery with the black. This method was lost hundreds of years ago, but he has figured out how to do it. And convincingly."

"And this forger—"

"Forger? Is it all so simple for you?" interrupted Kostas. "This man is an artist. A Greek! What is the difference between this artist and the man who made the bell krater five thousand years ago?"

I paused. "Five thousand years?"

"Exactly. Five thousand years." Kostas, who was driving poorly, pulled suddenly to the left, sweeping across oncoming traffic, and came to rest abruptly on the opposite sidewalk. Thus beached, we got out of the car. "We are all children of Pheidias!"

"Kostas," I said. "I'm an antiques dealer. It's possible that we don't have the same approach."

Kostas burst out laughing. "Don't worry. We still have some old things lying around. Faces staring up from the bottom of the ocean. Sometimes they come up in the nets."

He opened the door to the restaurant and ushered me inside.
"Things with the fishes. Heads of marble. Jewelry."

"Really?"

"You don't believe me?"

We both sat down at a table. "Where is this?"

"Aspros."

It was exactly what I thought he was going to say.

Kostas ordered all the food. I was delighted to start with octopus, a
glossy, purple, suckered monstrosity, but I was not prepared for it
to taste exactly as its appearance suggested. Kostas and I must have
looked like two old cats, chewing and chewing in silent concen-
tration. At some arbitrary point I decided to wash it down with wine.
There was a salad topped off with sheep cheese and capers, and some
little balls flavored with dill that looked like crab cakes but weren't.

"You like that?" asked Kostas.

I took another bite and nodded.

"You will eat a lot of that in Aspros."

"What is it?"

"Why?"

"So I can order it."

Kostas cocked his head to one side. "It is *revithekeftedes*."

I nodded at the small appetizer of the large name.

"Much of the food here is Asprian. The chef is from Aspros.
Usually, the best chefs are. They are good at *stifado*, any stew. . . ."
Kostas looked at me. He seemed dissatisfied.

"I'm sure their stews are marvelous."

"So agreeable. I expected you to argue with me over everything,
like your uncle. How I miss him!"

"I'm sure you do," I said. "I'm starting to miss him too."

Kostas glanced over to see if I was being ironic. I was not. "Is it
all right for you to leave Monday for Aspros?" he asked.

"No problem," I said. "What is the day today?"

Kostas laughed. "It is Wednesday."

The main courses arrived and I found myself discussing the particulars of my education, my involvement at the auction house, old Grolsz, whom I missed, my wife, whom I didn't. "She and I," I said, consciously holding Kostas's eyes, "grew apart." I'd almost added something about *growing apart* being an American phenomenon but had grown tired of blaming my culture for everything wrong with my character.

"Your voice changes when you talk about this wife you had, this job, as if you are making it up."

"I'm not," I said. I did not feel defensive. He was reacting to the reticence in my voice.

Kostas chewed his food, studying me. I shrugged, a man with no answers, and he set down his fork.

"What did I say?" asked Kostas.

"I don't understand."

"You are sad all of a sudden, quiet."

"It is the jet lag Kostas, and this wonderful food and the brilliant wine." I raised my glass and drank.

"I asked you about your wife," he said. "How are you supposed to enjoy your food?"

I smiled. "It must be very exhausting for you, being that perceptive."

"And you are always hiding, which is also tiring." Kostas topped up my wine. "If Nikos were here, he would be angry."

"Why?"

"He thinks I am nosy." Kostas considered this. "I *am* nosy."

I laughed.

"And where is my son anyway? He comes into the kitchen reeking like a Turkish whore. I am trying to enjoy my coffee. I say, 'Nikos, what is that smell?' and you know what he says? 'Papa, it's French.' So I say, 'What is that French smell?' And you know what he says to me? 'Papa, it is cologne. Sometimes you are so unsophisticated.' Do you wear this?"

"Cologne? No." I did occasionally wear cologne, but knew this would be a difficult position to defend. "Sometimes I use aftershave, but it's mostly alcohol, so it evaporates."

Kostas nodded so seriously that I knew he'd already forgotten his question.

"Tell me about Aspros," I said. "I've never heard of it, but if you look at the map there it is, right by Páros, right by Náxos."

"You have never heard of it, but once the island was very rich. There was silver, there, and gold. But the mine flooded, and Aspros had to find other ways to get money. Now it is not such a rich island, but the cheese is the best in Greece, and perhaps it's better to have good cheese than silver."

"Why?"

"Because everyone enjoys cheese, but only the rich enjoy silver." Kostas winked at me. He took a forkful of cheese off the salad and ate it with gusto.

"Didn't the Asprians have a treasury in Delphi?"

"Yes," said Kostas. "You know a lot about history."

"About art."

Kostas shrugged, as if to say it was the only kind that mattered. "So you know it was Apollo who flooded their mines."

"No."

"It's like this: every year the people of Aspros would give Apollo a solid silver egg as a tribute. Then one year, they got tired of this and gave him one that was only silver-plated. Apollo was angry and destroyed the mines. So you learn a lesson from this."

"Don't make Apollo angry?"

"No. Asprians will try to pass off something fake, even to a god. You don't stand a chance."

"Then why not send me to Náxos, where they're excavating? Why not send me to Páros or to Santoríni?"

"Why send you there? Aspros is all yours, no one watching, no one competing, and all the same history. The Minoans were there, the Macedonians, even the Egyptians, and later—like all the islands— the Venetians."

"And now me."

"There he is," said Kostas abruptly, and stood up, pushing his chair back. Nikos was conferring with the maître d', and Kostas gazed in awe at the miracle of his beautiful son. I had never seen such adoration of anyone for anyone and wondered at how Kostas managed to control all this emotion, put it away as Nikos approached the table.

Nikos looked down at his father. He picked up a napkin and wiped the corner of Kostas's mouth. "You ate everything."

"You are late."

Nikos shrugged. "Is there more food coming?"

"Of course, but what you have done to get such a big appetite, I do not want to know."

Nikos sat down beside his father. "How was your day, Rupert?"

"I went to Pandróssou Street and was not robbed. Nor did I buy anything, so I was not fleeced."

"What is this *fleeced*? Like the Golden Fleece?"

"It means *cheated*," said Kostas.

"I ran into Steve Kelly in a café at the foot of the Acropolis and might have gone and seen the Acropolis, but I had a couple of drinks instead."

"Good choice."

"And your father here is dispatching me to Aspros."

"When?" said Nikos. "On the Monday ferry?"

Kostas nodded.

"I will go with you!" said Nikos.

Nikos turned to Kostas, and they conferred quickly in Greek.

"Tomorrow I will take you to my tailor, if you like. We will have some shirts made," said Nikos. "And pants."

Kostas rolled his eyes.

"What?" asked Nikos. He looked at his father. "This is not the old days in Turkey where you had your good pants and your bad pants."

While Nikos ate—he insisted on fish, which Kostas refused to order anywhere he could not see the ocean—I found myself drinking more. The wine went down like water, fresh and light, not like the syrupy chardonnays and phlegmatic cabernets to which I was accustomed. Kostas left after coffee, but Nikos, who had a couple of stories to share about Sue and Helen, ordered some whiskey.

"They are gone," he said. "I took them to Piraeus today and put them on the ferry for Rhodes."

"And does that make you sad?"

Nikos poured a drink for himself, and then one for me. "Why be sad when you can be happy?"

"Or drunk?"

Nikos laughed. "How was dinner with my father?"

"Good," I said. "He loves you."

"Of course," said Nikos. "Doesn't every father love his son? Doesn't your father love you?"

I remembered that Nikos and I did not know each other very well. Finally, I said, "You forget about being a son when you become a father."

"You have a son?"

"He died," I said.

Nikos nodded and there was emotion in his eyes. He watched me.

"A yachting accident. I wasn't there. Now there's an advantage to being poor. How many poor children die in yachting accidents?"

"He could not swim?" asked Nikos cautiously.

"He was two years old." I finished my glass. "I've had dogs live longer than that. All my dogs lived longer than that."

We were quiet for a long time. I was walking that gulf of blackness, whose perimeter I constantly traveled.

I said, "I don't know why I'm telling you this."

"I do," said Nikos.

"You do?" I asked, not bothering to disguise the contempt in my voice.

"Yes. It is summer and you are in Greece. It is guilt."

We looked at each other for a moment. I could hear my heart's passive beating in my ears, the slow involuntarily, hauling of oxygen.

"Take me home, Nikos."

"Back to the hotel?"

"Yes. I want to be alone."

We were silent in the car. The streets of Athens were garishly lit and alive. I was thinking about nothing. Every now and then the small child face would show itself to me and then disappear, leaving clothes, toys, sandals, the boat. I remembered his laugh, but then I didn't trust myself to admit if I'd forgotten its specific music. It could have been any laugh. And then we were at the hotel and Nikos was opening the car door for me and I realized that I had been carrying myself like a very drunk person because I was too deadened to feign sobriety. I pulled myself together on the curb.

I said, "Good night, Nikos. Thank you."

Nikos looked at me directly and honestly. He said, "I don't know how you live with that. How do you live with that?"

And I said, "I'm not really sure."

Nikos put his hands on my shoulders and shook me affectionately. I nodded, a fractured person, as he took his car into the widening abyss of night.

5

Thursday seemed very bright, since I had missed morning and rolled out of bed shortly after noon. I was slightly offended that Nikos hadn't bothered to come by to introduce me to my latest hangover, but I quickly realized this was respect; the last thing I'd said to him was that I wanted to be alone, and if he was as expert in matters of the human heart as he seemed to be, he would think it considerate to hold off until a time when I could present myself with proper dignity.

I showered and dressed but decided to forgo shaving for the moment. I wasn't up to calling for Yorgos and the clay pitcher. My beard had come in thick and insane-looking and my eyes, bloodshot, were a peculiar antifreeze green. I looked depraved—I was probably still drunk—and I knew I should move quickly to food before the real enervation struck. In this state I stepped from my door and for the first time wished that I were back in New York, where I could get my eggs and toast and hash browns at the diner with no struggle, where the coffee would come liquid and steaming and endless. Now I wasn't sure if breakfast was available anywhere. Did the Greeks even eat breakfast? I could get a gyro, maybe. Who knew?

"Brigg!"

I heard the accusation and saw Steve Kelly standing at the end of the corridor in his undershirt and baggy pants, his feet bare, the red hair curling on the tops of his toes.

"You look like hell!"

"I'm aware of that."

"I didn't think it was possible. I should call up Alexandra."

"Alexandra? From the café?"

"She was quite taken with you, but right about now, she might actually think favorably of me."

I smiled. "I don't suppose you'd be willing to escort me to a plate of eggs and some coffee?"

Steve Kelly consulted his watch. "If we leave right now."

"Why? Where are you going?"

"North."

We stopped by Steve's office, since he had to pick up something before his trip. I stood outside the elevator beside a glass partition, smoking, watching the quick conversation between Steve and his editor, a blond Englishman with a patrician leanness to his face and an oddly wide yet thin set of hips. The editor's pants looked like they'd been stretched over a coat hanger. The elevator doors opened, casting a reflective light on the glass, and I saw for one moment my Hyde-like appearance—a hunching post-drunkenness—then the elevator doors shut again and the reflection was gone and in its place the very civilized and questioning face of the editor. He and Steve were both talking and looking at me.

There was a moment where I imagined the editor saying *Right!* and Steve responding *Okay!* Then Steve was sent off, a new batch of papers in his beaten-up leather satchel, new information percolating in his brain. He pushed through the door. He had an unlit cigarette in his lips and it wiggled up and down while he spoke, as he shuffled through his satchel in search of a lighter. We waited for the elevator.

"He's all right," he said, about his editor. "A bit uptight, but miraculous with language. I've seen him get information posing as a Turk. From the Turks."

"Is he one of those Oxford types?"

"He did go to Oxford."

"Probably started out in classical languages."

"Actually, yes."

"And why is he out here, everyone wonders, rather than back home with Genevieve, who has waited all these years for him, ever since university . . ."

"Now I'm out of information."

The elevator arrived and we got in.

"But he'll never go back, not as long as Dimitri—"

Steve smiled broadly. "That's where you're wrong."

"Am I?"

"His name is Iannis. And he's on the payroll as an informant." Steve shook his head at me, impressed. "That's uncanny. How did you do that?"

"A life spent looking at fakes."

"You think my editor's a fake?"

"That depends," I said, "on whether you're Iannis or Genevieve."

From the office, the restaurant was only two blocks away. Steve ordered for me in Greek and got me my eggs; he was eating a deep-fried piece of cheese. We were the only people there.

"So what's north?" I asked.

"North? Oh, yes. I'm researching a story."

"Where are you going?"

"Oh, you know. . . ."

"You're going up to the Albanian border."

"There are many things in that direction."

"Oh, absolutely," I said. "There's Poland. And Finland." I salted my eggs.

Steve looked pointedly at me. "There's a band of Communist rebels, around twenty men, and they're causing trouble."

"What sort of trouble?"

"That's what my editor wants me to find out."

"Sounds like a story," I said.

Steve watched me chew my food. "What are your plans for the next few days?"

"Aspros on Monday and, until then, drinking a lot of water and napping."

"Well, Brigg, I'm passing through Delphi. You could ride up with me, and catch the bus back."

This, of course, was a great opportunity. What educated traveler makes a trip to Greece without longing to visit the navel of the earth? But I was not in very good shape. Even after the eggs, I felt hollow. My brain seemed to have swollen painfully within my skull, although—ironically—I had no capacity for mental process. All this made taking a long drive seem ill-advised. But was there really a choice? I didn't want to be cursing myself, come afternoon, waiting alone like a desperate woman for Nikos to call. If everything went well, Steve and I would get to Delphi in four and a half hours.

We left the restaurant and found the car, which was parked in front of an elegant apartment building.

"Whose car is this?" I asked.

"It's Custard's car."

"Custard? Who is Custard?"

"My editor. He lives here." Steve pointed with his cigarette at the building.

"What's his first name?" I laughed. "Let's take Custard's car to Delphi!" I said. "No really. What's his first name?"

"Timon."

"Timon Custard?"

Steve did not seem to find this as funny as I did, although he probably had at one point. Or maybe he had been alone when he learned it, which always dilutes the humor.

We drove to Kostas's neighborhood next. I couldn't remember when I'd agreed to go to the tailor with Nikos. It might have been that day or the day after, not that Nikos would hold me to it, but running off without letting the Nikolaideses know where I was going would have been inconsiderate. When we drew near—I used the Acropolis to orient myself—Steve yelled up to an old woman who was hanging wash on a third-floor balcony, and she, with a few lazy gestures and some thick-tongued toothless speech, directed us the final steps. Nikos and Kostas were both out, so I left a note with the housekeeper explaining that I planned to return on Friday.

I fell asleep shortly after we left the city limits. Steve was reciting Greek sentences over and over, the subjunctive, or something like it, substituting nouns in and out, moving the stresses around. As I nodded off, I entertained a small hope that I was being taught Greek in my sleep, but who knew what Steve was asking. I guessed, "Who is supplying the weapons? Are you with ELAS? How old are you? Have you traveled far to fight this, to fight for the Communists?"

When I woke up, I was alone in the car and Steve was across the road conferring with a Greek man, lean, with intense eyes. He had an enormous diagonal scar that cut his face in two pieces, right through his mouth. He gestured with his hands at the horizon, up the street where a lone goat chewed , and then at the trees that were shivering their leaves. A truck came up the road, groaning through the gears, kicking up dust. There was some honking, some congenial cursing. The truck was carrying young soldiers who stood, uncovered, in the back. In the brief time I saw them, smoking, smiling, they looked like a fairly happy crew.

I thought the polite thing to do would be to leave the car and go and smile at Steve's friend, keep smiling, and then pretend to be profoundly interested in something: the trees, perhaps, or the goat. I imagined Steve making something up about how I was interested in goats, how rare they were on the streets of Manhattan. Was this his fascinating goat? But the old nausea was back, and before I could decide what to do I found myself purging out the door of the car and onto the dirt. Steve and the intense face-slashed man laughed with undisguised amusement.

Feeling slightly better, I got out of the car and wandered over.

The man smiled an off-kilter smile, and I saw his long yellow teeth. He said, "Drinking is good!"

And I said, "If you'd said that last night, I would have been inclined to agree with you."

Steve translated for me, the man looked at me, and I smiled quickly—expressively, as if it were a word and not a smile—and the

man laughed out loud. The goat, frightened by his laughter, let out
a series of sharp desperate bleats and took off over the rise in the
road.

"Do you know where you are?" Steve asked.

I looked up the street, where the goat had disappeared, and down
the street, where the truck was a diminishing spot of gray dust. "No.
And I find that question odd."

"Thebes," said Steve, "is that way." He pointed with his thumb
over his shoulder. "And Delphi"—he made a gun out of his hand and
pointed with his forefinger—"is that way."

"Ah," I said, "and where's Livadiá?"

"To the south," said Steve.

"Is this the place where Oedipus was to have slain his father?"

In response to the question, the Greek yelled, "Oedipus! Laios!"
and expressively dug into the dirt with the heel of his boot. He then
made a slashing motion across his throat. The Greek then said something else and smiled intensely at me, nodding and nodding.

I looked to Steve. "He's offering us a drink, isn't he?"

"Yes, he is," said Steve.

"I really don't need one."

"Hair of the dog."

"That's for headaches." But I really was grateful for the offer,
because I was not ready to get back in the car and I could probably
get juice or at least some water. The man placed his hand firmly on
my shoulder, and I responded quickly, "*Evkaristó. Evkaristó polí.*"

"Very good," said Steve.

"And how do you apologize?"

"*Signómi,*" said Steve.

"Let's hope I don't have to use it."

The man's name was actually Adonis, and if his face had not been so
terribly scarred it would have been fitting. He took us to his house
and we sat on a terrace in the late-afternoon sun. I was drinking very
weak ouzo and snacking on some pistachios. I couldn't converse at

all, but every now and then I would spout the name of some character from Greek tragedy, just to let Adonis know I was there and had
respect for him.

"Antigone," I said.

He nodded solemnly.

"Electra," I said.

And he threw his arms open wide and his face filled with
emotion.

There was a fuchsia blooming on the wall of the house, and bees
levitated and descended in the blooms. Adonis's wife was talking to
a very old woman—their voices carried out from the kitchen—and
the talk of the young woman, followed by the talk of the old one,
seemed almost like the strophe and the antistrophe of a chorus.

Adonis and Steve did not mind my silence. They were involved
in an intense discussion, but about what? "Well done" was said, possibly twenty times. I wondered what it meant in Greek, but then I decided it was someone's name. Well done: Weldon. Common enough.
I wondered what this Weldon was up to. And I heard the word *kerma*,
which I knew referred to me. It's amazing how sensitive one becomes
to gesture when speech is foreign. The two men kept glancing at me,
smiling in a reassuring way, which had the opposite effect.

"We should go," said Steve. "We'll make Delphi in time for
dinner."

I shook Adonis's hand. He seemed genuinely sad that we were
leaving. "Thank your wife for her hospitality. It was wonderful to meet
you," I said. I looked over at Steve, so that he knew to translate.

On the way to the car, I asked Steve who Weldon was.

"Weldon?" Steve was surprised and tried to seem casual.

"You were talking about him."

"Ah. He's an American artist."

"And your friend," I said, gesturing over a heap of manure in
the road, "he's a collector?"

"We keep track of all the stray Americans," said Steve. His eyes
twinkled.

"And what does *kerma* mean?"
"*Kerma*," he said, "means coins."

I tried to nap again in the car. I thought it might save Steve the worry of my throwing up again, but he knew the worst of my illness was over. Call it experience. I gave up on the nap and lit a cigarette. I lit one for Steve too, and we enjoyed a half hour of easy silence.

"I'd like to thank you for bringing me up here I pictured myself a complete loner on this trip," I said.

"What, you mean in Greece? It's impossible to be alone in Greece."

"If it were possible, I'd be a good candidate for it."

"You? Oh, you're one of those."

"One of what?"

"One of those social loners."

"What's a social loner?"

"You think you're completely self-sufficient and avoid the company of others, but you're actually very approachable. Even fun. At least funny. A social loner."

"A romantic stance?"

"Absolutely."

"Perhaps." I considered. "Or maybe I'm a circumstantial loner."

"Oh," said Steve, "the divorce."

"Yes, that and the fact that I spend my life with furniture."

"And coins."

"Yes."

"How'd you get into that? Furniture. You look more like a lawyer. Or a professional ladies' man."

"Very funny." I tossed my cigarette out the window. "I got a job straight out of college with an antiques dealer. I was good at languages, particularly German. This was in 1955. He had a number of pieces that had come over in the early thirties, wealthy Jewish families wanting cash. Many of the more valuable pieces he'd hung on to, thinking that in better times people might want them back."

"Was he Jewish?"

"No." I smiled. "Many people assume he is, but he's a Catholic from Bavaria."

"So why didn't he sell the pieces?"

"Frankly, I think it was guilt."

"And where did you come in?"

I shrugged. I'd asked myself this many times. "I did have some other duties, but mostly I researched the fate of the owners of some of the pricier things, the Fabergé eggs, the paintings. . . . I remember a Louis Sixteenth sideboard, gilt. . . ."

"Did you find any of these people?"

"I found one. He was in Israel. When he heard I still had his chair, he called, weeping over the phone. We packed it up and sent it to him. The chair had belonged to his father. He remembered him using it. He kept saying, 'He used to sit there.'"

We both fell quiet after this. Maybe it was the thought of all those people survived by their furniture. But also we had entered the mountains, and the winding roads and cypress trees were silencing in their own way. I felt I was driving into the past. There was some patchy fog, and Steve rolled down the window. At one point, we nearly hit a small herd of goats shepherded by an angelic dark-haired boy with eyes like a Byzantine icon. Another time, a truck was barreling down the road with no headlights—a common practice to avoid wear on the battery—and only Steve's honking and his flashing our own lights alerted the driver to our presence as we pulled off, dramatically, to crouch by the shoulder of the mountain.

"Tell me we're nearly in Delphi," I said.

"We *are* in Delphi," Steve replied, and soon I saw a small cluster of buildings and a plunging cleft between the mountains.

By the time we reached the hotel, there was only one room left. There were two narrow cots in the room, a shower off of it, a small window with a large view of the diving valley and the far sparkle of the Gulf of Itéa. Steve immediately left for the bar. On the way in, he'd noticed a large contingent of backpacking American girls, all long hair, shorts, and direct gazes, and he was in a hurry to buy them some drinks lest they evaporate, unmolested, into the fog. There was that quality of things being not quite as they seemed, a fairy-tale quality. I was exhausted, ready to shower and brush my teeth. Steve had instructions to wake me for dinner, but I knew he might get sidetracked and wasn't that concerned. The water in the shower was freezing and that, combined with the stiff clean bed linen, sent me into a profound sleep. When I heard knocking on the door, I was not sure where I was. The room was dark, the light mountain air unfamiliar.

"Come in."

There was a pause.

I felt as if I were rising from the bottom of a bathtub.

"For God's sake, the door's not locked."

It opened; and instead of Steve I saw the narrow shoulders and long hair of one of the girls, backlit and offered in silhouette. She stepped into the room.

"Hello," I said. "Did Steve send you?"

"I came on my own," she said.

I sat up in bed. My eyes had adjusted a little. She had broad cheekbones, cat eyes, black hair. She sat on the foot of my bed, calculated immodesty. I wondered how old she was.

"What time is it?" I asked.

"It's eleven."

I realized all of a sudden that I was starving. I hadn't eaten since the eggs in Athens. "What's your name?"

"Jeanne."

"Well, Jeanne," I said. I got out of bed in my shorts, practical immodesty, took my pants off the chair, and put them on. "I'm hungry and I need some food."

She stood up and went to the door. I put on my shoes and my shirt as she watched, slyly, over her shoulder.

"Let's go," I said. I buttoned my shirt on the way down the stairs.

Steve was holding court in the restaurant. He sat at a table with a half-dozen girls, Jeanne's friends, with his arm casually slung around a thin blonde. I took a seat at the table.

"There he is!" said Steve, with suspicious exuberance. "My good buddy Rupert."

The girls studied me, but Jeanne sat close on my left side, her bare thigh creating an even pressure against my pant leg. "I'm not sure if this is what Mr. Custard had in mind," I said.

The waiter, a teenager in jeans and T-shirt, was orbiting the table. We made eye contact. "Can I get you something to eat?" he asked.

"Yes."

"There's eggplant with some meat, very popular and quick."

I nodded in assent.

"And I'll bring another glass and some more of the red?"

"Bravo," said Steve.

"His English is very good," I said.

Jeanne put her hand on my arm. "We've been teaching him," she said.

Steve leaned across the table and stated, with undisguised glee, "They're bacchantes from California."

"Well," I responded, "I'm a sybarite from New York."

Jeanne didn't say much, which was fine with me. Steve liked his position as the center of attention, and I was busy eating anyway. Jeanne watched me, her wide unblinking eyes fixed on the side of my face. I could tell that Steve was starved for American company, but I felt violated at having been discovered by my countrymen and the loud English, although often funny, seemed intrusive, as if it shone a klieg light on us all, exposing us as confident, condescending, and rich. Hangovers depressed me. I was on my fifth glass of wine when I realized I had entered a phase of misanthropic inebriation. I looked over at Jeanne. She was conferring with a friend of hers, a regular Diana with strong features and muscular arms, and the two were looking at me. I returned their gaze, eyebrows raised.

"How long have you been in Delphi?" I inquired.

"About three weeks now," said the Diana.

"One would think the sights would be done with by now."

"The sights keep changing," said the Diana, and smiled. She whispered something in Jeanne's ear. Steve had pulled out his wallet and was counting out bills for the evening's libations. I was now better at the drachmas than I had been and noticed he was carrying quite a lot of cash.

"What do I owe you?" I asked.

He looked at the stack of bills. "If you get the room, we'll be even."

I put my hand on Jeanne's thigh and squeezed it. She didn't seem surprised. She said, "We're all going for a walk."

"Among the ruins?" I raised an eyebrow ironically, and Diana and Jeanne exchanged a look. "I think I'll retire to my room."

I stood and picked up a near-full carafe of wine and a couple of glasses. I looked at Jeanne, pointedly excluding her friend from my field of vision, and said, "Care for a nightcap?"

Jeanne thought about this. She looked over at her friend, who seemed encouraging, and smiled for the first time all night. I didn't like her when she smiled. She went from being an almost emotionless object to an eager teenager.

"How old are you?" I asked.

"Twenty."

"Really?"

She stopped smiling.

"Enjoy your walk," I said, addressing the table. Steve downed his drink and gave me a thumbs-up. I made it to the stairs and, when I turned, Jeanne was following.

I think the wine had reactivated the whiskey from the previous night, which must have somehow still been in my system. I can't explain my behavior any other way. I knew that a depraved sexual encounter with a girl ten years my junior was the only thing that would make me more depressed than I already was, and that appealed to me. There was something refreshing about not having to seduce her with pretty compliments and patience—she took her clothes off

shortly after entering the room and didn't even bother with the glass
of wine I poured for her—and she responded quite enthusiastically
to my suggestions, which was a bit of a novelty and sent me in some
recently unexplored directions. She misconstrued a certain aggressive bitterness on my part for passion and although I might have scared
her she was too self-conscious about her age and inexperience to let
it show. I passed out at some point and she did too.

At about five o'clock in the morning, I heard a disturbance in the
hall and woke to see Jeanne going through my suitcase. She had her
underwear on, and a sleeveless top, but for some reason had left her
shorts on the floor by the bed. I reached for my undershorts which
were also on the floor, but had not managed to get them on when
the door slammed open. Steve was standing there in a state of disbelief. There was a sticky gash on the side of his head that must have
been quite sore. It had emptied a considerable amount of blood onto
his shirt. Jeanne stepped back from the dresser. We all must have
looked at each other several times, around and around, until my mind
finally processed the information that Jeanne, or whatever her name
really was, had my wallet.

"Grab her!" I said.

Steve, clumsily, wrapped his arms around her. At this point,
Jeanne let loose a powerful shriek and I heard doors slam open, footsteps down the hall. I jumped out of bed, naked, and ran to assist. At
this point we had a good audience and it looked very bad for us. Jeanne
bit Steve's arm, but he hung on. I managed to pry my wallet out of
her hand.

"Let her go," I said. Jeanne took off, running down the hall in
her underwear. I took the towel off the back of the door and covered
myself, but I knew it was a bit late for that.

"Tell them she stole my wallet," I said. I tried to smile in a reassuring way.

"She stole his wallet," he announced.

"I meant for you to translate that into Greek."

And he did. The proprietor of the hotel came up and we made our explanations. He was still a bit suspicious and kept looking at Steve's head.

"Tell him we mean to report this to the police," I said.

Steve translated. The proprietor's mood changed suddenly and he seemed very much in a hurry to get away. He left. I sat down on the bed and opened my wallet.

"Well?" said Steve.

"It's all there," I said.

Steve picked up Jeanne's shorts and held them up. "I have a feeling that, between the two of us, you had the better evening."

"Did they jump you?" I asked.

"I think so." Steve went into the bathroom, and I knew he was looking at his head.

"When did you figure it out?"

"What? Oh, about the girls?" Steve laughed. "I think it was when you said 'Grab her.'"

He came out of the bathroom, shaking his head in disbelief. "I was actually worried about them. I came to passed out next to a pile of goat feces with a bloodied rock—my blood, next to my head. I thought we'd all been attacked."

"Bacchantes," I said.

"From California," Steve added.

Steve refused to see a doctor and I didn't have the energy to argue for it. I helped him clean his head and he assured me that, after the amount of alcohol he'd consumed, no germs could possibly survive. Still, we did buy a bottle of rubbing alcohol, which I poured over the cut as he stood outside the pharmacy, his head tilted to one side, holding the wall for support.

"Fuck, fuck, fuck, fuck, fuck," he said. I replaced the cap on the bottle and handed it back to him. "Better than coffee," he said.

"Any dizziness?" I asked. "I wouldn't want you to drive off a cliff."

"I'm fine," he said. We walked to his car.

I took out my wallet and looked at the cash. "How much is the bus going to be?"

"Can't be much more than fifty drachma."

I counted out about three hundred drachma. "Is this enough?"

Steve took a hundred and handed the rest back to me. "My ac-commodation is covered, and I honestly don't think I should be trav-eling with that much cash." He got into his car and started the engine. "Will I see you back in Athens?"

"Probably," I said. "I leave for Aspros on Wednesday."

I watched Steve disappear up the road. He honked a few times and waved out the window and I, with my book on monuments, began the trek to the oracle.

Delphi was saved by natural disaster, specifically earthquakes and the resulting landslides. Earthquakes accomplished for Delphi what vol-canoes had accomplished for Pompeii. The great works of art were hidden in the folds of the earth, as if Apollo himself had chosen a few key pieces to make the march through the ages, and there they slept, while above, on the surface, everyone from Nero to the Van-dals hoarded and crushed what remained. I thought of this as I looked into the eyes of the charioteer, who now stood chariotless and alone. There is something joyless about survival, even that of a gorgeous sculpture. The museum was crowded, people having rushed indoors to hide from the punishing sun. Looking at the charioteer in here with all the people made me feel almost sorry for him. It was a bit like viewing a tiger at the zoo.

The friezes from the Asprian treasury were in the next, less crowded, room. I had long wanted to see the eastern frieze with its spray of gods and goddesses, superheroes of old: Athena with her owl; Apollo with his lyre, marching onward and into the past. I became conscious at this point of a man who was standing a little too close. I could feel his breath on my neck. I turned to look at him.

"Some say," the man began, "that although the dates have not been officially disputed, 525 B.C. is too early by a half century."

"Excuse me?"

"The treasury," the man said. "The style of the carving is too advanced."

I looked back at the frieze. Perhaps it was a bit ornate. "Then why not date it later?"

"Because," the man said, "the Asprians were sacked by the Samians shortly afterward. They took everything. Perhaps you know Herodotus?"

"Not as well as I did ten years ago, but this all sounds vaguely familiar."

"After the Samians attacked, the Asprians would not have had the money to make such an exquisite treasury."

"What do you think?" I asked.

"What do I think?" the man said. "I am a complete stranger. How could that possibly be of interest?"

Chastened, I returned my gaze to the battle of the gods and the giants.

"The Asprians," continued the man, "actually consulted the oracle. They wanted to know if their wealth would last. The python told them, *When there are a white prytaneum and a white agora in Aspros, watch for a wooden company and a red herald.*"

I waited for the explanation. The man seemed quite fixed on the marbles, however, and needed prompting.

"What did the prophecy mean?"

"The Asprians didn't know what it meant either. They went ahead and outfitted their agora and prytaneia in Parian marble. And when the Samians showed up in their wooden ships painted vermilion, they should have been careful. They should have loaned the ten talents the Samians asked for. But they didn't. And that was the end of the Asprian wealth."

"I thought they flooded their mines," I said.

"Another theory," said the man, "unless you are Pausanias, in which case the flooding and the sacking are the same thing. Pausanias refers to the Samian invasion as a flooding."

"You are well versed in antiquities," I said.

The man smiled. "I *am* an antiquity."

"You are French," I stated.

"Yes."

"An archaeologist?"

"Yes."

"Perhaps," I suggested, "it would make more sense if you told me about yourself."

The man laughed. "I'm old. It might take awhile."

"I'm not doing anything," I said. "I want to see the site, but it's a bit hot right now."

"Good," said the man. "Join me for a light lunch, and then afterward I will escort you."

"That's very kind," I said.

"Perhaps," the man said. "But there is this"—he lifted his cane for me—"and I don't think I'll make it up without a little help."

My host, who introduced himself as Henri Michaud or, as I called him, Monsieur Michaud, had been a part of the original excavations. He was there for fifteen years, starting in the early 1890s, and at this point—short car trip to the village of Aráhova—he must have been close to ninety years old. His uncle had been a senior member of the French Archaeological Society, and Monsieur Michaud had accompanied him to Greece. Michaud's mother was eager to separate him from his sweetheart at the time, to whom he was overly attached, and who was also the maid.

"I started out carrying buckets of dirt. I learned the Greek of the time and studied the Greek of the past at night. I left for two years to take my exams and earned a degree."

Monsieur Michaud stepped out of the car. He said something to the young man who was driving and tossed him a coin. There was some good-natured banter back and forth. The restaurant was cheerful, in stark contrast to the view, which offered an uninterrupted dive into a ravine. I ordered grilled lamb.

Michaud had a salad. "Nothing cooked anymore," he said. And then leaned in, whispering, "It's the raw food that's kept me alive." He ordered some white wine and we drank it.

"Where are you staying?" he asked.

"At the Apollon."

"So you are in Delphi?"

"Yes."

"We built that town," said Michaud. "There was once a village over the site, called Kastri. We moved it to where you are staying. Delphi."

"And everyone just moved?"

"We paid them. There was one woman, however, who did not want to go. She lived in a shack, you know, nothing, but it was hers and she liked it. We tried reason but she didn't lack for anything and was happy where she was. Then one day she gets up and says she's moving. Of course we want to know why, and she says she had a dream that there was a young boy drowning in a sea of green beneath her and he was begging her to set him free. This, of course, terrified her. When she was gone, we were free to excavate in that area, and that is where we found the charioteer."

There was a moment of silence. It was a good story, hard to follow up.

Michaud said, "I have spent my life unburying things, but soon I will be buried, covered up." He was amusing himself. "This is my last trip to Delphi."

"You don't know that," I said.

Michaud looked at me as if I were a fool. "At my age, death is one thing you can be sure of."

Michaud insisted on treating me to lunch. He called for the young man, who appeared instantly, and soon we were driving back to the oracle. The heat was still powerful and, after the museum, the site did not hold my attention. Ruins were, after all, ruins, bleached by centuries, exuding a dignified despair.

Michaud glanced around him as if every rock were an old friend. There was something in the heat and the deafening drone of the cicadas that lent the ruins a sinister edge, made it seem more of the god Pan and his jovial mayhem than Apollo and his moderation. I could see how a place like this could drive people mad, or at least make them drink more than was sensible.

"Can I give you a hand?" I asked Michaud.

"Up to that rock there, which is by the temple of Apollo," he said. He tucked his hand firmly in the crook of my elbow, nodded, and we began moving slowly upward. The marble under foot was polished to a reflecting sheen, and I was afraid I might slip and take both of us down, there was a steepness to the place that made it possible for one to fall for an uninterrupted mile.

"I was looking forward to a little tour," I said. I looked over at my companion; he seemed pale. There was shiny film of perspiration on his forehead, but his hand was cold.

"The rocks speak for themselves. As for me, I have said too much already."

"Too much?" I protested.

"You have only been around me for the last hour. You have missed the ninety years during which I have spoken endlessly." He gestured at a bench that was mercifully shaded by a stone wall and a narrow cypress. "Go up," Michaud said. "You don't want to miss the theater."

I helped Michaud to the bench. I looked down at the road and thought I saw Custard's car, parked at a short distance, barely visible. I wondered if Steve had returned, but a moment later, when I looked again, the car was gone. Michaud sat and I continued higher, zigzagging up the Sacred Way, past the Temple of Apollo, up to the theater. From there I could see the entire site. Groups of tourists stood in the oppressive heat, staring at the blazing rocks. I looked down to Michaud; he appeared to be sitting quietly. Then I saw him fall to one side, as if the urge to nap had suddenly overwhelmed him. A woman rushed over, and then her husband. People began to cluster around and I knew something had happened. I thought I'd run down

to join them, but felt strangely incapable. I kept thinking of the face
of the charioteer peering through the earth, an image that had become intertwined with the burial of my son, as if he were waiting in
the rich Connecticut earth, calling for me to set him free. I sat on a
marble step, comfortably shaded, watching as if it were a performance.
A few minutes passed. Our young driver ran up to Michaud, but by
now a small crowd had gathered. I imagined that he grabbed Michaud's
hand. Maybe half an hour later, two men appeared with a stretcher
and laid Monsieur Michaud on it; when they carried him down, a
sheet was pulled over his head.

I woke from my stupor at this stage and got to my feet. I thought
I would run after them, tell them something, but I didn't know
Michaud. He was not my friend. He was a fellow lover of art, a man
who had treated me to lunch.

I made my way back to the hotel a half hour later and was relieved to learn that there was a late bus I could catch back to Athens.
I would have time to bathe and have a drink, and then it would all
be over, nothing but a darkly pretty dream.

6

Nikos stared at me across the bolt of cloth. "Rupert, what is wrong with this?"

"It's a bit shiny, isn't it?"

"No," said Nikos. "No it's not." He said something to the tailor, who smiled and set it aside. "I'm having some pants made out of it."

"I prefer linen."

"More linen? It's like a tablecloth, all that linen."

"All right," I said. "I'll have pants out of that stuff too."

Nikos smiled.

"But tell him to cut them wide. I like a nice long rise, none of the nut-hugging stuff you go in for. And I don't like pointing my toes like a ballerina to get my pants on."

Nikos translated as accurately as he could to the tailor, who started laughing. He yelled at his assistant, who quickly appeared with a tray of ice-filled glasses and a bottle of Metaxas.

"When is all this stuff going to be ready?" I asked.

"Day after tomorrow. I'm paying extra for it, and I'm one of his best clients. He's the only tailor around here with so many Italian fabrics. And he's a relative somehow. My mother's cousin's cousin's uncle-in-law or something." Nikos shrugged. He swigged the Metaxas, and the tailor immediately refilled his glass. The tailor said something to Nikos, but he was looking at me.

"Do you need any ties?"

"I was hoping I wouldn't need any. Not on the island, surely."

"That is true. You don't need ties on Aspros."

Nikos stood, said some final salutations, which I followed up with a *kali spera* and we were out on the street.

"You haven't said much about Delphi," he said.

"I told you about Steve Kelly and the bacchantes. How much more could happen in twenty-four hours?"

Nikos shrugged in acceptance, but he knew he had not heard everything. "Your uncle called while you were gone. He wanted to know how you are doing. He is a very good uncle."

I studied Nikos, but there was nothing ironic in his presentation. "He is an exceptional uncle," I said.

"He wanted to know if you'd made any progress."

"And what did you tell him?"

"I said that Greece was good for you."

"I don't think my well-being was the subject of his inquiry."

"There you are wrong," said Nikos. "I think it's what really interested him."

At this point, it was probably about two-thirty—lunchtime—so we headed to the Pláka for some food. There was a restaurant Nikos favored for its eggplant salad, which, with some wine, sounded good to me. I picked up a newspaper on the way.

Nikos had just finished ordering when he noticed a business acquaintance of his father's at the next table.

"The man is a bore, but it would be rude for me not to sit with him for awhile."

I held up my paper. "I'm quite capable of occupying myself," I said.

On the front page was a headline: CAR BOMB ON ALBANIAN BORDER KILLS SEVEN.

And the byline? *Steve Kelly*.

There were several things wrong with this. First of all, the day that the bombing was supposed to have occurred, in the wee dawn hours, was probably around the same time that Steve was waking up in the ruins of Delphi, himself a ruin of Delphi, on his way to report this story. How could he have known it was going to happen? Maybe this strange act of serendipity had happened in his favor. Or perhaps Mr. Custard was psychic. Nikos returned to the table and I held up the paper for him to see.

"Your friend reporting on the Communists again," he said, unimpressed.

"Again?" I looked at the paper. "Is there anything suspicious about this?"

Nikos tapped a cigarette on the table and then lit it. "Yes, there is. The Albanians don't have cars to blow up. Now, if it was a goat bomb—"

"A goat bomb?"

"SEVEN KILLED IN GOAT BOMB. It would resonate with Greeks, but, as I'm sure Steve Kelly has told you, his articles are picked up and printed everywhere. I doubt that Americans would respond to that. . . ."

"You don't think there was a bombing, do you?"

"I'm not sure. Why was Steve Kelly headed there? Maybe he was tipped off. You said he spoke to someone on the way up, someone with information."

"Why would he make it up?"

Nikos looked at me incredulously. "How can there be peace-keeping if there is peace already? It is your government that does this. They own the Greeks. They own our economy. Without America, we would be Albania. Every now and then, we are re-minded of this."

The food arrived and Nikos dropped a piece of bread on my plate. He spooned a small mound of the salad next to it. "You look depressed, Rupert."

"No, maybe a little naïve." I shook my head. "I don't think Steve's CIA."

"He doesn't have to be," said Nikos. "The paper he works for is all propaganda."

"Then why does anyone buy it?"

"They know things before they happen." He winked at me. "It's like tomorrow's news today."

I had trouble sleeping that night. I didn't care what Steve was up to, but his keeping me in the dark seemed ungenerous. Had he found his band of rebels? At some point, I fell asleep. I was having a dream that involved a goat, some dynamite, and a pair of tight shiny pants when I was awakened by the ringing of the phone.

It was a woman.

"*Guten abend*," she said, and, still in German, "I hope I haven't woken you up."

This of course surprised me.

"No, no," I said. I always lied when people woke me up. I wondered who was on the other end of the line.

"This is Elena Nikolaides. Kostas has asked that I call because there is a man here with a number of small pieces," she continued in German. "Some things he thinks are valuable, but there is a plate he needs you to look at. He has sent Nikos over on the motorbike to pick you up."

I waited for Nikos on the sidewalk and enjoyed a cigarette. The light was on in Steve Kelly's room. He must have returned while I'd been asleep. The clack of his typewriter sounding on the street was quietly reassuring. America was awake and in control everywhere.

Nikos pulled up on the motorbike. He closed his eyes hard and then opened them. He had a sort of smile on his face that spoke more of resignation than pleasure. "Get on, Rupert," he said.

"What's going on?" I asked.

"There is a—what do you call it—gravedigger?"

His English was worse in the middle of his sleep hours.

"I think that's probably a grave robber."

"Yes," said Nikos, unimpressed. "Small things. I don't know why my father has to wake you up, but when someone wakes him up, he takes us all with him. My mother. Me. You. Who knows who else he feels he has to share this with?" Nikos gestured with a grimace that made his discomfort clear.

"Did you see the objects?"

"I know nothing about old things," he said.

The grave robber was with Kostas in the study. He was standing in too-short pants, and no socks, his leather shoes caked with mud. He looked balefully at Kostas, who was eyeing a coin while referencing a large and, to all appearances, unhelpful book.

"Rupert, look at his coin," he said.

He handed it to me. "Well," I said, "it's electrum and Greek, but from the region that is now Turkey."

"Genuine?"

I took a closer look. "I think so. Second century A.D. Where did he find it?"

"He says near Epidaurus."

"You don't believe him?"

"Look at him," said Kostas. Kostas said something to the man, and he quickly knelt down and began unfolding a worn wool blanket. There were a few things hidden in its folds. The glory of the find was a small plate in two pieces, figures in black outline on a white ground. I hesitated to pick it up first—to look excited—because I knew there was some bargaining ahead. Instead, I picked up a simple steel comb. There was still a hair in it, long and gray. I showed it to Kostas.

"Maybe fifty years old," I said.

There was a clay lamp, simple, of the kind often found in graves, for use with olive oil. I looked at it but had absolutely no way of dating it. "Fourth century A.D.," I announced.

Then I picked up the pieces of the plate. I held them together. The image was that of a maid and her mistress. The maid carried a water jug and the mistress, hand pointed downward in some generalized imperative gesture, held the maid's gaze. The two looked at each other across the empty field of the white grounding, across the fissure that halved the plate, with a steely intensity. It was this gaze that held the plate whole. I felt a value here, although I wasn't sure if it was just in the beauty of the piece—there was something modern in the simplicity of the lines and the overall effect—or in its hailing from antiquity. I set the pieces down and picked up another coin, another Turkish piece.

"Does he speak English?" I inquired.

"I doubt it," said Kostas. Nikos yawned.

"Can I speak with you in the living room?" I said to Kostas.

Nikos perked up a little. He had been leaning against the back of a chair, but now he looked at me closely. "I could use a cigarette outside, in the air," he said.

Kostas followed me onto the front step. "Well?" he asked.

"All those things have a place and a value, except for the comb," I said.

"Good," said Kostas.

"How much is he asking?"

"Not a whole lot. Maybe five hundred dollars. I'll talk him down."

I lit a cigarette and pondered this. "It's not much."

"What is bothering you, Rupert?"

"Kostas, all those things could be from Epidaurus. The coin is Turkish, but coins are made for easy transportation. And the comb makes me think he *did* dig all this stuff up. But the plate?"

"It looks like a good piece."

"Well, that's just it. Very nice, but what is it doing with this other stuff? And is there more? It seems likely, if he pulled it out of the ground, that he was digging in a previously undisturbed location. Where's the other stuff?"

"He may be hired by someone excavating the site, and this is all he has managed to hide."

"All right." I nodded to myself. "It's just the kind of thing I was looking for. My uncle will love it."

"Is it real?"

"It's beautiful, and for five hundred dollars, who cares?"

Kostas looked at me with a tolerant yet uncomprehending gaze. "So I buy it?"

"Yes," I said. "Yes, you buy it."

"Now what is wrong?"

"That plate. Remember the dealer I spoke with on Pandróssou Street? He knew of some equally impressive pieces that I think were excavated from the same area."

"You think they come from the same place?"

"Or close by, but the other pieces were of a different, more primitive style. This plate is probably Athenian. It looks like something done by the Achilles painter."

"Why?" asked Kostas.

"Well, the depiction of the maid and mistress for one. And the way the women are shown in profile, but their bodies are natural and twist into space in a three-dimensional way. And the white grounding with black."

"Maybe it *is* the Achilles painter," said Kostas.

"If it were the Achilles painter, it would be worth an awful lot. But some things are off."

"Like what?" asked Nikos.

"I think he would have painted this on a *lekythos*." The Achilles painter preferred jugs.

"Maybe it was someone who was his student," said Nikos. "Anything is possible. I don't understand what the problem is."

"All pulled out of the same area at the same time, but differing in style." I thought for a moment. "Am I questioning good fortune?"

"Yes," said Nikos. "Your uncle is getting a classical plate that we can restore very easily. Just be happy."

Kostas paid the man and sent him off into the darkness. We sat on the terrace having a drink. Even Athens was quiet at this hour. The only sounds were the diminishing rumble of a motorcycle and a cat that yowled a couple of times, but had little to say.

"How will you get the plate to my uncle?" I asked.

"I don't want to take any chances," said Kostas. "Tomorrow, I will have the designer from the factory come here. I will get him to make maybe a hundred replicas. I will pack this plate together with all its children—and let my brother know where to find it."

I had solved the problem of finding breakfast in Athens by never rising before noon. Yorgos had me figured out, and by the time I called for my coffee and shaving water, he must have had it waiting; the two jugs took exactly as long to arrive as it did to take the stairs from the first floor.

On Monday, I had showered and put on my trousers and an undershirt and was rather proud of myself for being able to attribute this particular late rising to work rather than drinking. I heard the knock and when I opened the door found Yorgos, the coffee, the hot water, and Steve Kelly all waiting for me.

"Hello," I said.

Yorgos pushed his way in and set the hot water in the bathroom, leaving the coffee on the desk.

"That's an awful lot of coffee for just one person," said Steve.

"Help yourself," I said.

Steve had the morning's paper tucked under his arm and handed it to me. "Thought you might like to know what's going on in the world."

"Like the car bomb?"

"Oh, that," said Steve.

"Did you actually see it?"

"I saw what was left of it." Steve poured some coffee into a glass, leaving the cup for me. "You know that after the war the Greek-Albanian border moved south. There are many Greeks stuck in Albania. Not that long ago, we had a major civil war on our hands. Now, a lot of the Communist sympathizers are contained, but you know how it is."

"No, I don't."

"We'd like to think that any possibility of a Communist take-over had died ten years ago, but you hear things to the contrary."

"Not enough to topple the current government, surely."

"Maybe not, but there are quite a few people who want abso-lute stability. Remember, this is one country profoundly affected by the Truman Doctrine. No one wants to see that aid dry up, and every-thing comes at a price."

I picked up the paper, scanning for Steve's byline.

"Try page four," he said.

I read.

NATO MILITARY LEADERS DISCUSS
BALKAN DEFENSES

ATHENS, June 15—Top military leaders of the North Atlantic Treaty Organization from Greece and Turkey met here today to discuss "current defense problems" in the Balkans. The meet-ing was attended also by Gen. Frederic J. Brown, Commander Allied Land Forces Southeast Europe; Maj. Gen. John F. Seitz, U.S. Chief of Staff Allied Headquarters, Naples; and Maj. Gen. Leuhman, Commander Sixth Allied Tactical Air Force.

I looked at Steve over the top of the paper. "Why is *current defense problems* in quotation marks?"

"Custard's choice of punctuation."

"He's a very creative editor," I said.

Steve smiled cryptically. "Yes, he is."

I had a decent, if limited, understanding of Greek politics. I knew that after World War Two, the United States, under the Truman Doctrine, had flooded certain countries with cash, countries that had dangerous Communist leanings; Greece had been one of these coun-tries. I also knew that the Greek resistance, quite effective in blow-ing up bridges and disrupting German supply routes to North Africa, had leaned toward communism, and during this time, with King

George II and his lackeys known to be in Egypt, the public had become more sympathetic toward their dynamite-wielding countrymen
up in the mountains to the north, who lived, as did the other Greeks,
from day to day with the twin threats of starvation and capture. Together they knew the value and cost of liberty. In 1963, the average
Greek remembered what it had been like to live under the fascism of
Metaxas and was less tolerant of the extreme right than was King Paul,
who considered a right-wing government the most reliable way to
maintain stability and throne. The Americans and English shared this
opinion.

I could have pursued politics with Kelly, but I had just enough time to
run down to Pandróssou Street and talk to the shop owner before Nikos
came to get me at two. My ferry left from Piraeus for Aspros at four in
the afternoon. Kelly had been on his way to the office to see Custard
and was only stopping by for coffee—and to show me his impressive
scar, which was healing rapidly and, thanks to his ruddy complexion
and flaming hair, seemed to blend in with the rest of him. He had
pushed up his bangs with his hand so I could take a better look.

"I keep thinking I must have learned something from this, but
I don't know what it is. Don't travel with so much cash? Avoid
bacchantes?"

"Some things you cannot prevent, Steve," I said, sounding
mature.

"How long are you going to be gone?"

"I'm not sure."

"If you're gone too long, I'll come looking for you."

"I don't have the address of where I'm staying."

"Don't worry about that," said Steve. "Finding you won't be a
problem."

I had been in Greece less than a week, and somehow this seemed
both impossibly long and impossibly short. I could now make the

ten-minute walk to Pandróssou Street without really thinking about where I was going and no longer felt conspicuous, although I'm sure that I was. I headed straight for the antiques dealer. By the time I reached the store, it was just after one and the store was closed. I thought he might have been at his siesta, but the previous time I'd visited had also been around one. I remembered this because Nikos and I had ordered lunch at noon and he had joked that this was my effect on him because no real Greek ate lunch that early.

But now the shop was deserted. I put my face to the window and detected no movement inside and although I knew it was un-likely that the man would leave the more valuable stuff lying around in view of the street, I still scanned the dusty shelves and cluttered tables for some pottery of value. When I finally stood back from the window, I saw a cobbler watching me. He sat on a little stool ham-mering on a sandal, and when he saw I'd noticed him he applied himself to his work, tapping and tapping, his mouth full of tacks. I crossed the street and watched more closely. I wondered if he spoke English.

"Is this entertaining for you, my making this shoe?" the man said.

"No," I replied. "Was my looking in that window entertaining for you?"

The man emptied the remaining tacks from the side of his mouth and regarded me calmly. "That store in general has much going on. I sit here all day. Occasionally girls come and buy all kinds of sandals. They buy them for the whole family. Sandals pack flat and they're cheap. But when nothing is happening, I watch that store."

I looked at the sandals that were hanging on the door, just to the left of the shop's entrance. I picked up a large pair and looked at them.

"Do you think these would fit me?" I asked.

"No," the man said. He got up from his stool and went into the shop. I followed him. "These should fit," he said, handing me a pair of very plain sandals: simple crossing straps on a wide flat leather sole. "Long and skinny for your long and skinny American foot."

"You forgot white," I said, looking at the sandals.

"What do you mean?"

"My long and skinny and incredibly *white* American foot. I'm heading to the islands today, and I think it's been close to four years since I exposed my feet to the sunshine."

The man smiled and I saw that, despite his diminutive stature, he had huge teeth. In fact, his whole mouth was enormous, but covered up by the drooping wings of his mustache. "Do you want those?" he said, pointing to the sandals.

"I think I do," I said. "But I really would like to know if you saw anything of interest happening at the antiques store today."

The man nodded, thinking, as he wrapped up my sandals in a piece of paper and tied it with string. "He is usually open now, but late last night someone was banging on his door."

"He lives there?" I asked.

"Over the store, like me, over this store."

I looked to the back of the shop and noticed a narrow staircase leading upward. I also realized that the smell of frying onions and sausage, something I'd attributed to a nearby restaurant, was coming from upstairs.

"How late last night?" I asked.

"I don't know. Late. I was asleep, but I looked from my bed out the window and saw him open the door. There was this man banging. He had some things, heavy, tied in a big cloth."

"Were his pants short?"

"Who, the man with the big cloth?"

"Yes."

"I think so, but that does not mean much, not here where so many people don't have money, not like in America."

"We rich Americans make a point of wearing very long pants," I said, "so long they drag behind us and make us trip."

The man laughed again, loud. I saw his mustache part and his enormous teeth. "Yes," he said. "The man had short pants, and today the shop owner does not open his store. There must be some connection."

"I wonder what it is," I said.

I paid for my sandals and wished the man a pleasant day.

"Enjoy the islands," said the man. "Do not burn your feet."

By the time I'd stopped at the bakery for a cheese pie and made the walk from Monastiráki nearly all the way to Syntagma, I had left myself ten minutes to pack. Since I was taking nearly everything, it wasn't difficult. It wasn't like living in New York with my eleven linen-blend sweaters, my evening jackets, five pairs of seersucker pants. Packing here was easy. The clothes from the tailor had been delivered to the hotel, wrapped neatly in brown paper, and the package went straight into the suitcase. I packed my book on coins but left the others; as Nikos was planning to go back and forth from Aspros to Athens, he could always bring them to me. I opened the package with the sandals and tried them on. They fit well. I wasn't used to seeing my feet in sandals and they looked very pale. I realized, for the first time, that my toenails seemed to have been placed on my toes at angles. I wrapped my wingtips in the paper and put them in the suitcase too. I cleared off the little counter by the bathroom sink and it filled my shaving kit.

It was time to close everything up. I looked out the window and saw the taxi waiting outside the hotel. I wondered how long it had been there, but then the driver honked loudly and Nikos leaned out the window. I waved. I realized I was excited, like a schoolboy off to camp.

I barely had enough time to get in the taxi next to Nikos and shut the door before we sped off to Piraeus. Nikos had his address book open on his leg and was entering a number from a scrap of paper. He did this with great attention; to look at his face one would think he were performing surgery. He finished, put the cap back on his pen, and looked over at me.

"What has happened to your feet?" he said.

"It's my new look," I replied. "Sandals."

"You look like John the Baptist," he said.

"He's my fashion icon."

Nikos laughed and shrugged. "You look like a tourist."

We did well for time until we got to Piraeus. I could not tell the sidewalk from the street, because every inch was covered with people and vehicles in a generalized, indistinct way. An enormous ferry had come in from Crete, and everyone—grandmas, donkeys, old men wearing vests, young men carrying caged birds, children in strollers or strolling, young women—was in the road and in the path of our taxi. There was some aggressive horn honking, and a number of expletives delivered by the driver and seconded by Nikos. Nikos finally said, "It would be better if we walked. It's maybe two hundred meters that way." We left the taxi and jumped into the stew.

The ferry office was crowded with backpackers who didn't understand their dimensions, or didn't care, and insisted on turning one way and then the other. I was pressed up against the wall, but I watched Nikos walk right up to the counter, past all of them. His Greek and his good looks were enough to make the young woman listen, and I watched him get our tickets with a certain amount of pride in privilege. I was not fond of the revolving backpackers, who seemed sanctimonious and negligent with their personal hygiene. The first of these was conjecture, but the second amply proven.

Nikos returned, bearing the tickets.

"I hope you got first class," I said.

"Of course," Nikos replied.

The ferry, the *Aphrodite*, was relatively new. We had about twenty minutes before it left. We had been doing very well for time until we'd been forced to abandon our taxi, and now it seemed that we were in a cycle of hurry like madmen, wait patiently. We almost ran to the ferry terminal, pushed our way on board with everyone else, and were busily trying to stow our luggage when a man in uniform—very naval in appearance—approached Nikos and with a weary voice began to explain something to him. I watched, hoping for some miracle of comprehension, when the skipper, if that's what he was, fixed his sad eyes on me and said, "No."

"There is a problem with the engine," said Nikos. "We will be here forty-five minutes."

"Oh, is that all?" I said. "Let's go have a cigarette."

Nikos nodded and we made our way to the deck. The weather had cooled off a bit and the temperature was pleasant. The wind whipped my hair into my eyes.

"Does the sea make you sick?" asked Nikos.

"No," I replied.

"Well, on a day like this, it will make everyone else sick," he said.

I looked at the waves. The water was a bit choppy. "It doesn't look that bad."

"Not here, but wait until we get out farther. Then the fun begins." He smiled at me and put his hand on my shoulder. He then mimed some fairly large waves, shaping them out of the air. "The Cyclades is notorious for this, sometimes from nowhere. Poseidon gets mad."

I wanted to get going, eager for it, the sea god's anger, the white-capped waves, the salt-scrubbed rocks. I watched the travelers navigating the port below, and then a couple, two young women, one dark and one fair, pulled themselves out of the crowd.

"Look, Nikos," I said, "it's Sue and Helen."

Nikos looked down at them. "Helen," he said, with conviction. "What time is it?"

"I think you have a half hour until we leave."

"Come," he said. "We'll take them for coffee."

"I'd rather wait for you here. Though if you *really* want me to come, I will."

"All right," Nikos said. He was out of cigarettes, so I gave him a couple of mine and waved him off. I saw him disembark and then call to Sue and Helen, the little cluster of conviviality the three of them made, and they all wandered off.

Nikos must have been gone only ten minutes when I heard the sound of the engine roar into life. At first I thought they must be warming it up or checking it; after all, the delay had been due to engine trouble. But then I felt a shudder of motion. Nikos was nowhere in sight. I rushed inside and pushed my way down the stairs, past the tide of people coming upward. I found the sad-faced skipper, who was taking the last of the tickets.

"Excuse me," I said, "but is the boat leaving?"

"Yes." He looked at me slightly askance. After all, boats were meant to leave.

"But my friend went ashore. You said it would take forty-five minutes to fix the engine, and no more than twenty minutes have passed since then."

The man regarded his watch. "Yes."

"My friend is missing the boat."

The man looked at me sympathetically and nodded. "Yes."

"Yes, what?"

"Yes, your friend is missing the boat." He patted me on the shoulder kindly and returned his attention to the tickets he'd collected. I rushed back upstairs and onto the deck. I still felt that I could get Nikos onto the boat somehow, that if I saw him it would make the difference. But by the time Nikos appeared, he was very small, and I only recognized him because no one else had reason to stand at that particular edge of Greece for quite so long.

I was very upset at losing Nikos. I supposed things like this happened all the time. My uncle had warned me about the ferries. He'd said, "Mind the ferries," but hadn't explained what I should do to counter their inconstancy. I hadn't even brought any good reading material with me. At an English bookstore on Venizelos Street, I'd picked up a couple of novels by Lawrence Durrell, even though one was about Rhodes and the other about Corfu and had nothing to do with the Cyclades, but I'd left them on my bedside table. I stayed outside, watching the ocean. At one point, a woman came on deck and leaned on the railing a short distance away. I considered starting a conversation—she was wearing khaki pants and a white shirt with

some sort of scarf and didn't look Greek—but I missed the moment
and she went back inside.

I went in too and wandered around first class. Someone had
abandoned a newspaper, the *Guardian*, and I took a seat by a window and read the whole thing, even an in-depth report on a cricket
test where the Brits had taken on and been beaten by the South
Africans. Exhausted, I suppose, by that riveting account, I fell asleep.
When I woke up, two hours had passed and I was ready for a drink. I
headed for the bar. Something about the seas—I could see quite a
few people outside clutching the railing, and it wasn't for the view—
made me decide to get a brandy. There was something healing about
it, something almost temperate.

The brandy appeared in a regular tumbler with some ice. I preferred tumblers to snifters. Snifters always made me feel self-conscious
and reminded me of Kiplinger Sand, someone I went to college with.
Kiplinger insisted on having people over to his room for drinks. He'd
serve outrageously expensive brandies, always in snifters the size of
goldfish bowls. I went for the drinks, not that I was wild about brandy,
but he always had plenty of it and was very generous. He liked me
because I knew girls at Barnard and was invited to everything. Kiplinger
had not been blessed with good looks. He had the long ugly teeth of
the American aristocracy and sunken cheeks, rather like a cadaver. I
was shocked when I met his mother, who looked exactly the same
but was somehow almost attractive. Kiplinger had spent the spring
break of his junior year in California, and when he returned, the
brandy was gone; he had taken to wearing black turtlenecks and
smoking marijuana, with which he was equally generous, providing
I took him to parties.

I had run into Kiplinger at a divey Irish bar in Chelsea shortly
before I'd left for Greece. I'd stopped in for a drink after appraising
an armoire up the street. Kiplinger was with an extremely attractive
and very young woman, and both of them were drunk.

"Still selling furniture, Rupert?" he asked.

Kiplinger was now making movies. He'd lost the black turtleneck and was in an absurd salmon-colored jacket and no tie, which

exposed the protruding shelf of his collarbone. He was drinking some narcotic Argentenian liquid that was all the rage on the West Coast. He treated me to some of it, and the effect was a floating numbness quickly followed by the sensation that someone was stabbing my eye with an icicle.

"What are you doing here?" I asked, gesturing at the bar, which really catered to old men.

"This is the only place where I can get this," he said, raising the pleasing poison. At the time I hadn't questioned why that particular bar would serve this stuff, but now it struck me as absurd.

I was still thinking about Kiplinger, wondering what on earth his films were like, when the woman in khaki pants appeared beside me at the bar. She smiled at me and I smiled back.

"Hard to figure out what to do when you've forgotten your book," I said.

"Reading on a boat makes me feel queasy," she replied.

"I'd like to get your drink," I said. "What are you having?"

"Water," she said wryly. She revealed to me a fistful of pills, impressive and varied.

"I suppose you don't need a drink, not when you've got all that."

She was about ten years older than I was, attractive and seemingly intelligent, with a sharp nose and lively eyes, like a dark-haired Janet Leigh. She looked at me with frank suspicion. "Yes, I suppose I've got everything covered."

"Where are you going?" I asked. I was good at this, wearing women down.

"Aspros," she said.

"There's a coincidence. I'm going there too."

"Is it really a coincidence?" she said. She smiled disarmingly. "After all, that's where the boat is taking us."

"Isn't it also going to Mílos?"

"Yes," she conceded. "But what is there in Mílos? The Venus is at the Louvre."

I was going to ask her what there was in Aspros, but the bartender was waiting. "Glass of water for the lady," I said.

She took the glass but hung onto her pills. I don't suppose she
wanted to drink them down in front of me. "Thank you," she said.

"I hope I run into you in Aspros, " I said.

"It will be impossible not to." Another smile and she walked off.

Contrary to what she'd said, there were a couple of things worth
seeing in Mílos; I'd thought about stopping there. Mílos had a few
archaeological sites of some value and an interesting set of catacombs.
I threw back my brandy and waved at the bartender, who saw me but
was having some sort of baffling encounter with a group of French
tourists. I considered the wisdom of drinking at my usual pace. Maybe
this was a good time to cut back. I did have a job to do, but there was
so much luck involved in finding artifacts that it was hard to convince myself that being sober was worth much. After all, even the
Venus de Milo had not been excavated but rather unearthed in the
process of plowing a field. The date for that was 1820, and the reason the statue had ended up in the Louvre was that it was first claimed
by a French naval officer who witnessed its discovery. I wondered what
the French naval officer was doing in the field, and then what he was
doing on Mílos.

The bartender, having finally liberated himself, was pouring
brandy into my glass. "Do you know why the French were on Mílos
in 1820?" I asked him.

The bartender shrugged his shoulders and looked down the bar.
"Why do they go there now?"

I finished my drink and headed to the bathroom. I was just wash-
ing my hands when I heard a static bellowing over the PA system.
This was accompanied by the sounding of the horn and some odd
grinding of gears. I realized we were coming into the harbor. On the
ferry, numerous people were gathering their things, pushing their way
to the luggage rack. I checked my watch. We'd been on the ferry for
just over four hours.

There was a fierce struggle for the luggage and I was very worried that I wouldn't make it off the boat. As I was trying to get Nikos's

suitcase, a man reached over my head, and for a few tense moments I found myself surrounded by his armpit. When that was over, I pushed my way back onto the deck. I wondered what Nikos had in his suitcase. It felt like it was full of rocks. After all this rushing, pushing, and cursing, I was surprised to see that we were still some distance from shore. I found my skipper, who was regarding the distant twinkle of lights with a deep melancholy.

"Why are we stopping here, when the port is way over there?"

"The harbor is too shallow for this boat," he replied.

I wasted a minute waiting for him to explain further. "How do I get ashore?"

He nodded at me, looked down at the two suitcases, picked mine up, and walked quickly to the other side of the ship. Then, cavalierly and in his customary silence, he tossed my suitcase over the side. I knew better than to shout at him. I had understood nothing for so long that constant bewilderment was beginning to feel almost normal. I rushed to look over the side, and, sure enough, there was a smaller boat, filling up with luggage and passengers. A young man was stowing my luggage beside the other cases.

There was a rope ladder dangling down the side of the ferry. An old woman had reached the bottom of the ladder and was trying to figure out how to make the final transition from the ferry to the smaller boat, which rocked quite violently in the chop. There were a few suggestions here and there, and finally two sturdy men stood up and with their hands raised and readied, like soccer goalies, waited for her to abandon the final rung of the ladder. This she did, they caught her, and a small cheer rose up. Then someone said something, and all eyes turned to me. At this point I was quite happy to stay on the ferry. The two sturdy men had stood up again and were readied. The rope ladder didn't fill me with confidence and the woman, although old, was small and light. I considered jumping, but instead dropped Nikos's suitcase—it was too heavy to carry down the ladder— and descended quickly, trying not to think. My sandals were slippery, and a couple of times my feet shot out from beneath me. It was with some relief that I reached the boat. I made my way to the rear after

stepping on a lot of feet and a little boy stood up to give me his seat.
After some rapid-fire suggestions on the part of his mother, who was
holding a birdcage in her lap, he sat cautiously on my knee.

The boat ride was short, too short, and I was not yet ready to abandon our noncommittal floating, neither here nor there, when we
reached the pier. I clambered out, struggling with Nikos's suitcase and
my own, and contemplated the open harbor, the gentle rise of buildings, and the approach of night. There was no one to meet me and
even if someone had been there, I wouldn't have recognized him. I
was sufficiently obvious in my solitude, my vacant gazing, to let someone know that I was indeed the stranger they were supposed to meet
up with, but soon the crowd thinned and I gave up. Maybe Nikos
was supposed to contact someone when we arrived. I was hungry,
ready for a drink, ready for a shower. Nikos had told me that I would
be the guest of his cousin Neftali at her vacation home, which was
on the path from Stavri to somewhere else, but of course I'd forgotten the name of the second town and wasn't all that sure of the first.
Neftali spent the summer going back and forth from Aspros to
Mýkonos, where her husband came from, but she was mostly on
Aspros and managed the house. And there was a cleaning lady, a cook
who showed up for lunch, and a girl from the village to do the laundry. The caretaker lived two houses away and was married to the
cleaning lady, or something like that, but Nikos had told me all this
over drinks on the evening I'd come back from Delphi, and although
I'd put on a good show, I'd been overwhelmed by my "abstract fu-
ries," and then by the combination of whiskey and wine. I only remembered a few things. Neftali was American-educated—her father,
Kostas's brother, had moved to New York when Neftali was eighteen—
so she had many American friends, some of whom were staying at the
house. One was in publishing, traveling with another man. And there
was an artist with his wife. The artist was someone Nikos thought I
would recognize, but he could only remember his first name, Jack. He
was married to an Amanda, and the two fought a lot. I tried to come

up with some contemporary artists, but I didn't deal with anything contemporary and had never seen a piece more recent than a Miró pencil drawing from the late thirties come through the gallery doors.

I decided to eat at the second of the two restaurants by the harbor. By the time I'd settled in, lit my cigarette, and arranged my suitcases, it was almost ten. I decided to get a hotel and deal with finding the house and Neftali in the morning. A woman came out to take my order and I asked for some red wine and the stuffed eggplant.

"Do you know where I could get a room?" I asked.

"Room," she repeated.

"Hotel," I tried.

"Hotel!" she said. "*Né, né. Aspete moment.*"

This sounded promising. I didn't really care where I stayed. The food came out quickly and, since I was starving, I applied myself to it. I wondered about my lady of the khaki pants. Where had she gone? Wasn't this a small island? There were only two restaurants and the other was right beside this one, marked off only by a different choice of tablecloth. She wasn't there either. What did it matter? She hadn't responded favorably to my offer of a drink, and that's probably why I was still thinking of her.

When I was done with my dinner, the woman came to clear my plates, accompanied by a teenage boy. He picked up the suitcases and said, "*Zimmer.*"

I insisted on carrying Nikos's suitcase, because it helped justify my anger at having been abandoned. I knew it was petty. Of course he should have been running after Helen. Why should it bother me to be alone on this strange island dragging Nikos's eighty-pound suitcase down a twisting alleyway of whitewashed buildings where, no doubt, this innocent-looking youth with the big cross dangling around his neck would assault me with a knife and take all my money? I transferred the suitcase to my left hand, but when the boy began heading up a set of narrow stairs, I had to hoist it in my arms and embrace it.

After ascending for maybe twenty steps, some wide, some steep, the young man put down my suitcase and said "*Camera.*" He unlocked the front door and gestured for me to enter.

I followed him down a narrow corridor to my room. I could hear someone snoring in the dark, presumably in another room, and this punctuated the silence. The boy set my suitcase inside the door, opened the shutters, and disappeared, closing the door behind him. I put Nikos's suitcase down and went to look out the window. There was a little cascade of lights down to the harbor and then the infinite darkness of the night ocean. I could hear waves knocking some wooden boats together on the pier and somewhere, far away but carried by the breeze, drunk and without accompaniment, a man was singing a traditional Greek song. I kicked off my shoes and took off my clothes. The bed was hard, like a small sack of flour, and I was wondering how one was supposed to sleep on such a thing when, exhausted, I passed out.

The next thing I knew, someone was knocking on the door and a young man's voice called me to breakfast. I dressed quickly without bathing. I could already feel the heat slowly building and thought about going for a swim before I continued my search for Neftali and the others. Maybe Nikos had arrived. There was some thick coffee, fresh bread, butter, jam, a boiled egg, and a piece of yellow cheese. I was drinking my coffee when the young man came out of the kitchen with a fatty brown sausage. He had one for me and one for the couple who sat at the other table, dressed for hiking. They wore stout ugly shoes and knee socks. The man was done eating, he seemed like someone who ate in a quick, militaristic fashion, and was reading aloud from a bright blue Fodor's guide.

"This is where the infant Perseus came to land in a chest, with his mother Danaë, who later married the island's king, Polydectus; and it is here that, when he came to manhood, he petrified the ruthless king with the head of the gorgon Medusa." He set down the book and nodded, satisfied, at his wife. Then he looked over at me politely and said, "Good morning."

"Hello," I said, "Good morning to you both."

"Are you traveling alone?" the man inquired. He was English.

"I have some people I'm meeting, whom I hope to find soon." I smiled and began to spread jam on my bread. "Funny. I was listening to you read, about Danaë and Perseus, and I thought that island was Sérifos."

"It is," the man said.

"Are you going to Sérifos?" I asked.

The man and his wife exchanged a quick look. "This is Sérifos," the man replied.

I put a piece of bread in my mouth and chewed.

"Where did you think you were?" he asked.

"I was under the impression that I was on Aspros, and am now wondering why I thought that." I smiled abruptly. A part of me blamed this man for my landing on the wrong island, and I was having a hard time remaining pleasant.

"Do you need to be on Aspros?" asked the man.

I nodded.

"There's the *Diana* today, that goes to Mílos, and I think a boat from there goes to Aspros sometime this afternoon."

"He's very good with schedules," his wife explained. "We were just on Mílos."

"Would you know what time the *Diana* is arriving today?" I asked.

"I'd say in about fifteen minutes, maybe twenty."

I noticed he was looking over my shoulder out the window and turned quickly. Sure enough, there was a ferry steaming into the harbor.

By the time I reached Mílos it was 2 P.M. and I had fifteen minutes to make my connection. It occurred to me that I might be making good time, but then I remembered that I was a day late. The ferry from Mílos to Aspros was only a couple of hours but I'd been in motion for almost a day, managing to circle my destination without actually getting there, and my patience was nearly gone.

I thought of Xerxes flogging the Hellespont. He was on his way from Persia to conquer Greece when he discovered that his bridges, necessary for getting his troops from Asia to Europe, had collapsed. Xerxes' first move was to decapitate his engineers. His second was to submit the channel to a brutal lashing. The third was to toss in a set of shackles specifically cast for this purpose. When I'd read this in Herodotus as an undergraduate, it had been explained to me that this image of the deranged Persian emperor in the throes of hubris was what made the Greeks embrace reason. This same fear of chaos had led an artist to reduce a figure to its basic geometric elements. This made sense in the context of the classroom. But from where I stood, deck, Aegean, at sea again, I was beginning to feel the need to embrace the chaos. Flogging the water seemed reasonable. I thought about the archaic sculptor who had responded to the same anxiety, a generalized anxiety of spirit, by representing a horse as a series of triangles.

7

Aspros was a beautiful place. I could tell that at a distance, from the otherworldly sparkle coming off the mountains, the hush that fell over the people on deck as we drew closer. Fish sped through the water at the side of the ship like spits of silver, and I thought I could smell jasmine—clouds of it—coming off the land. I was drugged for a moment, dizzy with anticipation, but there was a bitter taste at the back of my throat. I felt someone watching me and turned quickly, but no one was there, only a mother fixing the collar of her son's shirt, a little boy who looked straight into my eyes and then down at the tops of his shoes. I kept looking at him, until I felt that my looking—his mother was furtively watching me—was unwelcome. The engines groaned like a beast awakening, and then, with a great cough of oily smoke, they were quiet. I lined up with the other passengers, carrying the two suitcases. I made the descent by rope ladder into the smaller boat and for one moment had the desire to let go, to fall into the water and drown.

As we were transported to shore by the smaller boat, I saw a familiar figure—Nikos—his arms folded in front of him, his face dark with concern. I wondered what was bothering him because I knew he was looking for me and was immediately cheered. I saw him pick my face out of the group as we approached, and there was a momentary flash of joy, but this was followed with something less indulgent.

"Rupert!" he shouted at me from the pier. "Rupert, what have you been doing?"

I ignored the question. I was struggling with his suitcase, struggling with mine. He helped me get the cases out of the boat.

"Aspros is lovely," I said.

"I am sick with worry," he said.

"How are Helen and Sue? I hope you gave them my best."

Nikos regarded me and smiled. "They are in the best of health."

"Your suitcase," I said. "I can carry mine." I began walking down the pier.

"Where were you, Rupert?"

"Sérifos."

"Why did you get off there?"

"I thought it was Aspros. I wasn't really paying attention."

"I didn't know what had happened to you. I thought maybe you got off again in Piraeus and were waiting for me for the next boat, but Olivia says she thought she saw you on the ferry." He switched his suitcase to his left hand. "But then you disappeared."

"Who's Olivia?"

"My friend." Nikos shrugged. "Neftali's friend, really."

"How did she know it was me?"

"This thing," he said. He poked my chin with his forefinger. "She said you offered to buy her a drink."

"So that's Olivia," I said. "Aspros *is* small." I wondered how Nikos had described me. "How did you get here so fast?"

"After the boat left, I found another for Páros and then I hired a *kaïka*. I was here last night."

"Well, there was nothing to worry about. I can take care of myself," I said.

"Rupert," he said, with appalling sincerity, "you got off on the wrong island."

I looked up the street, then back down. This street, at least, looked much like Sérifos. "What are we waiting for?"

"The taxi. He'll take us." Nikos gestured up the mountain. A twisting path of shallow steps marked the ascent.

"He's going to drive up the steps?"

"Yes. He has one of those Russian jeeps."

"Couldn't we stop and have a drink here?"

"Everyone is waiting for you," said Nikos. "They are not eating their lunch."

"But what if I hadn't been on that boat?"

"I had a feeling," said Nikos. He pinched my cheek.

The Russian jeep, made for hardship, bounced up the steps. The road was made for donkeys, and on the way we passed two of them. First there was a young man on a gray donkey, bouncing along, and then an older man dressed in similar clothes on a slower heavier animal. It was as if I were driving in hyper-time, and that the older man was the younger a few years down the line. I looked back at the port, down at the enchanted harbor, where a few boats bobbed by the pier. The harbor itself protected a shallow lagoon and the water there, underlit by white sand, was an unreal turquoise. Children swam and made sand castles, and a few were wading through the shallows with nets.

We turned a corner and the whole scene disappeared, curtained by the mountain. Now there were steep fields, olive terraces, sheer rocky drops with dirt clinging, and clinging in the dirt everything grew: grapes, figs, peaches, showy bougainvillea, and deadly oleander. We made the hairpin turns, bouncing upward, and Nikos said something to the driver. I guessed it concerned the baggage, because Nikos kept indicating our suitcases with a flat-palmed open hand, a gesture that I used to invite women onto the dance floor. There were a number of Venetian-style dovecotes, host to many doves. A black goat with a bell around its neck appeared at the side of the road, watching us with yellow eyes as we passed. A few dirt roads led off the main thoroughfare, but one sensed, in the tin-roofed shepherd huts and fenced-off caves, that people lived as they had for many years and probably didn't venture into town all that much.

"This is Stavri," said Nikos. We drove across a narrow bridge and the driver pulled over. The town square was not much of a town square in the Italian sense. There was no piazza, although there was a small park with a few trees and some dusty lawn, and in this was a cannon and a small pyramid of cannonballs, a memorial to some forgotten or remembered war.

"We get out here," said Nikos. "He's going to bring the bags. There's a back road, but we should walk."

I got down from the jeep and looked around. There was a restaurant with a grill, a bakery, and a pharmacy, where Nikos stopped. "The one pharmacy," he said. "If you need anything, maybe you should get it now." There was also a post office, a bank, and a kiosk. I bought some cigarettes and a package of gum.

"How far is the walk?" I asked.

"Not far, and straight, but people get lost."

"Is that a definite?"

Nikos shrugged. "Clive got lost the other night, but maybe he was lying."

"Who is Clive?" I asked. Nikos took a path to the left, and we began climbing the steps.

"Clive is young, in his twenties. He's traveling with Nathan Hoffman."

"Why does that name sound familiar?"

Nikos shrugged. "He's from New York, a publisher. He's rich. He and Clive are—how do you say . . . . ?" He raised his eyebrows and smiled with significance.

"I don't think you do," I replied.

Nikos laughed. "They were fighting last night. I think when Clive gets drunk and can't find his way home, that maybe he doesn't want to go home."

"Who else is in the house?"

"Jack is the artist I told you about in Athens." Nikos looked to see if I remembered, and I did. "Jack Weldon. Do you know him?"

"The name sounds familiar, but I can't think of what he paints."

"He's a sculptor," said Nikos. He looked at me with significance and added, "He's here with his wife."

"And what does she do?"

Nikos started laughing in a slightly uncomfortable way. "Amanda
Weldon. She's magnificent." He said this in a very detached way. He
was not emotionally involved, and the word *magnificent* might as easily
have referred to a car.

"And they're all friends of Neftali's from New York?"

Nikos nodded. "Nathan is one of her best friends."

"And what about everyone else?"

"Clive is Clive. He's not from New York. I don't know if he has
any money, but he has that American way that lets you know that,
somewhere, someone was rich."

"You don't like him?"

"That is not what I said," said Nikos. "He makes me laugh, but
he's very loud. When Clive is around, everyone is just watching
Clive."

"Who is the woman I met on the ferry?" I asked.

"Olivia? She lives in London."

"Is she married?"

"Widowed, I think twice." Nikos laughed. "Stay away."

"And that's everyone?"

Nikos thought a bit. He stopped and leaned over a stone wall
where a peach tree was dropping its fruit. He picked a peach and
handed it to me. "These people have been together for a week, and
if they are together, just them, much longer I think they will start
killing each other. When I got here last night, I was a hero. No one
wanted to talk to the others, just to me. 'Nikos, where is that jacket
made?' 'How remarkable to think of getting the laika in Páros. Tell
us again how you did it?'"

"And you and Amanda?" I said.

Nikos raised his finger to his mouth and looked around, hands
opening at his sides in mock alarm. "It is stupid of me. Amanda is
very beautiful, but this Jack is like a crazy man. He goes and drinks
with the fishermen, this one man who is also crazy—an Aspros man
named Thanasi who makes pots—he says they are both artists, but
this guy has only a few teeth and no shoes. Jack brings him back to

the house, yelling something about Thanasi being the only real man. It was funny, because Nathan and Clive like boys, and they started laughing, and maybe he meant to insult me, but I just hid behind Neftali, like I did when we were children. He challenged us to fight Thanasi, but no one wanted to fight Thanasi, and Thanasi didn't want to fight."

"What time was this?"

"I don't know. Three o'clock in the morning?"

"You were all up?"

"Only Neftali and Olivia had gone to bed. I was very happy that he wanted me to fight Thanasi, because when he started screaming outside, I was still with Amanda."

I started laughing. All this bad behavior was making me inordinately happy. A donkey started bellowing somewhere, and when it stopped I realized there was music in the air.

I listened for a moment and then said, "Is that *I Pagliacci*?"

"Yes," said Nikos. "It is coming from the house."

"Caruso?"

Nikos fixed me with a look. "You care about this?"

I shook my head.

"We are nearly there," Nikos added.

The path had flattened and was wider. Now the houses were bigger, Venetian style, not the quaint white cubes of traditional Cycladic architecture. Nikos stopped at a house fronted by a tall whitewashed wall. The music was louder here, and I heard someone swearing, and another person laugh. The gate was iron, solid and painted—freshly—in a deep green.

Nikos looked over at me, straightened my collar, and brushed off my shirt. "Are you ready?"

"No," I said.

He pushed on the gate, which swung inward.

The music was loud and no one noticed us at first. The house was perfectly symmetrical, with wide steps leading up to an enormous wooden door. People were standing in the yard to the left, in the shade of an almond tree, mostly clustered around a small table.

A young man with longish blond hair stood off to the side. He was wearing white pants and a white shirt, unbuttoned too low. He was smoking a hand-rolled cigarette. "Just let the Caruso finish," he said. This had to be Clive. "Honestly, Amanda, f I have to listen to *Lakmé* one more time, I'll kill myself."

"I like *Lakmé*," said a voice, one that I recognized. It was Olivia. She was seated in a lawn chair off to the side wearing a straw hat, the kind used by donkey drivers, and a pair of large sunglasses.

"That's because you're a lesbian," said Clive.

Nikos said nothing but went to his suitcase, which had been delivered and was standing next to mine, just inside the gate.

"Last night you called me the Black Widow," Olivia said, laughing. "Which is it?"

"You kill your husbands because you're a lesbian," said Clive.

A man whom I guessed—correctly—to be Nathan stepped out from behind the table. Seeing us, his face lit up. "Nikos is back, and he's brought Robert."

"Rupert, actually," I said. I walked over quickly and extended my hand.

Nathan shook it. "I am Nathan, and I'm delighted to meet you. I think I know your wife."

"Ex-wife," I said. "That's why I recognized your name. You do that fund-raising thing. Musical instruments for the underprivileged."

"I'm Clive," said Clive.

I shook his hand.

"I'm glad you're here," he added. "We need some fresh blood."

"I think the term is new blood," said Olivia. She got up from her chair. "I'm ready for that drink."

"What drink?" I said, although I'd anticipated the joke.

"The one you offered me on the boat. What was it, a brandy?"

A woman who must have been Amanda Weldon was standing over Nikos, who had opened his suitcase and was rifling through it on the lawn. She was very tall, nearly six feet in her flat sandals, and was wearing cropped pants. Her hair was a disheveled blond mess. She looked Amazonian. She was standing just in front of the suitcase, kind of hovering over Nikos in a way that looked both threatening and possessive. I looked over at Clive and he raised his eyebrows.

"Did you find what you're looking for, Nikos?" he said.

"Yes," said Nikos. "And I think they all made it in one piece."

Apparently what I had been carrying all over the Cyclades was Nikos's record collection—or, more specifically, Kostas's collection of Victrola disks from the thirties and forties. The object of everyone's attention was a portable Victrola, an old one, with a big horn-shaped speaker and a hand crank. Clive had found it under his bed, along with about ten records, mostly opera, and for the last four days the group had been occupied by a constant bickering over who got to listen to what. Neftali had sent word to Nikos that more records were needed, and he had complied.

"I wondered why your suitcase was so heavy," I said.

"Why didn't you open it? It wasn't locked," he replied.

I had never considered opening Nikos's suitcase and I realized this was one of our cultural differences. The Caruso ended then, and Clive went to lift the arm.

"Don't touch that," said Nathan. "You've scratched nearly all of them."

Clive lifted his hands and stepped back. From what Nikos had told me of these two, I had expected a different dynamic. I'd thought Nathan would be overweight or bald and that Clive would be his opportunistic boy-man, but it didn't seem that way. Nathan was the better looking of the two, although he must have been close to fifty. His nose divided his face like a knife and his brow crossed it, making a T. He really did have chiseled features and classic proportions. I wanted to go at his face with a compass. His hair was black shot through with gray; thick, it seemed to stand straight up naturally but was forced along a perfect line of part.

"Is everything all right, Robert?" he asked.

"Rupert, Rupert," I said. "Yes."

Nathan smiled, and I was treated to his perfectly square teeth.

"Well, what have you got?" asked Clive.

Nikos was holding about five of the dozen or so records. "Bix Beiderbecke, and this one I don't know." He handed the record to Clive.

"Oh my god," said Clive. "It's Al Jolson."

Clive took it quickly to the Victrola and put it on the turntable. He invited Nathan to set the needle down, and Nathan did. After the initial crackle and hiss of the Victrola warm up, the garden filled with Jolson's warbling, pitiful yowl. The song was "Carry Me Back to Old Virginny," to which Clive, apparently being from Virginia, knew every word.

"Carry me back to old Virginny," he sang in a high-volume whimper, "that's where the cotton and the corn and taters grow. . . ."

I looked over at Nathan and he was laughing. Nikos was speaking to Amanda in a rather stiff, overly polite way.

"Olivia," I said, "I need a drink."

"I was about to go in and make some martinis. And you should meet Neftali. She's been worried about you." I picked up my suitcase and followed Olivia up the steps to the front door. She pushed the door open and it swung inward, silently. Inside the house it was dark and still. Clive's awful singing and a low, dirty laugh that had to be Amanda's, seemed instantly far away. Down the corridor, I heard two women conversing in Greek and the sizzle of something cooked at a high heat.

"Neftali." called Olivia. "Rupert is here to meet you."

Neftali appeared in the doorway of the kitchen. She was wearing wide-legged white pants and a fitted sailor-style shirt. Neftali was not a small woman, but she was beautiful and she knew it. Her hair was pulled back tightly off her face and she had a thick fuchsia lipstick on. "There he is, the one Nikos loves so much."

She came up to me and grabbed my upper arms and squeezed. Then she kissed both my cheeks. "Come," she said. I followed her into the kitchen. She was peeling some charred eggplants while an older woman, probably the wife of the caretaker, tended to something frying in a pan. Neftali looked at me purposefully. "You have to talk to Nikos," she said, in an anxious whisper. "He must leave Amanda alone. Jack will kill him."

"Where is Jack?" I asked.

"He's still asleep."

I nodded. "Why don't you talk to Amanda?" I asked.

"I don't know her," said Neftali.

"So it's Jack who's your friend?"

"He's a genius," she said, as if to explain his presence and the possibility that she didn't like him. "They were supposed to return to Hydra, but Amanda has convinced Jack to stay another couple of days." Neftali shook her head. "This will only bring trouble. Talk to Nikos. He will listen to you."

"I'm not really sure he will," I said. I moved next to her and began peeling one of the eggplants. Olivia was dropping ice in a pitcher.

"You keep doing that, I'll get the garlic." Neftali nodded at me. "You'll think I'm a bad host for making you work, but remember I lived in New York, and she—" Neftali gestured with her head at the woman at the stove—"no one's really sure, but I think she's in her eighties."

The woman looked over her shoulder and smiled at us, and I nodded back.

Olivia had finished making martinis. "First one's for you," she said, pouring it.

"Thank you."

"Very handy, aren't you? Your mother brought you up well."

I looked at the eggplant, which was turning into a gray and seedy mound of glop on the pan in front of me.

"Actually, I never knew my mother." I smiled charmingly. "Or my father."

"Really?" Olivia looked at me, possibly sympathetic, possibly suspicious, but at least interested.

"I was brought up by my uncle," I added.

I had determined these precise sentences and how they ought to be delivered while still in college. I knew how to say them without being self-pitying or hostile and without divulging too much. I took a sip of the martini.

"What is this?" I said. "This is no martini. This is a glass of vodka and—see—it's managed to kill this olive." I pushed the olive down and it bobbed, lifeless, in the glass. "Are you trying to get me drunk?"

"No," said Olivia. She smiled stiffly and walked out, carrying the pitcher of martinis. I knew other people needed drinks, but I also knew she was fleeing my presence and had some secrets of her own.

Lunch was served in the yard on a wobbly table, covered with a white cloth. Neftali fussed around, shaking her head at the plates, at the table, at the chairs. "This house was built in 1825," she said, "and we have owned it the whole time and replaced nothing." She held up a fork that had tarnished to a pinkish sheen. "I wonder how old this thing is?"

"Rupert can tell you," said Nikos.

"Yes I can." I took the fork from her and studied the handle, the imprint, the quality. "This is Italian and dates from about 1870, maybe a bit later."

"That comes in handy," said Clive enthusiastically.

I handed the fork back to Neftali.

"Well, you wouldn't want to eat off a fork without knowing how old it was, would you?"

We all turned to see the source of this booming voice, and there he was, standing on the steps of the house in bare feet, rough cotton pants, and no shirt. It was Jack Weldon.

"Well," said Nathan, who was sitting to my right, "that's an appealing introduction, isn't it?"

Jack walked slowly down the steps and took the empty seat next to his wife. He kissed her on the cheek and leaned over the table, his hand extended. "I'm Jack," he said. "I'm a sculptor."

"I'm Rupert," I responded, shaking his hand. "I'm a fork expert." I let the moment hang for a moment and then smiled.

Jack squeezed my hand a little too tightly.

Jack Weldon was a man of convictions, mostly political, and he liked to hear himself talk. He hated the Greek king and hated the current government for being controlled by the Americans. He believed that the common man in Greece lived in a state of complete oppression. As he held forth, we passed the platters of food up and down the table. I had just remembered where I'd heard him mentioned when he slammed his hand down on the table and yelled, "We're all complicit!"

I knew Jack Weldon not from conversations about art in New York but from Steve Kelly. It was Jack that Steve and Adonis had been so interested in—he was the focus of their conversation—on that day when we had stopped near Livadiá on the way to Delphi. I made a mental note to tell Steve, next time I saw him, that Jack was nothing but hot air and ego, a waste of time. I looked over at Nikos. He was sitting across from me, as was Jack, with Amanda between them. Nikos gave me a knowing, slightly terrified look.

I turned to Jack and said, "You're a bit like a modern-day Byron."

"That old fag? He was carried off by his own shit."

I looked over to Neftali, who put her forkful of veal back down on the plate and shook her head.

"Well," said Nathan. "That's quite an epitaph."

"Can we please talk about something that doesn't make us fight?" asked Amanda.

"Something less contentious," added Nathan.

"Than Byron?" Clive laughed. "How can we be fighting about Byron? Are we even fighting? And I thought he was sleeping with his sister."

"Someone should tell a story," said Amanda.

"Or a joke. Rupert, do you have a joke?"

"I don't tell jokes," I said earnestly. "Honestly, even when people tell jokes that I know are funny, I have to make myself laugh. I don't really understand the process."

Nikos waved at me with his knife. "Tell them about you and Steve Kelly in Delphi."

"Steve Kelly the journalist?" asked Neftali.

"Yes," I said, "the same. And I will tell this story, but Nikos, you have to promise me that when I leave bits out, you're not going to say, 'You left something out.'"

"There are," said Nikos, "women present."

"I don't know if I should tell it," I said.

"Tell the damn story," said Jack.

I looked over at Olivia. I knew there was no point in telling it unless I included the part about me naked in the hallway while Steve wrestled the girl for my wallet. I drained my martini and the glass of wine that was next to it and jumped in, leaving out only the fact that I had been in a dark mood at the time, skirting an even darker depression.

Lunch lasted nearly two hours, and by the end I was fiercely tipsy and bold. Most people seemed to be retiring to their rooms—I was sharing a room in front with Nikos—but he'd made a point of asking me if I was going to nap and I'd intuited that this meant he'd rather I didn't. He wanted the room to himself. Jack was going to the beach for a swim, but he didn't ask for company and no one, me included, had felt like accompanying him. Clive and I were the last people at the table.

"Where is the beach?" I asked.

"It's not walking distance. I usually hitch a ride, but if a few people want to go, we get a taxi." Clive rolled a cigarette and offered it to me. I took it. "If you want to go for a swim, I'll go with you. There's a little beach by the fishing village I've wanted to try out. You might be good company for that."

"Do you think Nathan will want to go?" I asked.

"No," said Clive. "He naps religiously. That's why he still looks like that. And he doesn't smoke. But most of all," said Clive, "he only goes to the one beach where the ferry came in, because that's the only one with restaurants and therefore bathrooms."

I went to get my trunks and a towel. I didn't have the right kind of bag to put them in, but Nikos had a canvas knapsack that he loaned to me. He had his shoes off and was lying on the bed.

"Neftali knows what you're doing," I said. I found my sunglasses and put them on.

"She disapproves," said Nikos.

"She's scared that Jack will find out."

"So am I," said Nikos. But he made it seem as if the whole situation was beyond his control.

Amanda was coming up the stairs as I went down. "Jack took the Vespa, so you're going to have to hitch." She smiled her gorgeous, large-toothed, all natural smile. "Clive started ahead. He said he'd walk slowly so you could catch up. Okay?"

I forced a smile back. I didn't like Amanda and I wondered why.

When I caught up with Clive, he was sitting on the wall of a small chapel conversing with a young Greek in jeans and a T-shirt. The Greek, who was close in age to Clive, was clearly interested in whatever Clive was offering. They had an ease with each other that let me know that they were not meeting for the first time. I announced myself with a loud hello when I was still quite a distance away. I waved my arms. I hadn't been on Aspros long, but I knew I didn't want to be sneaking up on people.

"I'm Rupert," I said. I extended my hand.

"This is Tomas," said Clive. "He has to make a delivery in Faros, and he said he'd drop us off."

"That's very kind," I said.

"Yes," said Tomas. "Very kind."

Tomas didn't know much English, but I could see he was a fast learner. He had a small pickup truck and I volunteered to ride in back. The truck was carrying nets and although there was a faint fishy odor, I didn't mind sitting on them.

The sun was shining brightly but I had my sunglasses, and we sped around the curves, past the olive terraces and herds of goats.

But there was something nagging at me, some residual guilt. And then I remembered the date. It was July 14. I had bought a ferry ticket that morning, so the date should have been in the forefront of my mind. July 14 was my wife's birthday.

One year ago I had been at Saks, choosing the evening purse that I bought for the occasion. It was black, elegant, with all kinds of fancy whorls of jet embroidered onto it. I liked it because it seemed almost flapperlike, not that there was anything flapperlike about Hester, but she was hard to buy for. Rather than trying for something she might actually like—that might be an outright failure for having been a borderline success—I bought something I would find attractive on a woman. And this was doubly ridiculous, since Hester and I had been separated for a year.

The woman who assisted me in the purchase was young, attractive, and flirtatious. Usually, this didn't bother me, but I was reliving my failures of the last few years, starting with the wreck of my marriage, the loss of my son, and all the women whose lives I had lately tried to destroy in a desperate attempt to keep myself afloat.

"I like the metallic ribbon with the blue paper," she said.

"That's very nice," I replied.

"Is it for someone special?"

"Yes," I said. "My mother."

I offered to take the woman for a cup of coffee, and she went to find someone to cover for her. I could see them assessing my virtues in one of the mirrored pillars. Then, to save time, I'd headed for the Plaza, where I was meeting Hester for dinner. It wasn't hard to convince the girl to come upstairs with me. And she wanted to be seduced, which made it almost boring. I promised I'd call her, wrote her number down on a pad by the hotel phone, and left it there for the cleaning lady. The girl went off in a state of confusion and I showered, then had to put the same clothes on, which is always unpleasant. Hester was in the lobby heading for the restaurant when the elevator doors opened, and I annoyed the woman who was riding with me when I hit the button for the basement without letting her get off.

I turned to look at Clive and Tomas. Clive was talking and talking, and Tomas, who had enormous black eyes and the eyelashes of a camel, was smiling at him in a calm way that, to me, meant he only understood every third word out of Clive's mouth. I shifted on the nets. The sun felt good. I knew I was getting grilled, but here in the open air, the Plaza and that terrible salesgirl with her expensive matching underwear and powdered skin, my own sweat, the impossible luxury of the feather pillows, the sounds of doors closing up and down the hall, and my Hester—that cold vessel of grief—striding into the lobby. . . . I could almost forget it all.

Clive stuck his head out the window and yelled, "Is everything all right?"

And I said, "I think my feet are burning."

"What?"

"I think I'm burning."

"I can't hear you."

"I'm burning." I'm burning. I'm burning. I'm burning. I'm burning. I'm burning.

Nothing seemed to be happening in Faros. There were a couple of men by some colorful boats mending nets. People seemed to do an awful lot of net mending but not much fishing. A woman in black in active conversation with herself was picking capers from the flowering vines that clung to the wall.

"*Yásas*," said Clive as we passed.

"*Yásas*," said the woman, and smiled very wide. I supposed we were entertaining in the same way that encountering rare fauna was entertaining.

The path was narrow and somehow I was leading.

"Where am I going?" I asked Clive. It sounded like a larger question.

"Just follow the path. We're going over this rise here, and then the path leads down to a pebble beach. And there's a charming little church." Clive kept talking, but I was thinking about Hester and I wondered what was happening, if she was thinking about me.

I hadn't wanted to take her out for dinner that night or buy her a gift, but my Uncle William had insisted.

"Rupert, she's suffering too. When we don't know what to do, we do what's polite. That's all the guidance we need."

Uncle William didn't believe in psychotherapy. I wondered if he'd even heard of it, apart from Freud jokes. Instead, he maintained that if we followed protocol and observed good manners, our lives would achieve the tidiness that some people sought in therapy. Mostly he was right about the importance of good manners. However, in this particular application—Hester's birthday—there was the biting of presence hypocrisy.

Clive and I reached the top of the hill and stopped to enjoy the view. A natural rock promontory extended like a tongue into the bay, and built on this was a small white chapel with a blue dome. There was also a complex of low concrete buildings leading out to the chapel, all whitewashed.

"That's a little monastery," said Clive. "You can get a room there and some travelers do."

"Doesn't sound like much fun."

"Well, it might be in a Chaucer sort of way, but then again there is the hair thing."

"What hair thing?"

"They're all Orthodox. That's a lot of hair.'

I said, "Did you bring anything to drink?"

"I did," said Clive. He pulled out a bottle of white wine. "And I remembered the corkscrew."

I'd really meant water but was pleased to see the wine. We sat down on my towel—Clive had forgotten his—underneath an olive tree and began passing the bottle back and forth.

"Nikos says you're here to look for works of art," said Clive.

"He said that?"

"Yes."

"He must be drinking too much."

"Does that mean you're not?"

"Do you mean looking for art, or drinking?" I gestured for the wine. "What does it look like to you?"

"You make a convincing bon vivant," said Clive.

"As you know," I said, nodding, "we the few, the privileged, need a sense of purpose. It's all that Protestant vigor and distrust of sloth, so whatever we do we have to pretend it's in pursuit of something worthwhile. And the only thing so profoundly abstract that we can bend it to our will and make it fulfill all our needs, including those of productivity and civic duty, is art."

"You're very cynical, Rupert."

"Only when I'm talking about myself." I took a gulp of wine and it went down easily. "And what about you? Are you a cynic?"

Clive shook his head. "I wish I was." He looked at me for a moment and grew serious. "I'm a romantic." He stood up and grabbed the hair on the sides of his head. "What am I doing?" he asked the sky. He then turned to me and repeated the question.

I didn't know what he was talking about, but I took a guess. "How long have you and Nathan been together?"

"Are we together?" asked Clive. "Am I being funny, or am I being tedious? Am I young and full of life, or am I uncultured and immature? Nathan invited me to come and I would have been an idiot not to, but it doesn't mean anything, not to him."

"What makes you say that?"

"Because Nathan has someone else, who is mature and cultured and almost as exquisite to look at as Nathan. But not quite. No one is."

"But Nathan invited you," I said. I wasn't exactly sure what to say. I didn't like giving anyone advice and found my role as Clive's confidant a bit premature.

"I'm boring you," said Clive apologetically.

"No, no," I protested.

"Yes, I am, and I don't take it personally. I bore everyone after a while."

I did feel bad for Clive. He was young and emotional, and I wanted to have him back where he'd been that afternoon, singing off-key imitations of Al Jolson. Or maybe I was being just like Nathan. I didn't know.

"Who is Nathan's other . . . friend?"

"I'm not supposed to mention his name," said Clive. "He's a writer." Clive set about rolling himself a cigarette. "If you think I'm boring you, you can't imagine what I'm doing to myself."

"It's a beautiful day," I said. "Enjoy yourself."

We'd been sitting under the tree for a little over half an hour when Clive got up to take a leak. The wine seemed to have hit him hard. He must have drunk a lot at lunch and this last bottle had been all he needed to cross into a rather sloppy state.

"Rupert, you've got to come here," he said, from behind the rock.

"No, Clive, I don't," I responded.

"I think you should. Jack's down there in a boat, and he's doing something suspicious."

I got up and walked around the rock. Clive was now crouched behind a bush and I followed his lead and crouched beside him. Clive was right. Jack was in a rowboat with a man who looked like a fisherman, and they were paddling up to some caves in the rock face, caves filled with water and inaccessible by land.

"Who's he with?" I asked.

"I'd say that's Thanasi," said Clive.

"The real man?"

"The same."

The sea was a bit rough and a few times I thought the boat was going to smash against the rocks, but Thanasi managed to jump out, holding the rope. He looked around then helped Jack out. They went into the cave together, stepping and climbing from rock to rock. The whole thing looked dangerous.

"Do you think there's any dry space in there?" I asked Clive.

"I wouldn't think so," he said.

"Any fish?"

"You're asking the wrong person. But the locals don't fish in the caves."

Ten minutes passed with nothing happening. Clive was still rather drunk, and said that we were like the Hardy Boys. I'd never read the Hardy Boys, but he was insisting passionately that this was very similar to one of the books and was about to launch into a detailed description of the book's plot when Jack left the cave. He was empty-handed and seemed to have a hard time getting out among the rocks. He was almost crawling.

"I wish we weren't hiding," said Clive.

"Why?" I asked.

"Because I'd like to yell down and tell him what a sissy he is."

Jack was followed by Thanasi, who was picking his way across the rocks with considerably more skill, despite the fact that he was carrying a net on his back that appeared to be very heavy.

"What's that?" asked Clive.

It was impossible to see, but Thanasi was struggling with it. Thanasi set the net down in the boat very carefully and the two men began to row off.

When they were gone, we went down to the beach. I wanted to swim out to the caves to get a better look, but they were much farther out than they'd looked from a distance, and the tide was in. Clive had a snorkel and mask back at the house, and he said it might be better if we came back on another day. For one thing, we didn't want to be in the cave if Jack returned. And all the wine we'd consumed did introduce the possibility of drowning.

After soaking awhile in the water, we got out and followed the path back to town. Clive was a bit more sensible after the swim and surprisingly quiet. Tomas's truck was still parked by the harbor. Clive went into a store and bought a couple of bottles of beer and we sat on the pier with our feet in the water waiting for Tomas to show up, watching the fishing boats come in and a few young people strolling about, arm in arm. Everyone greeted us and I felt lucky to be there. About a half hour later, Tomas returned and we got back into the truck. I lay on the nets contemplating the cloudless sky. By the time we reached the house, most people were stirring to life.

8

The next day I was very sunburned, especially on the tops of my feet, and could not wear shoes. I, therefore, could not leave the house. I spent the majority of the day padding after Olivia in my bare feet. Later, we sat on opposite ends of the couch, reading books. She was in the middle of *Moby-Dick*, and I had found some paperbacks of Neftali's from her high school days, stashed in a box in the closet with the croquet set. One was *The Girls of Delta Delta Delta*, which was wonderfully lurid. I read to Olivia the account of the mayhem following a panty raid by Sigma Chi. The book took me about three hours to read, and after that there was a horror tale—*The Cave of Count Carlos*—that involved sex slaves and human sacrifice. As Neftali passed by on the way to the kitchen, she told me it had been one of her favorites. Olivia tried to make it seem that I was driving her nuts—I insisted on reading all the really good parts out loud—but I knew she was captivated and her progress on old Moby was extremely slow.

The next day, Olivia wasn't feeling well and was in bed all day. I was able to wear my sandals again and so had ended my brief captivity. I went to a small museum in the old town, a couple of miles away. The walk was good for me, and the solitude, and looking through the glass cases gave me focus. There was the hand of a statue rescued from the water, which, despite its pocked appearance, asserted an affecting beauty in the gentle bend of its fingers and the relaxed yet questioning poise of the musculature. It reminded me that some things were still valuable.

I swam some more and tried the various beaches. Nikos and I
took the Vespa into the harbor town and bought drinks for some
Swedish girls; then waved them off as they boarded the ferry. When
we returned, Clive was wading through the underbrush that surrounded the east wall of the house, holding a lighted candle. Nikos
asked him to stop. It was very dry, and the risk of fire was quite real.
And there wasn't much water on the island this time of year. What
was he looking for? We learned that Clive had been playing the Al
Jolson record, and Jack had yelled something about "Don't you know
what's happening in Alabama?" to which Clive had responded, "I
make it a point never to know what's going on in Alabama." And
then Jack, very angry and alive with sanctimonious verve, had
snatched the record off the Victrola and Frisbied it over the wall.

"He's rather strong and the thing flew," said Clive. "It might still
be in the air."

So we took his candle from him, blew it out, and promised to help
him look for the record in the morning. But there was no sign of it the
next day, until we saw two children rolling it down the steps, and before we could recover it, the disk was smashed into a thousand pieces.

I got up late the next day, around eleven. People were awake and
Clive was setting up croquet on the lawn. There was an Ink Spots
song playing on the Victrola, and I wondered how long it would last
with Jack stalking around. Nathan came to stand at the window beside me. He handed me a cup of coffee.

"Thanks very much," I said. "Do you know how to play croquet?"

Nathan laughed. Clive seemed very serious about setting up a
proper course. "What would we all do without Clive?" he said.

"It wouldn't be as much fun," I agreed.

"No," said Nathan, "it would be tedious. As it is, I sometimes
feel I'm trapped in an Agatha Christie novel. There's a part of me
that keeps waiting for someone to die. There's a tangle of motives
here, a lot of desire."

"That's the publisher in you talking," I said.

"Drink your coffee," said Nathan. "Olivia is looking for you. She's in the kitchen. She wants to make everyone omelets, but she doesn't know how to cook."

After lunch, Nikos, Clive, and I went to the beach. Amanda showed up after an hour and she and Nikos set off for a walk together. Amanda had taken to calling me "Rupie," rather like the Indian currency, and seemed to resent the fact that I wasn't flirting with her. I was beginning to wonder if she wasn't that smart. Amanda was actually a great manipulator, but because of her natural beauty and unkempt appearance—Nathan called her "Amandirt"—no one really thought of her as being that clever.

Clive and I, apparently equally concerned that we might find ourselves stranded on the beach with no wine, had brought two bottles and a bottle opener apiece. We kept thinking that Amanda and Nikos might come back to join us, so we kept opening bottles, and by the time we got back on the Vespa—it was somehow decided that Clive should drive—we were zigzagging dangerously and at one point nearly collided with a truck full of watermelons. Shortly after this, a possibly suicidal goat wandered onto the road.

"Did you see that?" yelled Clive. He was outraged, as if the goat had intentionally cut him off.

By some miracle we got home safely, and as I wove my way up the stairs trying to avoid Olivia, whose voice was floating out from the kitchen, I nearly collided with Jack.

"Where's Amanda?" he said.

I looked over my shoulder drunkenly. "She was at the beach with us."

"That's why I'm asking you where she is," he said, angry.

Clive was standing at the foot of the stairs. He said, "Let me make you a drink, Jack."

Jack shook his head. He looked like he was ready for a fight, but then I heard Amanda's voice outside. "Jackie?" she called.

I wanted to find out what Nikos was up to, but instead managed the last few feet to my room. Neftali was passing by in the upstairs corridor, and I made her promise to wake me in half an hour. It

was already six and I wanted time to shower and put myself together
before we wandered in to Stavri for dinner.

When I awoke to a knocking on the door, it was pitch dark and I
had no idea where I was. Someone was calling *Rupert* through the
door in a voice I didn't recognize.

"Come in," I said. "Just a minute."

"Well, which is it?" came the voice.

"Come in," I said.

The door swung open and standing there, backlit by the hall
light, was Nathan. "Wakey, wakey," he said. "It's nine o'clock."

"Nine," I said. I sat up and put my feet on the floor. "Neftali
was supposed to get me at seven."

"Well, she didn't," said Nathan. "Everyone's gone into town for
a pre-dinner drink, but you and I will join them as soon as you're
dressed for dinner."

"Do I have time to shower?"

"Of course," said Nathan. "I'll meet you downstairs."

I took about twenty minutes to get ready. The night had cooled
things off a bit, but it was still warm. Nathan was on the couch downstairs reading a manuscript—loose white pages—and had a pair of
glasses on. I snuck up on him, but even in his solitude he was completely poised.

"Hello, Nathan," I said.

"There you are," he said.

We began walking to Stavri. The moon was full and lit the path
with a natural brilliance. Jasmine grew over the walls, and the scent
and beauty of the walk seemed almost studied.

"Neftali didn't want to wake you," said Nathan. "We figured you
needed your rest, and I wanted some time alone. That house is like an
asylum half the time. Between Clive and Jack and Amanda, it's impossible to read anything. Clive takes it personally. Neftali sees it as a sign
that she's being a bad host, and Jack and Amanda are always fighting."

"Jack's a lot older than Amanda, isn't he?"

"Amanda was his student. He was teaching in Florence, and she was there on her junior year abroad—from Smith, I think. She still paints, on occasion." He gave me a cold smile to let me know that this was not a talent of hers.

"She's attractive," I said.

"Your friend Nikos thinks so." Nathan stopped to admire a wall overflowing with jasmine. He picked a sprig and smelled it. "But you," he said, "prefer Olivia."

"She's nice," I said, in a pointedly bland way. I realized this was the first time that Nathan and I had really conversed.

"Olivia's second husband and I were good friends. He was Scottish, a dealer in rare books. I spent many pleasant hours in the offices of his shop in London. When he died, five years ago, she was completely alone. I wanted her to move to New York. She's originally from Boston, but she hadn't bothered to keep a life in America, so she stayed in London."

"They had no children?"

Nathan gave me a penetrating, questioning look. "No," he said.

"And what about her first husband?"

"He was a fighter pilot. She was eighteen." Nathan seemed mildly disgusted by the whole affair, as if its romantic tint made it a little tasteless. "I think she was married for almost two years, but she never lived with him and they spent a total of eleven nights together. Something like that." Nathan grew suddenly introspective. "You should get Olivia drunk and ask her these questions. When she's talking about her life, it's terribly funny. When I'm telling it, it sounds like some horrible Greer Garson vehicle."

"I find Olivia very entertaining," I said. "Neftali too." I was being noncommittal.

"Neftali defines generosity," said Nathan. He said this with such conviction that it seemed the first time those words had been used on anyone. "She invited Olivia at my request and has treated her with real warmth and tenderness."

We were both quiet. I found it odd that Nathan would have such compassion for his friend just because she'd been widowed. Hadn't that been five years earlier? We walked for about five minutes in silence. I'd been waiting for Nathan to ask me about Hester, not that I liked talking about her, but this state of expectancy was excruciating.

"You're a very polite man, Nathan," I said.

"Yes, I am." We had reached the foot of the pathway and were across from the park with its cannon, and the pharmacy. Nathan rested his hand on my forearm with a studied even pressure.

"You see, I know about your tragedy." He looked me straight in the eye. "I know from Hester. I just didn't know that your marriage had ended."

I nodded, not sure of what to say. "Of course Hester would tell you," I finally said. I found it strange that she had been able to speak to Nathan about our son but not our marriage, and then reasoned that she found the divorce more embarrassing than tragic.

The silence was not awkward, but heavy on us both. Nathan patted my forearm quickly as a way to remove his hand. "The restaurant is just past the pharmacy," he said. He knew he was rescuing me. "There's a lovely view of the mountains, and on a night like this, with the moon full, it's really quite stunning."

Of course Nathan knew, and once again I was Rupert Brigg, resident of New York City, expert in decorative arts, divorced man, once a father. And that's why he hadn't said anything to me for the last couple of days, because Nathan was an expert in motive and desire—all the books he'd read had taught him that—and he could see I wanted to escape. I looked over at him and knew I didn't need to ask him not to mention the death of my son to the others, to let me lie on the beach, and drink too much, and chase after the occasional woman. I knew he understood and, in his own way, was sympathetic.

There was a large table set for our party at the back of the terrace. The moon hung like a huge gaudy bauble and the mountains seemed falsely cut out, as if it were all for a school play. Clive, Neftali,

Olivia, and Nikos were sitting, clustered together at the end of the table. They seemed a little subdued, and only Clive had wine in his glass.

"What's wrong?" asked Nathan. "Where are Jack and Amanda?"

"They walked off," said Neftali. She took one of Nikos's cigarettes and he lit it for her.

"You slept through it," said Clive. "Jack wants to take the eleven o'clock ferry tonight, but Amanda doesn't want to leave. They've been bickering all day, and just now they had a huge fight. Amanda took off running, and Jack followed her."

I looked over at Nikos.

"She's crazy," said Nikos. "She says these things . . . it has nothing to do with me. I told her she should go with her husband."

"I asked him to say that," said Neftali.

"And it made her crazy," said Nikos.

"I'm so sorry," said Nathan, addressing Neftali.

"I have to go to Mýkonos. My husband is waiting, but I'm too scared to leave them. They could burn the house down."

And then Jack and Amanda walked back into the restaurant. Amanda had her arms wrapped around Jack and her chin rested on his shoulder. A shorter woman would have needed to be piggy-backed in order to do this, but they were actually walking that way. They separated and sat in their chairs. Clive poured out a couple of glasses of wine, and we slid the glasses down to them.

"Jackie has to go. He has to get back to work. It's that way for artists. But he's going to let me stay another couple of days, and then I have to go too," she said.

"I have an idea for a project," Jack said, in a scratchy whisper. I caught Clive rolling his eyes. "The ferry leaves in forty-five minutes," Jack added.

There was a moment of silence, and I realized that Jack was waiting for someone to offer to take him. Apparently, real men didn't ask for favors.

"I'm sure," said Neftali, "that someone would be willing to take you on the Vespa."

She was desperate for him to leave, and he was already cutting the trip to the harbor kind of close. I regarded Neftali, who was looking at a cold plate of chickpea croquettes, upset at the prospect of appearing inhospitable.

"I'll take you," I said, "if everyone promises to save me a lamb chop."

"We'll save you more than that," said Olivia.

"All the tender bits are yours," added Clive.

Jack was only taking what he could fit in his knapsack; Amanda would bring the rest when she followed him to Hydra. The trip down to the harbor was serene. A light breeze was blowing and, despite the steps, which were like relentless curbstones, the act of driving was clearing my head. The sprinkle of lights let me know that it wasn't far, and if Jack hadn't started singing some strange blues song I could have forgotten that he was on the bike. We parked by a café, where we had a good view of the harbor, and Jack asked the one local policeman, who was drinking a coffee at the next table, when the ferry was coming in. Jack's Greek was very good—Nikos even thought so—and a part of me had to respect this in him.

"Ferry won't be here for another half hour," said Jack.

"Well, they're always late," I said.

"That's not late, not here," said Jack.

I really did dislike him. I felt the need to remind him that, even though I didn't speak Greek and live in Hydra, I did have experience—bad experience—with the ferries.

"Let me buy you a drink, Rupert," he said.

"I should get it," I said. "You're the one who's going on a trip."

"No, no." Jack yelled something to the waiter. I understood *whiskey*, and I was relieved that I wouldn't have to trundle out my patient tourist–waiter English in front of him. When the drinks arrived, Jack looked at me and a sudden glimmer of humor lit up his eyes.

"You're in love with Olivia, aren't you?" he said.

"Love is a big word," I replied. "I find her attractive."

Jack laughed into his glass. Olivia was beautiful, undeniably so, and I didn't flinch. "You don't know, do you?" he said.

I watched him across the table. He was enjoying himself. "Apparently not," I said.

"Olivia," said Jack, leaning across the table, "is dying. She has cancer. She spent all last year having parts carved out of her. And it's bought her some time, but there's no hope for recovery."

"How do you know this?"

"You don't believe me?"

I took a drink. I felt a bit light-headed, but there was no reason to feel defensive, although Jack was doing his best to encourage it. I just felt sad. "You're going to tell me to leave her alone because she's sick," I said.

"No," said Jack. "The kindest thing you could do is fuck her." He drained his glass and stood, shouldering his knapsack. "Just don't wait too long."

I stayed at the café and had another drink. Facing Olivia now required some degee of courage, and I'd never been good at courage. I decided to walk down to the little grocer to see if they had any peaches. Clive and Olivia loved peaches and had finished the last two over breakfast. The grocer was closing, but was very pleased that I was buying nearly all his peaches and what was left of his tomatoes. I was just returning my wallet to my pocket when I noticed Jack, quite a distance away on the pier. He was with Thanasi, who was helping him carry a crate or a box. There was some discussion going on and I figured the smaller boat had to be on other side of the pier, out of sight. After the crate was loaded, Thanasi and Jack had some sort of intense discussion and then the two men embraced in a way devoid of affection—a way that made me feel that something was at stake. I remembered the caves and the pebble beach and wondered what Clive and I had been up to for the few days that was so important that we'd never gone back.

Nikos and I spent the next day on the Vespa chasing down a couple of leads that Neftali had compiled over the last few months in preparation for our visit. One was a small archaic statuette that belonged to a once wealthy family. The man we spoke to was about forty and held a public office. According to Neftali, he'd been mayor of Stavri a few years ago and was hoping to regain that position sometime soon. The more we wanted the statuette, the less he wanted to sell it. He and Nikos argued passionately while I handled the piece. It had been badly damaged, at one point, and restored in a haphazard way. In addition, although the body and arms—reattached—came from the same figure, the head was not only not original but from a later period. When Nikos lifted his hands in frustration, I was almost relieved that we hadn't been able to purchase it, although Uncle William would have loved it regardless.

Our next lead took us to fields in the hills surrounding the old town. A farmer who had a few dusty acres of tomatoes and zucchini, but was mostly in sheep, had found a clay lamp while digging up a plot of land behind his house. There had once been a sheep shed on this land, but the shed had collapsed and the farmer had rebuilt it farther from his house. As I walked up to his cottage and passed the new shed, with the scent of sheep and a cacophony of bleating, this seemed to have been a rather good decision. Also, the old shed had been on a nice flat piece of land, perfect for planting, and in the process of readying it for just that, the farmer had dug up the lamp.

We sat on the steps of his house. I looked down at the old town, which had been built atop and all around a hill, and this hill sat surrounded on three sides by deep ocean that here sparkled a dark sapphire color. This farmer, although he had holes in his roof and the smell of manure, had one of the most beautiful views in the world. He had brought us some water and a plate of pistachios, and after talking to Nikos for a little while he came back out with the lamp. The lamp was plain but well preserved. I wasn't sure about its value, but it did look old. I set it down a short distance away and regarded it as I ate my pistachios, cracking them between my teeth.

"Ask him if this is all he found," I said.

Nikos turned to the man and they talked back and forth. The man was gesturing a lot and making faces, and I translated this to mean *I found this lamp. Why, don't you like it? It's all I have.* But then his face broke into a wide smile. Nikos said something else, and the man went back into his house.

"He has some pieces. He didn't think we'd want them because they're broken."

The man had a small basket with pottery fragments, one maybe three inches square that had a gorgeous octopus painted on it. I wondered what the best way to display a fragment like this was. I looked through the pieces, which came from at least three different pots.

"Does he have any more?"

Nikos and the man spoke for a while, and then Nikos got up. "He wants us to follow him."

We walked around the house to a little field. The zucchini plants were in full blossom and the tomato plants had started to bear fruit, although it was still green. And then I saw between the furrows, just sitting in the dirt, smaller pieces of pottery, as if the dry dirt had spat them out along with the vegetables. It seemed suspicious that he had a field full of pottery just for me. There was a fairy-tale quality to it that I didn't trust.

"Ask him why he's moved his shed," I said.

Nikos and the man talked for a while, and the man kept shaking his head.

"There was an earthquake and half the mountain slid down. This was two years ago. He was able to rebuild his house, mostly using the original materials that he found and carried back up the hill with donkeys. But the shed . . ."

"Amazing," I said.

Nikos looked at the scattered sheep manure, the farmer and his dirty shirt, the dust on his shoes. "Amazing?"

"Don't you see?" I said. "It's like Delphi. Who knows who once lived here, what's been hidden for all these years? The earthquake makes everything possible."

"You think there's more?"

"I want to dig up his field," I said.

Nikos considered the field with more respect. He spoke to the man and there was some back and forth of disbelief. Then the man said something quite nasty and angry, to which Nikos responded with a placid and sympathetic expression.

"I take it he doesn't want us digging up his backyard," I said.

"No, no. He just wants to harvest the zucchini first."

"How long will that take?"

"Another two weeks."

"Why don't we just pay for the vegetables?"

"I tried. He's charging too much."

"Nikos . . ."

"I'm not going to pay it."

"You're being absurd. It's Uncle William's money."

"And I am the one responsible to negotiate for it. This man is charging too much, and I am not going to let you throw your money away."

There was no point in arguing with Nikos over this, even if the money for the vegetables was probably half that of what Nikos paid to his tailor every month. This was an issue of pride, not just mine, but Nikos's, Neftali's, Kostas's . . .the pride of every Nikolaides since the dawn of time. But I was annoyed. He could have negotiated further for the vegetables, but despite his resistance to being overcharged, Nikos also found it distasteful to haggle. As if feeling this anger from behind—I was staring at the back of his head—he pulled the Vespa over suddenly, cut the engine, and turned around.

"What is two weeks? Look where you are. Now you can go to the beach, eat some food, talk to people."

"I am here to find art for my Uncle William."

"You should be happy that you have some time when you don't need to wake up before it gets too hot, where you're not digging through the ancient droppings of the sheeps."

I was quiet.

"I will buy you a drink," said Nikos, and he started the motor up again.

Nikos was right. Now that I had time to think after the initial excitement of discovery, it made sense to take the next couple of weeks to prepare. There were a few things I needed to figure out. I had no idea how old the fragments were. I'd have to find out about classical Aspros for that; all I knew is that it had been sacked by the Samians in 530 B.C. Most of this stuff was probably Hellenic or later, but I wasn't sure what made me think this. If I had been dealing with a dresser rather than pottery fragments, I would have been sure. I would have slid the drawers open, checked the dovetailing, checked for original fixtures, looked at the feet and other decorative elements, and determined whether the structural wood was white pine or maple. There was a real science to furniture, and that was because it was recent history. But the field was a mystery, a bunch of broken pots to be pieced together by consulting the jumble of broken memories that we referred to—with a willful and blind faith—as history.

Nikos and I stopped at a café in the center of Stavri. He ordered a plate of sticky cakes and a cup of coffee and I had a bottle of beer.

"Why are you so concerned what the exact of everything is? Do you think your Uncle William cares?"

I considered this. "No, I'm sure he doesn't. I'll type up some letters for him, give him a nice provenance for the stuff." I poured my beer into a glass. "You're right."

"But there is still something bothering you?"

I laughed. "Yes," I said. "I want to know how old the things are."

"Don't be that way, Rupert," he said. "There's no reason to worry. I know you like to do a job well, like me."

"That's the prerogative of those who work only on occasion."

Nikos smiled. "But that farmer with his sheep, he cares about the zucchinis and the tomatoes. He probably asks the same amount of money for vegetables as for pottery. So dig it. Buy it. And then you can do all the chemical things back in the States, find out how old it really is there. Now you just get your shovel and your bucket for sand and enjoy."

"How old do you think the pieces are, Nikos?"

"I don't know these things," he said. But for someone so disinterested, he was pondering something. Later, as we sat in the shade enjoying our cakes, I saw Olivia walking through town alone. She had a canvas shopping bag on her shoulder. She stopped at the grocers and looked at some pears, then went in to buy them.

"There's Olivia," said Nikos. "I'll get her."

"No," I said. "She's busy."

"Busy?" Nikos looked at me suspiciously. "Now you don't like Olivia?"

"She's ill," I said. "She has cancer."

Nikos was quiet for a moment. Of course he'd known. Neftali must have told him. But she probably made him promise not to tell me. Nikos was looking directly at me and I was doing my best to remove all expression from my face.

"All right," I said. "I'll get her."

Olivia was paying for the pears and a couple of tins of Italian sardines. We'd been eating the sardines on the terrace in the afternoon, and it seemed that, at the villa, if you did things more than once it became a routine that you could not vary. I knew Olivia had been memorizing key phrases from a language guide, but to hear her using it affected me. The woman gave Olivia her change, and Oliva said to her, "*Evkaristó*," in a determined and nervous way.

"You're showing us all up," I said.

Olivia was startled, surprised to see me there. "Hello, Rupert," she said. "Just in time to carry my bag."

I took the bag. "Nikos and I are at the café across the way."

"Yes, I know," said Olivia. "I saw you sitting together."

"But you didn't say hello?"

"No," said Olivia. She smiled a gorgeous, knowing smile.

"Why not?" I asked.

"Because you are avoiding me."

I suddenly felt both guilty and stupid. "Well, I'm not avoiding you now, and I have been very busy."

"Busy," she repeated. She looked over to Nikos, and he waved. "I could use a coffee," she said.

By the end of the week, Olivia and I had reached an uneasy truce. We were often in the same room, but all hope and banter was gone. It was Friday. I only knew this because Neftali had decided to take the ferry for Mýkonos in the morning, and that ferry left on Fridays. Now that Jack was gone, she didn't mind leaving. Apparently, none of the rest of us struck her as pyromaniacs. She left Nathan in charge, and we were all comfortable with that. Amanda was still lurking around the house and Nikos was still sleeping with her. I wondered when she was going to follow Jack to Hydra.

Old Amandirt was much easier to handle without Jack around. She didn't call me Rupie and sometimes read books, quietly, in the garden. She was still unkempt, which made Nathan suspicious of her, but she was much less contrived without Jack and even made jokes that were funny. Nikos, who I'd thought was on the brink of escaping back to Athens, now spent nearly all his time with her, which of course increased the time I spent with her. She and Olivia had done some things together, some short walking tours, and on this afternoon when the rest of us had napped—drinking four beers in the early afternoon had made napping a necessity for me that day—Olivia had taken a notebook and Amanda her watercolors and the two women had found a field suitable to their pursuits. Olivia had long wanted to try her hand at poetry, something that had been overshadowed by her marriage to the Scottish book dealer, who, although he gave her no children, had led a time-consuming and mostly entertaining social life. She had a blank notebook and her copy of Moby-Dick, and she spent her time filling the one and wasting the other.

We ate at the house that night because of Neftali's imminent departure. I didn't say much at dinner. I was wondering what I was going to do with Olivia. I think I'd been lazily pursuing her because she was attractive and kept moving away, and these two things had kept me in motion. But the notion of pursuing someone who was terminally ill was tasteless, and even though I could be tasteless—the girl in Delphi, the salesgirl at Saks—Olivia did not bring out that aspect of my character. We had had no physical involvement, which made things much easier. It was just casual flirtation, and as she was thirteen years older than me, how serious could I have been? But I could not get Olivia out of my mind. Her illness, rather than making her more alien, seemed to bond me to her. Her illness made me feel we had something in common, but what this was I did not know. I was not ill, not physically, but I did not care what I did with the rest of my life, and she did not have a rest-of-her-life to concern her, and maybe that made us compatible. Olivia caught me staring at her and held my gaze with frank concern. I smiled, but it was a bland smile, incapable of putting anyone at ease.

After dinner, Neftali insisted that Amanda show us her pictures. She had one rather large painting of meadow and it seemed to have been going well—nice impressionistic dappling, roughly sketched-in wall—until she'd overdone a pink flower in the foreground. The flower was flat and too large. Amanda seemed to have sabotaged her own painting. To look at it, one would have guessed the flower was the donation of some second-grader who felt the picture would be too dull without it.

"What do you think, Rupert?" asked Clive, after everyone was done with their compliments, including a "very nice" from Nathan.

"I'm better at guessing how old things are, so with this I'd say sometime between two and four this afternoon."

"Very funny," said Amanda.

"Go on, Rupert. Tell us what you think," said Olivia.

I realized that Olivia was mad at me, justifiably, since I hadn't responded in a very mature way to the news of her illness. By asking my opinion of the painting, she was inviting me to show the others what a little shit I was, and it was tempting to rise to the occasion, to make up something like *The banal beauty of the landscape is questioned by the intentionally naïve flower in the foreground*, but I wasn't feeling quite so ungenerous.

"It's clear this picture was done *en plein air*," I said, and smiled. "There's something genuine in the treatment of the light."

Amanda nodded, rather pleased with this. I looked over at Olivia and raised my eyebrows smugly.

"What about you, Olivia?" said Nathan. "What do you have to show for your time?"

Olivia laughed loudly. "I have a truly ghastly poem."

"You must read it," said Clive.

"God, no," she said. "In addition to being clumsy, it's also depressing."

"What?" said Neftali. "I'm sure it is a very nice poem."

"No, it's not," said Olivia. "It's like an ugly person walking along in cement shoes."

"Now you have to read it," said Nathan.

"It's like, it's like . . ."

"What?" said Nathan.

"It's like someone who always wanted to write poems for years," she continued with some emotion, "but always had the clarity of judgment not to do it, or at least to keep it to herself, and now finds that—"

"And now," said Clive, interrupting, "finds herself surrounded by a table full of people who all love her and, even if they don't, have had a bottle of wine apiece and wouldn't know what made a poem good or bad even when sober."

Nathan had grown introspective. I looked over at Nikos, and he said, "If you read that poem, I will sing, and I am a very bad singer."

Olivia had realized that she didn't have a choice, not without being labeled someone who took her poetry seriously, so she nodded at Nikos and said, "Who could resist that?"

"What's it called?" asked Amanda.

Olivia picked up her notebook and opened it. "It is called," she said smiling, "'A Cock to Asclepius.'"

"I already like it!" said Clive, and everyone laughed.

Olivia did read her poem and afterward I made her give it to me, and I have kept it folded in my wallet ever since taken out rarely,

because I'm scared that one day the words will be gone and I won't
have it anymore, that little document that changed how I thought
about my dear Olivia and the future.

Apparently, the final words of Socrates had been, "Crito, I owe
a cock to Asclepius; will you remember to pay the debt?" And this is
the poem:

> We don't die well. Even the best of us
> reduced to ugly children on our way
> to dust, hoping that this lengthy absence
> will function as a sort of presence, others
> paying our debts, moving the furniture, placing
> new place settings at the table. New!
> Since new it is. Not death—silence, really,
> our little implosion sucking those around
> them into movement, much—as when we lived—
> our little suns kept our friends revolving,
> blood asurge and surging. Still yes, but still
> space on the bed is charged as Malevitch's
> white field, the quiet of the breakfast table—
> your thoughts, replacing mine, now doubled, your
> extra sweater. Congealing casserole—
> my new blood, that bleating phone—new heart, your
> step and step, my new feet, endless walking,
> pushing always the space in front—my space.

Olivia read it in a halting way but still somehow too quickly,
and after, when I was still trying to figure out what the space at the
end referred to, she had already demanded that Nikos burst into song.

9

For the next two weeks the weather remained clear and hot, and I walked about with an image of the field in my mind: the dusty zucchinis and tomatoes, the thin-fleshed peppers with their narrow leaves—all those lucky plants with their roots plunged into the earth. Olivia said she recognized obsession, and this was obsession.

We were spending a lot of time together, and everyone—me included—was surprised at my seeming devotion. I was following her around, maybe even loving her. I knew I had given in to a pointless hope for our future and, with that, pity—not for Olivia but for myself. I'm not sure how Olivia felt. She hadn't hesitated when I'd followed her into her bedroom. There was an unshowy confidence in everything she did. Unlike other women I'd known, she didn't seem to care what sort of relationship we were having. Olivia was different. She never made much of her feelings, and I admired her for it.

In Neftali's absence, we all became brazenly immoral. I moved into Olivia's room and Nikos moved in with Amanda, even though our room was quieter, because Amanda's had a double bed. We agreed that when Neftali returned from Mýkonos in the next few days we would all go back to our old sleeping arrangements, so as not to create scandal. Neftali would no doubt recognize and appreciate the hypocrisy.

I wanted to get to work on the field, if for no other reason than to be occupied. Olivia's concern for her own health was now exacerbated by her concern for me, watching her struggle. A morning when she didn't get out of bed was a morning with me sipping coffee in the garden, worried, waiting for her to get up. If I'd been digging up the field, it would have been better for us both. A part of me was still angry with Nikos, who for all his good taste and love of beauty didn't seem to recognize the value of classical art. He refused to be humbled by it—to be humbled by anything, for that matter—as if having a face that women loved and clothes that men admired were enough.

"You're always like this, Rupert. Classical this, classical that. You have to stop. It's like me asking you to be a cowboy."

"It's not the same thing at all," I said. We were sitting in the garden together, and I was trying to convince Nikos to pay a visit to the farmer, who should have been ready to harvest everything.

"Why did you bargain and bargain with that annoying man in Stavri over the statuette, if you find haggling so impossible?"

"Bargain?" said Nikos. "With him?"

"I could hear it in your voice. You were arguing back and forth."

"No, no," he said. "We were talking about building a real road to the port, one that doesn't have steps for the donkeys, and then he said something about buses. He wants to have buses. Remember, he's running for mayor again."

But Nikos agreed it was probably time to check on the farmer. Besides, Amanda had gone into town to make a much-dreaded phone call to Jack, and Nikos didn't want to be hanging around the garden when she came back.

We had some trouble starting the Vespa. I was not good mechanically, and neither was Nikos, but he had more persistence. I stood for about ten minutes watching him try to get the thing going. He thought it might be the starter. A little boy with his sister came to watch and were joined a couple of minutes later by a dog. Nikos wiggled some wires somewhere, and the children watched with their unblinking black eyes. He tried again. The starter responded with a shattered whir that soon degenerated into a series of desperate clicks. Nikos jumped off the bike and walked away. He covered his mouth with his hand and shook his head, looking at the Vespa, seemingly offended and capable of violence.

I said, "You're thinking about Amanda."

Nikos looked at me. "No," he said.

"One more time, Nikos, and then I'll get help," I said.

He turned the key again and finally, miraculously, gorgeously, there was a larger, deeper, coughing purr. Nikos was victorious.

He gestured for me to get on the bike. "I am not thinking about Amanda," he said. "I am thinking about me."

I knew that Amanda was in love with Nikos, or at least the drama he created. I knew that Nikos liked Amanda a lot. She was fun, and the calculated stupidity that she used to keep Jack strung along was, apparently, only trundled out for this specific purpose. But Nikos was engaged, although to a very young woman he hardly knew, and had completely and happily accepted his destiny as heir to the export business established by his father. When it came time to settle down, Nikos was not going to feel the victim. I leaned in my head to shield it behind Nikos's shoulders and lit a cigarette. A dove flew by on its way somewhere, and I watched it for a bit. There was nothing to interrupt my view of its journey. I saw a cloud, rare thing, floating over the old town, and it created splashes of gray shadow on the whitewash, a sudden depth, but the cloud would not stay for long. In fact there was something unreal in its lonely shadowing. We reached the end of the gravel path that led to the farmer's house and got off.

"Is she going back?" I asked.

"Amanda?" said Nikos. "Of course she's going back."

"When?"

Nikos stopped walking. He pulled my cigarette out of my mouth, took a drag, and threw it on the ground. "Do you want me to be sentimental?" he said patiently. "Why?"

I shrugged. "Just making conversation."

"That means speaking without saying anything, yes?" Nikos shook his head. "She should be with her husband. Even she knows that."

"Good," I said.

Nikos really did believe in the sanctity of marriage. He even wanted it for me. Because Nikos wanted me to be happy, he thought I would return to Hester. Because he knew I missed my son, he thought I wanted another child. But he was wrong here. I never wanted another child. I would find myself staring at them, but the sound of their voices scared me. Their voices were the dark music of angels. The death of my own little boy had made them all—girls, boys, babies—otherworldly. But Nikos thought I wanted a child and Hester, and I understood, because all his problems would be solved or at least organized to some extent by the needs of family. He had no time for existential angst because he knew he was just a moment in the continuum of history, his story just a minute in the narrative of his family, and it gave him peace.

There were three donkeys tied to the railing outside the farmer's house. A young man was taking bundles of wood off of one and stacking them by a low stone wall. When the farmer appeared with a basket full of peppers, I was near speechless with joy.

"He says this is going to be taken away today, and that some plants are still—"

"Oh, for God's sake, Nikos, tell me it's over!"

"We can dig," he said. He patted my shoulder. "Are you happy now?"

I felt rather infantilized by the whole thing. I could see the farmer thought I was crazy, and this was good for me, because being disparaged by Nikos openly and sincerely made my excavating the field extremely lucky for the farmer, a wonderful serendipitous event: an earthquake had coughed up all these broken pots, and then a crazy American had shown up to purchase them all.

"I am happy," I said.

Nikos talked to the farmer as the donkeys were loaded down with vegetables. There was still some negotiating left and this, apparently, Nikos was quite willing to do. Nikos and I had agreed that it would be better to dig the field up quickly with about five workers than to draw it out and work with fewer. I knew that looting was almost irresistible and wanted to be around for all the active excavation. Nikos had warned the farmer that if things went missing, he wouldn't be paid. And then Nikos had gone on to give the man a gun, something used around the turn of the century for hunting hare, that he had found in the attic of Neftali's house. I'd never seen a gun like that, but it looked quite frightening, and that's all that was needed.

"All right," said Nikos. "Now what?"

"How about a celebratory drink?" I said.

"And this time," said Nikos, "we actually have something to celebrate."

We went to a café in the old town. It was across the valley from our field, and I could see that Nikos too spent most of his time watching our little plot of land in a proprietary way.

"I wonder how old the stuff is?" I said, for the hundredth time.

"I am," said Nikos, lighting a cigarette, "as you say, cautiously optimistic."

"Funny," I said, "because I was beginning to think you had no opinion at all."

Nikos agreed. "But I have a small reason to think this," he said.

"Why?"

"Well, I was thinking if all this pottery appears because there is an earthquake, maybe it is all there because of an earthquake. But no one has built there for a long time. The wall and the tower at the top of the mountain"—we looked across the valley, above the little sheep farm, and saw the ancient tower and the wall—"have been there forever, but once there was a house."

"When was this?"

"Who knows? We have so many ancient things everywhere that old things don't make us too interested. When the villagers say old, it might be four hundred years or four thousand."

"But you're cautiously optimistic. Why?"

"Because many people know that once there was an old house, but where did this house go?"

"Can't be that long ago," I said. I was already feeling disappointed, deflated at the possibility that a Venetian villa, since destroyed, was the source of all my artifacts.

"It could be very long ago," said Nikos. "Someone remembers the house, then some grandchild remembers the grandfather remembering the house, then someone finds a door and uses it for their own

SABINA MURRAY

house. It's there for four hundred years. Everyone says *Where does this old door come from?* and they say *Near the old town,* and when the door is gone someone remembers that."

"That sounds more like hearsay than provenance," I said.

Nikos smiled. "But there was a very big earthquake around 150 A.D., and that I am not making up."

"Well, I hope that's when it's from," I said.

"Memory here goes back a long time. The people don't change, so it's like the same people happening again and again," said Nikos.

"Like reincarnation?"

"What is this thing? I don't know, but I am sure I am not talking about it."

"What are you talking about?" This was one of those rare occasions when Nikos got philosophical, and I'm sure the thought was equally vague when expressed in Greek.

"I don't know." He laughed. "But things are talked about for years and years. A year on this island is not the same as a year somewhere else. It could be one minute, it could be a hundred years."

Nikos grew quiet. I could hear the sheep in the valley. I watched them hop among the walls in the distance, gray like the earth was gray. Somewhere a dog barked, and I saw a donkey making slow progress from the farmer's house. The sun was high now, and the air had a bleached quality to it. A cat, sitting quite still, suddenly extended its leg and began to lick it vigorously. The waiter, leaning on his elbow at the next table, swung his worry beads onto the back of his hand and then against his leg, over and over in a rhythmic clacking. The distant growl of a motorbike bounced along the valley, until the bike rounded a curve and sputtered into view.

"Do you think this place will stay like this?" I asked Nikos.

"Yes," said Nikos. "This is why all the foreigners come, and why all the Greeks leave."

We began digging the next day. Nikos had assembled his people, all relatives of Neftali's caretaker. This small crew of five workers included

Tomas. Clive had volunteered his time, insisting that I wake him early, but at seven o'clock he was impossible to move, and at eight, and when Nikos and I finally left the house at eight-thirty we didn't even bother to look in on him. Nikos had ordered some brushes and sieves over the last couple of weeks at my request, but I wasn't really sure how to go at it. I had no background in archaeology and realized I was trying to remember details from *The Curse of Mummy* and some higher budget mystery, name lost, that had featured archaeologists. I decided to rope off two areas, with me supervising one and Nikos supervising the other. This way we could keep track of things. I roped off two areas, each about six square feet, and then we split the workers—Nikos got three and I got Tomas and some teenager named Andreas who wanted to learn English—but when we all stepped into my roped-off areas it was on the crowded side. There was a pen a short distance away with a half-dozen sheep in it and when Tomas, casting a humored glance in that direction, made a joke, I understood and laughed along with everyone else, even though he'd made the joke in Greek.

"We will abandon this roped-off thing," I said to Nikos, "and we will return to the time-honored 'dig around and tell me if you find something.'"

By noon I had a nice collection of pottery fragments and was organizing them into little tin basins, trying to match pieces based on design or thickness, or what worker had dug them up in what area. The farmer came by at one point to check on our progress. He was smiling heartily and I knew it was because all we'd found was little, broken, and to all appearances, worthless; he had gotten the better deal and nothing, not even the glory of having an entire statue on par with *The Charioteer* pulled from the earth behind his house, could make him happier.

An hour later I saw Clive walking along the valley. He was unmistakable, even at a distance. The road curved a lot and even though, as the crow flies, Clive wasn't really that far off, it took him nearly half an hour to reach us. I would brush at my little bits of baked history and look up every now and then, to see how far he'd advanced. Each time he was a little bigger.

By the time he was standing opposite me, across the divide of table, he was hot, dusty, and not interested in the dig at all.

"Clive," I said, "Good to see you."

"Unbelievable," said Clive. "I was going to hitch a ride, but no one passed me, not even a donkey. Can I have a drink?" I gave Clive some water.

"Look at this," I said. I held the best fragment of the day, tiny but with a small flower design painted on it.

"Very nice, but actually that's not why I'm here." Clive looked very grave for Clive, and Olivia entered my mind.

"Is everything all right?" I asked.

"Well, yes. Sort of." He was trying to find a way to tell me, but knew that subtlety and phrasing were not his strengths. "Well, nothing to worry about."

I put down my fragment. "Clive, why are you here?"

"It's your ex-wife. She's turned up on Aspros."

"Hester?"

"Is that her name?" Clive had rolled himself a cigarette and he lit it. "You never talk about her."

I took the Vespa and dropped Clive at the villa before continuing on to the harbor, where apparently Hester was having a drink with Nathan. My thought the whole way to the port was that Uncle William was responsible for sending her. Her father was, after all, one of his close friends and he had expressed a strong desire for me to behave in a more adult fashion, to consider returning to my wife and work. Uncle William had to be careful with how he phrased such desires, as he did any time he began to sound paternal, because I had no tolerance for this sort of behavior and I had every right to feel this way. I knew protesting that I didn't want to be married anymore wasn't really very manly, but it was also treacherous territory on which to engage me in battle. At least for Uncle William. Perhaps he had sent Hester, above reproach in this regard, in his stead.

I parked a short distance away and began the walk to Nathan's regular café. I had been thinking about Uncle William precisely so as not to think about Hester, and it wasn't until I saw her—she was wearing a black dress, very plain—that it occurred to me that she might have a reason more compelling than our failed marriage to make the journey.

I watched her talking to Nathan, her back straight, every now and then angling her face to the side, a human imbalance that she corrected compulsively. I could tell she lacked sleep and knew something more than travel had caused this. I saw her reach her hands across the table like a cat stretching its claws; then she pulled them back quickly. No one was watching so why did she care? And then I realized that I was watching her, and then that she was watching me.

Nathan stood up as soon as he saw me. I knew his chair was intended for me and had an urge to run—yes, run—in the opposite direction. It was not maturity that brought me to the table, but rather the need to disappoint Hester, who probably expected bad behavior.

"Hello, Rupert," she said.

I bent down to kiss her on the cheek and formally shook hands with Nathan, who only that morning had greeted me by hitting my head with a newspaper.

"I should let you talk," said Nathan.

And then I was seated across from her and saying nothing and she was rolling the stem of her wineglass in her fingers, but when she looked up and held my gaze I could see she was trying not to cry.

"I have some bad news," she said.

I was dizzy, reliving that day four years ago when I had lost my son, but then I realized—a small kindness—that this could only happen once.

She looked at me, inhaled in a patient and disgusted way, and said, "My father has died."

I sat quietly for a moment. "Heart attack?"

"Yes," she said. "You don't seem that surprised."

"But I am, Hester. No one even told me he was sick."

Hester narrowed her eyes. "It was a heart attack."

"But why didn't you tell me?"

"Tell you what?" She glared effectively, then, waving her mani-cured hand sharply, summoned the waiter. "Another," she said, rais-ing her glass, "and a double bourbon on the rocks for him."

There was another moment of silence. I thought of Grolsz who had loved me and whom I had loved, but the moment was so ab-stracted by everything—the ocean, the teenagers playing backgam-mon, a sparrow fight in the eaves—that I felt I had to be making it up. I wanted to will the moment into the distant past, but the drinks arrived and Hester, purposefully and with seeming malice, took an impossibly small sip from her glass.

"You're wondering why I'm here," she said.

"Yes," I said, which wasn't exactly true but was what I ought to have been wondering.

"It's in his will. He asked to be cremated and have his ashes scat-tered, and he wanted you present."

I considered this. Hester had never stated, but had often thought, that her father preferred me to her. She had a few reasons to suspect this. I was male. I had a better sense of humor. I had done him the favor of marrying his daughter, who was thirty-five at the time and whom he considered beyond marriageable age. All this was running through Hester's head, and she was cornered by it.

"You brought the ashes here?"

"Yes," she said.

"Well, you've made it easy for me," I said.

"And if I hadn't?" She sighed. "I could have enjoyed having my father's ashes sit in the house until you were ready to come home and deal with it."

I lit a cigarette. "How is Uncle William taking it?"

She gave me an intentionally awkward smile. "Your father," she said, "is handling it very well."

"I'm sure my father," I said, holding her look, "misses Max very much."

There was another silence.

"I can take you for a drive later," I said, "and we can find a good spot to scatter the ashes. We can go up to one of the monasteries, or perhaps rent a yacht."

"Shut up, Rupert. Please shut up." She grabbed my cigarettes and she lit one. Hester was not usually a smoker. "I have to ask you something."

I was surprised that any questions remained between us, but I nodded.

"Where were you?"

"What do you mean?"

"Where were you the day that Michael drowned?"

"I told you," I said. "I was in a diner on the Upper East Side, having a cup of coffee."

"For four hours?"

"It's the truth."

Hester regarded me coldly. "I sat in the hospital by myself, then with my father, then with your father. Michael was so small and still . . ."

"Stop it," I said. "Please. Don't."

"Where were you?" she repeated.

I had always taken refuge in the fact that this was the truth: the coffee, the café, the location. I suppose I didn't want to admit that there was anything worse than a father losing his son, but being unreachable when it happened, not knowing for four hours was perhaps just that. "I was there," I said.

Hester exhaled through her nose. "I don't believe you," she said.

"Of course you don't, and I'll tell you why. Because you want to believe I was with another woman. But even if I had been off fucking someone, Michael's death still wouldn't be my fault."

Hester waited.

"Uncle William wanted Michael to call him *Grandpa*. Of course I told him he was stuck with *Uncle William*." I put out the last of my cigarette and immediately lit another. "I took it as an opportunity to ask about my mother, and Uncle William told me. He was—well, uncharacteristically vulnerable the day Michael was born."

"Why are you talking about this?" Hester asked.

"Haven't you always wanted to know about my mother?"

At the next table, someone won the backgammon and a small cheer rose out. Hester took another sip of her drink. "Who was she?"

"My mother? A dancer. A waitress favored by Uncle William. A transgression. Here I am." I smiled sarcastically, which I knew she hated, especially when I was using it to show the dark side of self-pity. "She had no desire to know me. I suppose he thought he was protecting me. He still sends her money."

"What does this have to do with Michael's death?"

"The day Michael drowned, I was at the café where my mother works."

Hester showed a little surprise.

"Where I used to go every Tuesday from about two to four in the afternoon. Sometimes longer."

Hester took a dry swallow. She tried to look angry; anger was the glue of her dignity. That there had been no other woman was straining her last reservoirs of strength. I watched the reasoning: that I was not the villain, that all the hatred of me that had sustained her since Michael's death was undeserved. I was not the naked and lunging animal. I was just a curious and sad man sipping coffee, watching a middle-aged and still attractive woman take orders, replenish cups, suggest pie, on what had been—that luckless Tuesday—a sunny day, stiff breeze, good for sailing.

Hester looked like she was appraising me, but she was really processing the information. Who was this ex-mother-in-law, the grandmother who had never—would never—know her own grandchild?

"Why didn't you tell me?"

"About what?"

"Where you were the day Michael drowned."

"I am telling you now," I said.

The fact was that Hester had never asked. I'm sure she thought it beneath her to go digging for details of what she was sure were her husband's transgressions. And a part of her felt responsible for this presumed philandering. What did she expect? She was older than I and on the plain side. I had been attracted to her wit and strength, which were fine for me yet never quite enough for her.

Hester served up a cold smile. "And that's what the truth sounds like," she said. That the truth might be unsatisfying had never occurred to her. "So what's she like, your mother?"

"I never spoke to her," I said. "I never had the courage."

Hester waved the waiter over again. She'd drained her wine and I knew—from drinking the stuff—that it wasn't strong enough. "What he's drinking," she said.

We sat there quietly for a while. Hester was wondering what had happened to our marriage. She had wondered for years about this other woman, this cheating wife or stupid girl, who had sabotaged our life and made it unfixable. And I had let the marriage fall apart, because Hester's grief was frightening and I lacked the courage to watch it. And I had my own grief, of course, but it was quiet, and alone I could take myself apart piece by piece.

"There was hope for us," she said finally. It was an accusation, but it contained an optimism for our future. "You know," she continued, "we need you at the shop. Without Papa, we're short."

This surprised me. "You've kept the books for years," I said. "You're better off without me in the way."

"But you're the best at appraising."

"Ah, yes, the foremost expert in dressers, handy to have around."

Hester shut up. She took a minute pretending to be interested in the ashtray by worrying a flaking chip. She stopped abruptly and trained her eyes on me again. "Nathan keeps talking about his friend Olivia in such a way that I've determined she must have some bearing on my life," she said.

I wanted to lie, but right then I didn't have the imagination. "I'm moving to Scotland with Olivia after I'm done with my work here."

"Are you going to marry her?"

"One thing at a time."

"You look very well, Rupert," she said. It was intended to humiliate, but I'd seen it coming. "How old is Olivia?"

"She's a year older than you."

This made Hester pause. She thought to herself and then started laughing, then laughing louder, hysterically. I watched her without moving. "You don't love her, and you didn't love me either," she said. "All you want is a mother."

There's a hit, I thought. "That's banal," I said.

"Oh, yes, nothing more banal than analysis." The alcohol was beginning to have some effect and she had melted ever so slightly. She said, "Don't you ever miss me, Rupert?"

I looked at her, the heart-shaped face, the weak chin, the once-golden hair that had faded to a pale ashy yellow. The pause bothered her, and she shook her head.

"I do miss you," I said.

"When, Rupert? When do you miss me?"

I thought for a moment. "I miss you now."

Hester was booked into a hotel in the port town, a decent place with its own bathroom and a small private balcony. Nathan took a room in the same hotel, since he thought someone should stay near her. Hester seemed on the verge of something that we all hoped was sanity but could easily have been something less desirable. I provoked her, so I was off the hook. Nathan hardly knew her—Hester really wasn't that close to anyone except her father—but he had met her. Nathan was really doing it for me. And for Olivia, who wanted me around. And I didn't want to be with Hester. I wondered at that younger self that had found her comforting.

Neftali showed up the next day on the 11 A.M. ferry. I was at the site all day, and by the time I returned home at six, dusty, frustrated, and sunburned, Olivia had filled her in on recent events.

"How was Mýkonos?" I asked.

Neftali shrugged. "I wanted to bring my son to meet you all"—Neftali's son was eighteen—"but he says Aspros is too boring. Of course, I could tell him some things that might change his mind, but then my husband might disapprove."

"If you were my wife," I said, "I wouldn't let you out of my sight."

Neftali looked at me with some concern. "I'm worried about you."

"Thank you," I said. "Please don't stop."

"Tomorrow you can borrow my cousin's car to find a place to throw your father-in-law into the ocean." She squeezed my arm. "Rupert, Rupert," she said. I knew I was supposed to tell her I was fine, but I liked her too much to lie.

I was grateful for the car because the thought of climbing around the hills with Hester on the Vespa wasn't really appealing. Hester wasn't that old—she was forty-two—but she had embraced middle age while still in her thirties and dressed like a younger Miss Marple. I went to pick her up at seven, and we drove to the one monastery reachable by car. The soil was dusty, like ash itself. We had to park the car by a bullpen, and the fact that an unfriendly bull was contained there by only the suggestion of a fence—he must have had a fear of sticks to stay—sent us back to the coast. I returned for the first time to the beach by Faros and we climbed the same hill that Clive and I had climbed on the day we'd seen Jack and Thanasi lurking in the cave.

Hester looked out at the water, the small chapel. A wind had picked up, and she raised her hand to the top of her head to keep the hair out of her eyes.

"I think this will do," she said.

I didn't tell her that we were standing just in front of a rock that Clive had urinated on, or point out the small pile of goat dung just to the right of her shoe. The breeze was blowing out to sea and, honestly, Max had been such a delightful person that had he been there he would have said, "Oh, just get it done. Then you can go have a drink before dinner. Hester needs one." And thinking about old Max saying that made my eyes sting for the first time. And it all came on me at once. There would be no more Tea Room lunches. There would be no more Christmas hams studded with stinking cloves. I would no longer pour out aperitifs into tiny crystal glasses because Uncle William wouldn't want the toxic syrups, not anymore, not without

Max, and who else drank them? No one would yell at me from the
back of Grolsz's, "Another new suit?" when I entered, because no one
would care. And he was one less person to remember Michael. And
he was one less person to know me, the old me, that for all the booze
and sex and love of Olivia, had never recovered.

Hester took the urn, which had been sticking out of her alligator bag, but after twisting off the lid, she hesitated. She wasn't surprised at my sudden grief. She knew that side of me and it reassured her. She had been waiting for it, needing it, since her arrival. She placed her hand on my arm and whispered, "Who would have thought that a man with a forty-two inch waist could fit in there?"

I took that as my cue to pull myself together. "Better throw it now, Hessie," I said, "before the wind shifts."

And when we were walking back to the car, I remembered, and I said, "I missed your birthday this year, but I did think about you."

And then I took her back to her hotel.

I should never have slept with Hester. I knew it was wrong, even as I took off my shirt and she undressed quickly and neatly, putting her dress on a hanger and that on the curtain rod with the same speed it took me to get my shorts around my ankles. Hester knew what she wanted in all things, and in this arena—the bedroom—what she wanted was quite a divergence from her socially impeccable, unyielding image. I'd wondered what was going through her mind, what she'd made of the last mouthful of bourbon that I took from the glass on the nightstand even as I laid myself on top of her, but she kept her thoughts to herself. I'd appreciated her silence because I was trying to deny that Hester was Hester, not because of her, but because of my son. Because I didn't want to remember him then. Not when having sex. The connection seemed—at least intellectually—absurd.

I returned to the villa at around nine the next morning. The Vespa was not in sight, and I assumed that Nikos had gone off to supervise the workers without me. I had a hangover and no cigarettes;

I could hear *Lakmé* spewing out over the wall, and it did not fill me with confidence. I pushed the gate open and peeked inside. The familiar donkey-driver hat was visible over one of the chairs, but Olivia was facing the Victrola and didn't see me. I wasn't sure what to do when Amanda swiftly and silently—she was barefoot—ran down the steps of the house and ushered me back outside.

"Where were you last night?" she said in a whisper.

I opened my mouth, shut it, and then said, "I was with my wife."

"Your ex-wife," Amanda reminded me.

"I take it Olivia's not very pleased with me."

"She's not mad at you." Amanda glanced at the house. "Olivia thinks she must have been out of her mind to get involved with someone thirteen years younger, who really doesn't seem the faithful type."

"But I am," I protested, "usually." I pondered this. "It was my wife, for God's sake. She was grief-stricken, and I was a mess, and it was stupid, but I didn't see a way out of it."

"Was she blocking the door, Rupert?" Amanda had a twinkle in her eye.

"What's the use?"

"I'm not about to give you a hard time," she said. "Olivia won't stay mad forever. She really does care about you. In fact"—Amanda moved my hair around; I supposed she was fixing it, but I hadn't seen it that morning and didn't know if it was messy—"Olivia thinks she's making unreasonable demands on you."

"So what do I do?"

I'd meant it as rhetorical question, but Amanda grew suddenly serious. She moved the gate open so that she could get a clear view of Olivia's back with her signature hat. "You go in quickly and, without saying anything, you sit at her feet and put your head in her lap. And she'll probably say your name, and when she's done that, before she can get another word out, you launch into an apology, and tell her how crazy you're feeling and how you don't deserve her."

I considered this for a moment. "I think you're right," I said.

"You're good for her, believe it or not," said Amanda. She pushed me through the door. "Quickly, before Clive shows up and ruins everything."

I did put my head in Olivia's lap, and she said I needed to wash my hair, and I apologized profusely and then confessed that, although I was apologizing, what I really wanted to do was complain about my wife and how could Olivia stand me when I was so selfish? She agreed that I was selfish. It was undeniable. But she also said she was sick of thinking about herself, sick of other people thinking about her, so maybe it was all right, and I told her I found it offensive that she thought of me as a distraction, which made her throw back her head and laugh, and she called me a *wife fucker* or WF, and only Olivia ever called me that.

The Vespa was dead the following morning, no clicking, no rattle, so it went to the one person who could fix it and Nikos and I walked. The walk usually took about a half hour and I realized how much I'd wanted time with Nikos. A stiff breeze was blowing off the water and keeping things cool. Hester was to leave on the evening ferry and I was glad for it. I thought of making an offering to Apollo, or perhaps Poseidon, to guide the passage of the *Aphrodite*, to keep the seas calm and the sun shining. To make it leave miraculously on time. To get her off this island and over to Corfu, where some English friend of hers named Eleanor, who was known to Nathan, kept a house.

We walked for a while in silence, and I could feel Nikos checking me every now and then.

"I'm just a bit depressed, Nikos. It's understandable."

"Yes," said Nikos. "What would make you happy?"

"Small happy? Athens four weeks ago. You and me, Sue and Helen, only this time I get Helen."

Nikos laughed. "And big happy?"

I shrugged.

"You don't know what makes you happy, Rupert. To me, if this was my life, I would think it was a problem."

I wondered. "I've never known. I only know when something's gone, far away, and then I can say it made me happy. I think I'm perverted this way." I walked a couple of more feet. "Nikos," I said, "I think I'm going to ask Olivia to marry me."

Nikos looked at me with concern. "Is that the smart thing to do?"

"Probably not," I said.

"Why marry her? There are no kids. You are already married once. Why?" Nikos shrugged in an exaggerated way. It made him look like a turtle pulling in its head.

"You wouldn't understand," I said.

I was struggling to understand it myself.

Part of it was Olivia's illness. Her circumstances were, in a fairly operatic way, alluring. Perhaps I could equate this with gallantry. I didn't want Olivia thinking about us as something with a shelf life. I remembered Uncle William grappling with his father's impending death, the flotsam of which no doubt clouded my dealings with mortality, any mortality, Olivia's included. My grandfather had died, shortly after I'd graduated from college, at the age of ninety-two. He was forty years older than Uncle William, and I think this age gap and the fact that Grandpa William was fairly spectral through all the years I knew him—and possibly earlier—might have created certain negative associations with the role of father. Uncle William never liked to visit Grandpa William in the nursing home, but he absolutely refused to go alone, and I was the obvious choice for company. We visited Grandpa William once a week on Wednesdays. His was a slow decline, but at some point after he turned ninety, I did observe that he had become unrecognizable and not quite a man. He was an amalgam of smooth nubs of skin and bone that made me think of heels and elbows. The nurses kept him very clean and his only smell was one that I attributed—although now I wonder why—to the palate of his false teeth, which the nurses must have popped in for our benefit. His constantly open mouth was sort of dry and it seemed unlikely that he used it for eating. He was frighteningly thin and small and reminded me of skeletons of prehistoric people, reassembled on lab tables; there was a certain "this skull goes with this collar bone" unity about him, although the final effect was not exactly a person. His eyes were still very much alive but had only one expression—bewildered fear. He seemed to be in a constant state of awe. At some point he became completely paralyzed. I remember going shopping for one of his final birthdays. I was stymied and called Uncle William for some guidance.

"He doesn't do anything, and whatever he might use—linen sheets, for example—is a bit macabre," I said.

"Don't get him sheets," said Uncle William.

"What are you getting him?"

"Golf clubs."

Uncle William saw nothing funny in this, although I did laugh on my end of the phone for a while, but after I hung up I realized he'd managed to convince me. I went out and a got an argyle sweater, a nice green one, that would look great on a golf course. It wasn't in good taste to remind people of their death when you were supposed to be celebrating their birth. I now saw the stinginess in getting chocolates for little old ladies on their special days, and it wasn't merely financial: it was a stinginess of spirit. Of course, when Uncle William and I showed up on Grandpa William's birthday and gave him the golf clubs and the sweater, he responded with the same bewildered terror about the eyes, as well as a moan, which started somewhere in the lungs, losing nearly all its strength by the time it left his mouth, as if it were the echo of something he'd said ten years earlier.

"I think he's pleased," said Uncle William.

Yes. I was a buyer of sweaters. It was the only proper thing to do.

I wondered how to communicate this to Nikos, who had been watching me as I pondered this. He kicked a rock and it went bouncing into a ravine, loosing some pebbles and sand. At the foot of the ravine, a donkey was grazing, accompanied by a few chickens. Suddenly offended, the donkey began honk-wheezing, louder and louder until, apparently pacified, it became silent again.

"If Olivia weren't ill," I said, "I probably would marry her. I can't be with Olivia without imagining a future for us. It's not fair to her."

"You are being generous?" he tried.

"God, does it sound that pathetic?"

"It sounds like . . .there's a good English word for it that means making excuses."

The word he was searching for was *justification*, but I didn't feel like having it pointed at me right then and I kept it to myself. Another word he might have thought of was *desperation*. Another word was *confusion*. And I was self-pitying and lost and, in addition to all these things, hung over. Again.

"I need Olivia," I said. "What else am I doing?"

"You are running away," said Nikos. "But even if you marry Olivia, Hester will still be there. Making your life crazy now isn't going to fix what has already happened."

It occurred to me to thank Nikos because he'd made sense of something that I had been unable to see clearly. But I didn't. He hadn't changed my mind. The wrongness or rightness of it—of anything—seemed irrelevant.

All day I managed to avoid thinking about Hester. This had been an exhausting endeavor, and by the end of it, as I showered off the dust and sweat, I was eager to put her on the boat and be done with it. But I wasn't ready to face her. Not really. When I appeared at the café for the changing of the guard—Nathan, sipping the last of a martini, ready to relinquish his chair—I could see she had gained hope for us. And now that I had relented once, that hope would be very hard to extinguish. I steeled myself and went forward.

Nathan and Hester made their goodbyes, complete with obligatory nattering about dinner back in New York. I sat down, waiting for it all to be over. I was sulking like a child, behavior I saved for Hester, I suppose, in the same way that Amanda did her sex-kitten cooing for Jack. Nathan finally gone, Hester turned her attention to me. I think she'd hoped for some tenderness, but she saw this particular slouch of mine as a sign that this was not the case. She sat down.

"I was hoping you'd come see me yesterday," she said.

I looked away. "I know," I said.

Hester looked down at the table and said in a small voice, "Well, that's that."

I felt bad for her then and hated myself. Maybe hate's a strong word. I hated Hester then. "What did you expect?" I said. "Why did you come here?"

Hester was thinking, wasting different possibilities. She looked up after a while. "Because, Rupert, you're all I have left." She looked off to the left as if that would let her escape everything—me, the restaurant, her life—but she had a few things to say and, with a ferry arriving in another half hour, this was the safest time to do it. "I thought I needed to know where you were that day." She shook her head, dissatisfied with her explanations. "And now I know."

"But that was never the question," I said. I was beginning to feel reckless. "The question is *Where were you?*"

Hester looked up. She knew she was in danger.

"Because that's the real question, isn't it? Where were you? Because you were on the boat, not me, and you should have been watching him. And you were there. You were. You were there, and you let him drown."

I put some money down on the table, although I didn't remember taking out my wallet, and left quickly. I wanted to get away as fast as possible because I couldn't stand the smell of it. I didn't want to be near such a ruined person. I also knew that I had destroyed any hope that Hester ever had of healing at that point. I'd learned over the last few days that her life would not mean much without me—without a few years to let her grow out of pain—but now I had killed any possibility of happiness. Any happiness. I might as well have killed her.

I walked up the hill through the village, taking the steps two at a time, until it was behind me and there was nothing but dirt and rocks and plants. I sat on the ground. I couldn't see Hester, but I knew what restaurant she was in, under which roof. I could hear a small voice speaking somewhere inside, saying that I still had time to go to her. The damage was done, but maybe there was a kind word to be said. And for a minute I saw Michael in my mind in a red sweater, and he wasn't just a reconstruction of shattered pieces of memory. He wasn't an amalgam but looked just as he had when he was in front of me. I could see his expectant half smile, although he knew he could get anything, because Michael was spoiled. And I was lying on the couch with a novel and he was playing with his trains loudly. Hester is at the door saying, "It's eleven. Nanny wants to go to bed." And I say, "Let her go to sleep. I can brush his teeth and put on his pajamas." And Hester relents and gives me a long-suffering look, although she's happy I'm willing to do this for our little son. She takes the whiskey tumbler from the side table and judges it. I say, "Looks like I need some ice." And she gets it for me. Michael, who has tired of the trains, is now supposed to be making a puzzle, but it's too difficult, so he throws the pieces at the big flowerpot, which is more fun.

And then there is Hester, walking along the quay, carrying her own suitcase, the suitcase I should be carrying for her. But I can't do it. I can't move. It's like Delphi and someone might need me, but I can't imagine making a difference to anyone. I am only a bird or a ghost or a tree. I cannot move. I can only observe. I am not living.

10

The ferry arrived and there was the usual bustle. Someone was reversing in a small pickup truck, either trying to get on the ferry or kill the elderly woman who refused to move. Cameras were out and pointing. People were hugging. I saw Hester waiting on the pier. Even if she had been wearing other clothes, I would have recognized her stiff spine, her thrown-back shoulders. Goodbye. Goodbye, I thought, but a part of me was sad because she was taking some of my old life with her, something I would not get back. I watched her climb down into the boat, out of sight. Then I saw Clive and, after him, Nikos. I wondered what they were doing at the ferry.

There were a few sheep, causing problems, and a donkey. The donkey, not in the mood for seafaring, was pulling anxiously at its rope. At the rope's other end, a man was struggling, and then the donkey—defiant swing of the head, monster teeth gleaming—escaped. I watched its mad dash, the men waving their arms; the women, mouths all Os of shock and wonder—then it reached the edge of the land. I saw the donkey's lowered head, the moment of indecision, then decision, and it jumped off the pier. For a timeless second the donkey was flying; then it hit the water with a tremendous splash. I held my breath, worried that it had broken its legs. But the donkey resurfaced, swimming, and then—as if dropped from the heavens—was wading through the children on the beach, and they were hugging it and slapping its sides, and a little girl ran over with a sprig of jasmine and tucked it into the bridle. And another little girl ran down from the restaurant and gave it something to eat—maybe a carrot? a cake?—and the donkey liked it.

I felt happy then—an awkward joy—and realized that the gravel was poking through the seat of my pants. I walked down the hill, back into town. Nikos and Clive were by the newsstand, and Clive was reading the paper. I could see by the way Nikos lowered his glasses and then put them back that he had been looking for me.

"Rupert," called Nikos, "did you see the donkey?"

"Yes, yes. Quite a jump."

Clive looked me up and down. "You look terrible. Are you hung over?"

"No," I said. "I'm hung under."

"What does this mean?" asked Nikos.

Clive wondered. "It means either he has a large penis or he wants a drink."

I smiled. "I'll take the drink."

Clive and Nikos were actually at the port to see off Amanda, who, in response to the latest phone call from Jack, had decided to leave immediately. She'd packed in a hurry and only just made the ferry. Nikos, although he'd been insisting that she go to Hydra for the last two weeks, had suddenly felt compelled to try and convince her to stay.

"She didn't say why?" I asked.

Nikos shook his head. "There was something wrong."

"No one knows much about Amanda." I waited for Nikos to disagree, but he didn't.

"She's up to something," said Clive.

I spent the next few days dividing my time between the site and Olivia's side, which seemed the safest places to be. Although Amanda had not been a regular drinking companion, her absence somehow disturbed the balance, and I found myself going to bed at the reasonable hour of 2 A.M. and often waking because I was done with sleeping. I hadn't asked Olivia to marry me, because it seemed ridiculous—I seemed ridiculous—in Hester's wake.

The site had not yielded anything exceptional, or even whole, and the little chips and shards of dirty pottery were no longer that compelling. The promise of a great find had dimmed. When Nikos and I referred to the "site" it now included the café across the valley, where we could supervise, although the workers at this distance were as small as ants. Nikos thought the whole thing was under control. He had decided that Tomas was a good supervisor and, to keep him in line, had dangled the prospect of a job in Athens and maybe even New York as incentive to find something. I agreed that this was the best way of having the dig yield something real.

Nikos was going to have to return to Athens to see Kostas, who probably just missed him but had sent a number of messages citing all Nikos's neglected duties, his spending too much money, his mother, his fiancée, all wondering what he was up to. He decided to go home for a week but kept not leaving, until one Thursday he packed a small bag and sneaked off without saying goodbye to anyone. Nathan and Clive were returning to New York in another ten days, and although it had seemed that the summer would go on forever, what was left was passing too fast. We made jokes about all getting a house together, a commune of sybarites, or meeting up again next year. No one believed it, though. And it covered up a sadness— an anticipation of nostalgia—made all the stronger by a few things: the ghost of angry Jack hovering over Amanda, Nathan's recent post-office phone calls to his lover in New York, Olivia's declining health.

Nikos was in Athens when Amanda returned. The rest of us were in the garden with the Victrola cranked and coughing up a Viennese waltz, and Olivia was killing me at backgammon. Neftali had Clive helping her with some potted geraniums that needed to be moved. Nathan was writing postcards, the sure sign of someone about to return home. There wasn't much light in the garden, and when the gate creaked open I couldn't make out who was standing there.

Then I heard Amanda's voice—"Don't make a fuss"—and before I could decide what she was talking about, she stepped into the light shining off the front of the house, and we saw what a mess Jack had made of her face.

Nathan stood up, and all his postcards slid to the ground. I didn't move, because I didn't know what to do other than make a fuss. Neftali was holding her breath, but Olivia got up right away. She ran over to her and put her arms around Amanda and walked her up the stairs of the house. She paused at the door and said, "Rupert, please bring in Amanda's bag," and then they disappeared inside.

Later that night I heard Amanda sobbing in the room across the hall, but it sounded almost staged to me. I could never be generous to Amanda. Too much of this, again, seemed within her capacity to control.

The next morning I had to walk into town to get another notebook. I'd filled mine with little sketches of the larger shards and guesses as to their provenance. I'd been looking forward to the walk, but after rounding the first corner I saw that I was behind Amanda. I could have waited to let her get ahead, but, as if sensing me, she turned. Her face was blue on one side and she had a cut above her left eyebrow. It looked as if she'd been in a barroom brawl. When I got closer—she was waiting for me—I saw that her lip had also been cut but was almost healed.

"Cigarette?" I offered.

She took it.

"Did Jack do that to you?"

"God, Rupert, how do you do it?"

"What?"

"You just asked me about Jack in the same tone of voice that you offered me a cigarette."

I thought, "Years of practiced patrician denial."

"You really think you've got my number, don't you?" said Amanda.

I regarded her. She looked more angry than wounded, more aggressive than needy. "If you want to be alone," I said, "I understand." I began to walk ahead.

Amanda watched my back for a minute, then said, "Yes."

I turned around.

She began to shake her head in an appealingly self-deprecating way, a predictable way. "Yes, Jack did this to me."

I waited for Amanda to catch up.

"He was drunk when I spoke to him on the phone, not darling-I-miss-you drunk, more why-do-I-even-bother? drunk. But when I got to Hydra, he was so deep into it that, I don't know, he didn't even recognize me."

"He's got a problem," I said, "and it sounds like you have some decisions to make."

"His problem is my problem," said Amanda. "He's my husband and I love him."

"Well, I can't argue with that," I said. I tried to make it sound clipped and proper, but Amanda saw the sarcasm.

"I won't argue with you," she said. "I know you don't like Jack."

"And right now," I held her chin, which was level with mine, "you're not in a very good position to defend him."

Amanda seemed inclined to be honest with me, but I didn't want to look into the depths of her relationship with Jack. Everyone hated Jack. Everyone said he was pompous, a poseur, and that the tiresome tough-guy routine, complete with macho dialogue, was contrived and offensive, but they always added the disclaimer, "He's a great artist." Clive and I, however, had decided that even his art was crap. This was a deep-felt conviction, although neither of us had ever seen any of his sculptures. And the fact that he was a wife-beater didn't surprise me at all. Clive had called him that one night—"wife beater!"— as Jack stumbled his way to a restaurant bathroom, but this was just Clive's sense of humor, not based on anything. Then again, no one was surprised that Jack had hit Amanda, and no one was surprised that she'd shown up again on Aspros. Amanda considered us family—we were safe—but I thought it was something more. I thought she needed people to witness her pulpy face as a sort of vanity. A true drama queen needs everything noticed, cooed over, regardless of the pathetic light she is thrown into.

That night Amanda, Clive, and I stayed in town after dinner for a few drinks. Olivia needed her space and didn't want me walking around the house, pretending not to be bored.

"I need a night of sitting on the couch reading one of Neftali's lurid books," she said. "Go on then." She waved me off. "Go make some mischief."

We went to the small fancy bar that served cocktails and ordered martinis. Actually, we ordered glasses of vodka, and then asked for them to bring a bottle of "martini" out so we could add a little. We'd learned the local martini was a glass of vermouth with an olive, but sometimes a caper, floating in it. We also dropped ice into it. I took a certain amount of pride in this, my very bad martini, as all those girls I'd known growing up had taken pride in their very good martinis. I thought that Amanda was drinking rather fast, but then I'd finished my drink before she had. Clive ordered another round and we made our drinks.

"I miss Nikos," said Clive.

"He'll be back soon," I said.

"But I might be gone," said Clive, "and he didn't even say goodbye."

"I'll give you his number in Athens," I said. I looked over at Amanda. "Do you miss Nikos?"

Amanda smiled. "What's it to you?"

I looked over at Clive, then back at Amanda, raising my eyebrows.

"You're very fond of him, aren't you, Rupert?" said Amanda. "A little too fond. And jealous of me?"

"What are you suggesting?" said Clive. He feigned shock.

I was amused. "I know what this is about, Amanda," I said, because I did. There had to be something wrong with me because I had never pursued her, hadn't even flirted passively, which I did with nearly all women.

"What is it about?" asked Clive, but Amanda and I just kept looking at each other.

Two martinis later, Tomas walked by with a few of his friends. He was clutching a paper bag with a bottle in it. After a quick exchange, Clive decided to join him. At this point, Amanda and I should have gone home, but we were talking about people from college, and we, predictably, had a few people we knew in common. One of them was Kiplinger Sand. I didn't know much about Kiplinger other than he was now in the movies, wore offensive jackets, and drank toxic South American liquors that he bought at Irish bars in Chelsea, but I found the conversation pleasantly shallow and thought, I suppose, that I should stay for another drink.

"A friend of mine went out with him a couple of times," Amanda said.

"Just a couple of times?"

"Well," said Amanda, "they had an encounter in the back of his car."

"You can't stop there," I said. "Amanda, subtlety is completely lost on me."

"I don't know. I guess it wasn't very good." She laughed, and I saw her big clean teeth. "Let's have another one," she said. The bartender had left the vodka, "martini," and ice on the bar, so we could make our own.

Sometime shortly after, we crossed the border. At one point I was still witty and neat, and the next I was slipping a bit off the bar stool, the room was spinning in the corners, and when I went to the bathroom I saw my face had taken on a vulgarity. I took a slightly longer way back to the bar stools. Amanda seemed a little slumped but pulled herself straight when she saw me. The bottle of vodka was empty.

"I think we're done here," I said. I paid up and we walked out. "We'll have a nightcap back at the house."

We turned off the town square and began walking up the path, up the steps. Amanda had my arm and was clinging to me. She was almost my height and her hands felt very big, especially compared to Olivia's. At one point, one of us, probably me, said, "Look at the moon." And the moon seemed very full and I wondered if it had actually been a month since I'd arrived, and then Amanda had lifted up my shirt and put her bare hands on my stomach, had worked them around to the base of my back, and we were kissing. And I was sitting on the low wall in front of the chapel, and it occurred to me that it would be better to be inside the courtyard, out of the moonlight. And then we were inside, and then Amanda unbuttoned her shirt.

"No," I said. "I can't do this right now." I don't know why nudity all of a sudden bothered me. Possibly discovery. Possibly Olivia. Some clear-minded guilt had exerted itself, but Amanda wasn't listening. She began to unbuckle my belt. "No, we are not doing this." I pushed her away and rebuckled my belt.

"Why not, Rupert?"

"Because we can't. It's not going to work."

Amanda stood looking at me, her shirt open. "Who wants anything to work?" she said. "Is it Olivia?" she added, with great condescension.

I was so drunk I remember being impressed with Amanda's ability to come up with that. She took my silence as acquiescence, and I must have done the same, at least for a couple of minutes. Amanda was strong and warm and she smelled wonderful. But then I wanted another drink. And then I remembered Hester, and Hester's face at the restaurant and what I'd said to her, and all of this wouldn't go away and I didn't feel like fucking Amanda just then. I pushed her away and said, "I can't do this."

And Amanda looked angry and said, "Mister Morals."

Which was something I'd never been accused of. I shook my head and said, "Not even you and I can fuck our way straight this time."

I realized I was sobering up ever so slightly, but the last of the vodka was only hitting Amanda now. I remembered the bottle of vodka, empty on the bar, and that it hadn't been that way when I'd gone to the bathroom, and that Amanda must have drunk it all, a lot, as if it were water. I was walking up the path again, buttoning my shirt, but Amanda caught up with me and I think I must have hated her because when she tried to kiss me again, I pushed her, and she fell off the path and against an olive tree. I didn't help her up. I started walking away as quickly as I could.

Then I went and woke up Olivia and said many things to her, some of which I actually remembered the next morning.

I woke up because the sun was shining strongly. I opened my eyes just a crack. I wasn't sure where I was and my first feeling, before recognition, was dread. Then I saw the little desk and all of Olivia's lotions and her pills on it, and then the bed creaked gently and I saw Olivia sitting on the bed at my side. I put my arm around her as she sat there.

"How do you feel?" she asked.

"I'm not sure yet," I said. "What time is it?"

"It's two."

There was a moment of silence that I wanted to last forever, and then Olivia said, "I'm going to go down for lunch. I'll be back in an hour. Do you want anything?"

"No," I said. I wanted to make conversation right then, as if to prove to Olivia that I hadn't been badly drunk, only extremely jovially drunk, which was why I could make light conversation now and didn't really have a hangover, but this was impossible. I let her go and then remembered Amanda. I wondered if she'd ever made it out of the branches of the olive tree, whether she'd made it home. Then Clive came in and sat just where Olivia had been sitting, and for a moment I was inclined to put my arm around him.

"What were you and Amanda up to last night?" he asked in a loud whisper.

I was still trying to reconstruct the events of the previous evening and was momentarily concerned that Amanda and I had indeed been fucking each other in the light of the moon.

"Why?" I ventured.

"Well, she's still not home yet. I was hoping she'd somehow come back and found you. But your room's empty. I really ought to go find Tomas."

"What does Tomas have to do with this?"

"Tomas and I were walking up the path and we saw Amanda. She seemed to have fallen into a tree. And then she and Tomas were talking, and all of a sudden I was going home to bed, and Tomas and Amanda were . . ."

"Were what?" I asked.

"I don't really know. Tomas had a bottle of wine. He and I were going to drink it together, then, all of a sudden, I was going home." Clive thought for a minute. "We really shouldn't drink so much."

Clive disappeared and I closed my eyes again. When I opened them, Olivia was back on the side of the bed. She was holding a glass of water. She was looking into it as if the glass possessed a divining ability.

"How do you feel now?" she asked.

"I'm all right," I said, but I wasn't sure yet. Olivia looked serious and it made me nervous.

"I have to ask you, Rupert. Is it true, about your little boy?"

I closed my eyes and when I opened them again, she had put the water on the side table and was crouching with her face very close to mine. "What if I made it up?"

"Why would you do that?" she asked.

"Handsome and damaged, Livvy. It's supposed to be irresistible."

"I don't know about irresistible," she said. She smiled and handed me the water. "It is dangerously attractive."

"I'll take what I can get," I said. I sat up.

Clive stuck his head in the door and said, "Is he up?"

"He is," I answered.

"Well, you better get dressed. Amanda still hasn't shown up yet. I think we should go to the site and ask Tomas what happened to her."

By the time I got on the bike it was almost five. Clive drove as fast as the thing would take us, which was at a dizzying speed down the hills and then excruciatingly slowly as we crested them. The workers were finishing up for the day, laying out the canvas tarps over the site, but I got a quick look at the pit, before it was completely covered; I saw that in some places they had struck rock, and this wasn't a good sign. Clive immediately began questioning Tomas, who was his friend after all. I would have been happy to avoid Tomas altogether at that point—it was some variety of guilt at having delivered Amanda to him—but I needed to ask about the dig. I walked over slowly.

"Amanda's all right," said Clive. "She's still at Tomas's."

To me these seemed to be mutually exclusive facts, but Clive seemed satisfied. Tomas looked positively smug. "How is she?" I asked.

"She is sleeping today a lot," said Tomas.

"Is she coming back to the villa?" I asked.

"No, boss," he said. "She does not like you very much." And he laughed.

Clive guffawed, but I was in no mood for this. "Tomas, are you striking rock?"

"In some places, there's the rock," he said, suddenly serious.

"Well, you better find something soon. You know, the dig's almost over."

"I don't understand," said Tomas.

"No dirt, no dig." I got on the back of the bike and Clive took off. I saw Tomas looking back at the pit. He knew he had to find something if he was to get the job in Athens, or even New York, where women like Amanda populated the streets. All those Amazonian blondes and all that money, but our little sandpit hadn't yielded anything marvelous. Although—and here I was cautiously pleased—we had a number of fragments that could be restored into a rather large bowl with nautical figures on it, a starfish, a squid, a dolphin; it was lovely and justified the whole process for me. But I wasn't feeling particularly generous to Tomas. I wondered first what Amanda had said, and then what she thought, and then—because I still wasn't sure—what had really happened between us.

Amanda did not come back the next day either. Clive said something about Tomas having tied her up in his shed, and I said she probably liked it. Clive wasn't any happier with Amanda than I was. He had been cultivating this friendship with Tomas for a long time and wanted something to show for it, but, since he and Nathan were leaving in a week, it seemed that all that cultivation might not yield the specific results that Clive had hoped for. Amanda's sleeping with Tomas annoyed me, although I'm not sure why. As far as I was concerned, she had wasted whatever limited goodwill she'd managed to accrue. When Neftali came in at lunch—I usually ate back at the house to be with Olivia—and said that Nikos was going to be on the seven o'clock ferry, I felt a little thrill of pleasure. Amanda's defecting to the working classes would disturb him profoundly. I took Clive back to the site with me, because he was bored, and we stopped off at the café in the old town for a drink first. I showed him my notebooks.

"You know, Rupert, you're an excellent draftsman," he said.

"I have no sense of depth," I responded.

"But the detail." He nodded at me encouragingly.

"Where were you when I was in the third grade?" I asked.

"Preschool probably. No, I was still at home."

We sat for a little while enjoying a drink, the quiet of it all, anticipating Nikos's return and gossiping in an enjoyable, unkind way. And then Clive jumped up and said, "I think something's happening over there."

"Where?"

"At the dig."

I looked over and it seemed, I couldn't see very well, that someone was swinging his shirt as a signal. There was a German couple at the next table and Clive asked to borrow their binoculars.

"They're waving at us," said Clive. "They're looking right over here and waving, and someone's holding something."

I grabbed the binoculars from Clive. I could see it, something round, something white. "I think," I said, the blood pounding in my ears, "I think they've found a head."

11

When I finally had that head in my hands, cradled in my lap—the thing was heavy—and I could see it up close, I knew I was holding a work of art. The head was of a young man, possibly from the second century A.D., and this was all good, because that coincided with the earthquake. The curls were beautifully rendered, almost soft. The eyes, wide set, had a strong brow that gave the appearance of concern, or at least focus. The lips were full, closed but not hard. This was a handsome head. I laughed, but only to myself. I looked up and the workers were standing around me. Tomas had his big camel eyes on me, his head angled as if he were looking around something.

"Very nice," I said. "This is beautiful."

"Maybe we have the rest of the day off," said Tomas.

"No," I said, "this is just a head." I held Tomas with my eyes. "Where's the rest of him?"

Clive leaned in and whispered, "Isn't it sometimes just a head?"

I nodded. "But Tomas doesn't know that."

Clive wanted to go back to the villa to share the good news with everyone, but I hadn't decided what I wanted to do, so we went back to the café. I had wrapped the head in an old sack and unveiled it ceremoniously.

"What do you think?" I asked Clive.

"Beautiful," he said,

"Is beauty everything?" I said. "I wish it were."

"That would make your life very easy, Rupert, but the rest of us have to rely on our wit."

"And virtue," I said. I turned the head to better see the profile.

"Aren't you supposed to be delighted?" said Clive.

"I am."

"Great," he said. "And now I hope you're going to tell me why you're behaving in such a strange manner."

I set the head up on the table so that it was standing on its neck. I turned it so that the eyes fell on Clive. The two regarded each other.

"What?" said Clive. "Is it a fake?"

"Doesn't look fake, does it?" I said.

"So what's bothering you?"

"It's not my art background this time, it's my knowledge of human nature. There are two ways that this head might have made it into the dig. One is serendipity. The other is Tomas."

"But it looks old," said Clive, "doesn't it?"

"Yes, it does. It's been weathered. Look at the curls."

Clive scratched at one of the curls, and a white powder came off.

"What is that?" asked Clive.

"That is . . ." I scratched some off myself. It didn't smell like anything, so I tasted it. "It's salt."

"Salt? Would there be salt in the dirt?"

"No. Where do we get salt?" I asked.

"Kitchens?" he said, with some irony.

"No, Clive, not kitchens." I'd finally figured something out, just a part of the whole but something intriguing. "Before the kitchen."

"What are you talking about, Rupert?"

"This was weathered in the ocean." I laughed. "I wonder if Amanda's in on it."

"In on what?"

"The head is big and round and heavy." I put my hands on his shoulders. "It's been under water, salt water."

Clive thought for a moment. "This has something to do with Jack?"

"He's a sculptor. Remember how I said all his work was crap? I
was wrong. He's actually very good."

"But why?"

"I don't know. But this head . . .it's the head of Antinoüs."

"What, the statue in Delphi?"

"Same person, but this head is a copy of just a head. I think the
real one is in Scandinavia somewhere. Except Jack's changed the
nose. It's a bit narrow through the bridge. Clever, clever, clever." I
scratched off some more salt and tasted it, just to be sure. I looked at
Clive. "Feel like a swim?"

When we reached the villa, only Neftali was home. She was with
the caretaker, supervising the scrubbing down of the garden furniture. I had been warned by Kostas to keep all important finds to myself,
especially if he was supposed to get them out of the country, so I didn't
say anything about the head. I hurried upstairs, holding it against my
chest, trying to look casual, but the thing was heavy.

"Rupert," she called.

"Yes, Neftali?" I tried not to sound guilty.

"Have you seen Olivia's hat?"

"That old donkey-driver thing?"

"She can't find it."

"I'll get her another one," I said.

"That's what I said." Neftali laughed. "But she said she liked that
one."

I got up to my room and hid the head, still wrapped in the sack,
under my bed. I felt like a twelve-year-old, stashing it there. Outside my window, I could hear Clive and Neftali discussing Amanda.
Apparently, the villagers had expressed some concern over her
behavior.

"It's really none of their business," said Clive.

"That's what I said," said Neftali. "They are all scandalized, and
they are all entertained."

I pulled on my swim trunks and grabbed a towel. I looked out the window, down at Clive and Neftali. "Come on, Clive," I said. "Get your trunks on, and don't forget your snorkel."

I had a cigarette with Neftali while I waited for him.

She said, "Is it true that you are thinking of asking Olivia to marry you?"

"Don't you start," I chided her.

"Nathan is worried," she said.

"Then Nathan can talk to me," I said.

Neftali made a disapproving face. "Don't be like that, Rupert."

"What do you mean?"

"With the wind blowing you here and there," she said. "Be strong."

"All right, Neftali." I patted her hand, but I could tell she wasn't finished with me.

"Why doesn't Amanda want to come back here?"

"Why should I know?"

"You were with her that night," she said.

"I really don't know," I said. Then Clive rescued me, appearing on the steps to the house with two masks and two snorkels.

"Look," he said. "One each. I forgot that Nathan had this stuff. He never uses it."

We took the Vespa into Faros and parked it in a small alley off the main street. Clive was worried someone would see it and know where we were. Of course, I argued this point with him. Who would see us? Who would care? We were just going for a swim to explore some local caves. Remarkably, neither of us had thought to bring wine.

The water was calm. From the shore I could see where the ledges of rock cut through the sand. I waded in with my mask around my neck, the snorkel in my hand. Clive was still on the beach. He was looking up at the rise, at the path we had descended to get to the water.

"What are you looking at?" I said.

"Just making sure we weren't followed," he said.

I put the snorkel in my mouth and lay on the surface of the water. All sound disappeared except for the slow draw and release of my breath. I kicked a little and spread my arms out. I looked at the floor of the ocean, maybe ten feet down, and watched a flounder skim the sandy bottom. Its eyes peered straight up into mine. I could have floated there all day, but suddenly Clive was swimming beneath me. I was startled and pulled my head out of the water.

"What are you doing, Rupert?"

"Nothing," I said. "Snorkeling."

"Let's go," he said. "What if someone shows up?"

Of course, the real secret wasn't hidden in the caves. The caves weren't the treasure trove of antiques, false or real, that Clive hoped for. He wanted us to be the Hardy Boys and wasn't very convincing when he tried to make this desire sound ironic. I knew he saw gold heaped in clinking, spilling mountains, chests with strings of pearls, fist-sized rubies, and probably a skeleton grinning beneath the rim of a tricorne hat. Even if he hadn't articulated this notion to himself, I could read it in his eagerness and knew that only disappointment awaited him. I, on the other hand, was looking to solve the mystery of Jack. Jack was now complicated and I was intrigued.

Of the two of us, I was the better swimmer and reached the caves first. Clive had suggested that we race and at some point I had been tempted to let him win. Clive brought out a side in me that few people did. But I got tired of swimming so slowly. I was momentarily concerned that all Clive's hand-rolled cigarettes had rendered his lungs useless, but he powered along in a sort of alternating freestyle, breast-stroke, dog paddle, and who cared what it looked like as long as he wasn't drowning? The waves by the mouth of the cave hadn't looked like much from shore, but here, up close, they were enough to smash us against the rocks. It took me quite a few tries to scramble onto one of them, where I perched like a seal waiting for Clive. I was wondering, of course, how he was going to make it back to shore. When he finally reached the cave—I helped him up and he sat—because there was not enough room for him to lie down—breathing wildly, the first words out of his mouth were, "I could use a cigarette."

* * *

Much is made of caves and entering them. A part of me would like to say that there, at the threshold, something of our innocence was still intact; that we did not know; and that our not-knowing had somehow kept us pure. But I wasn't Wordsworth paddling along full speed in his barque, and Clive—well, if anyone had blown his innocence it was Tomas, who had let Clive believe in a deeper friendship. Not that this sort of friendship wasn't possible, it was that anything was possible as long as Tomas could get off Aspros. Behind those unblinking black eyes and heavy lashes was a calculating mind, an aware individual who knew that his only currency was his good looks and a canny intelligence capable of making the quick decisions needed to advance himself in the world.

"Let's go in," I suggested.

The water was cold in the cave, and paddling around I suddenly remembered the moray eels that were sometimes speared as they prowled beneath the jetties of Faros. My eyes took a moment to adjust to the gloom, but then I saw a rock ledge, narrow but mostly dry, and I pulled myself up and out. There was a candle with a small square of folded oilskin alongside it. When I unfolded it, I found a dry box of matches. I lit the candle and the cave was dimly illuminated.

Clive stood unsteadily on the rock at the mouth of the cave. "Is there anything in there?" he asked.

"Are you scared, Clive?"

"Yes, frankly," he said.

"Don't worry about the eels," I said. I peered into the water.

"What eels?"

"The ones that aren't here." I shone the candle around. I couldn't see anything that struck me as out of place, but I didn't know what I was looking for. Clive paddled quickly across the cave and pulled himself out of the water.

"My foot touched something," he said.

"What was it?"

"I think it was a net. Maybe they've set a trap."

"Don't be ridiculous," I said. I held the candle up toward the mouth of the cave. An iron hook was driven into the wall and from it hung a net, very taut, holding something that was hidden beneath the surface of the water.

I swam over to the hook, leaving Clive to hold the candle. I put my feet on a submerged rock, and tried to pull the net up. It was too heavy. I swam down with my mask and made out some roughly round objects—heads?—that were being weathered beneath the surface of the water. I resurfaced.

"Clive, I need a hand," I said.

Clive put down the candle and gingerly paddled over to me. We pulled at the net and, with both of us straining at it, the objects started to rise. I saw a marble face begin to break the surface of the water.

I am not exactly sure what happened after that. I know Clive saw Thanasi rowing up to the mouth of the cave and shouted something, and this startled me so that I dropped the net. Thanasi began to row away, but then Clive was screaming and I realized his hand had somehow gotten pinned between the taut ropes of the net and the cold stone of the cave. His knuckles were grazed but I knew, from looking at them, that there was no serious damage. Trying to convince Clive of this was not so easy.

"You need to get a boat to get me back to shore."

"No, I don't."

"Yes, you do," he said. "I can't swim."

"All right," I said. "I will swim to shore. That will take at least twenty minutes. Then I will walk to Faros. That will take at least fifteen minutes. Then I will find a fisherman who is willing to part with his boat, or maybe I'll steal one. . . ."

Clive really didn't want to stay in the cave by himself. We took to the water. Luckily the tide was going in. Finally, with me swimming circles around him, Clive made it to shore.

He collapsed on the beach, lying there as if he were Robinson Crusoe.

"I'm never going anywhere with you again," he said. But he was already making plans. He wanted to come back with a boat so we could take whatever was in the net. I told him that was stealing, and he said it wasn't, because the heads were fakes. I told him taking the heads would be dangerous regardless of their authenticity. People who made fakes were probably fairly sensitive when it came to keeping track of their merchandise.

Clive moaned in an aggressive, frightening way the entire ride back to Stavri, but he was very happy when Neftali made a big fuss over his hand, and not terribly pleased with me. Neftali walked Clive into the house cooing and making sounds of disapproval. She said she would clean his knuckles well and make sure that there was no possibility of infection. Clive was of the opinion that his knuckles might already be infected, but the wound had had a good half-hour soak in salt water as he'd floundered to shore, and the possibility of infection existed only in his mind.

Nathan had a glass of something and rattled the ice cubes festively. "Neftali says the two of you have been acting very suspiciously today," he said. "What are you up to?"

"We're solving a mystery," I said. I waggled my eyebrows. "What are you drinking?"

"Vodka," said Nathan. He offered me the glass and I took a sip.

"That might hit the spot," I said. "How's Olivia been today?"

"Olivia looked all over but didn't find Amanda. Then she talked to some woman rumored to be Tomas's grandmother, and the woman shouted something at her."

"Actually, she hissed at me," said Olivia, who had walked up to us. "She hissed, and maybe she even cursed me."

"What on earth did you do?" I asked.

"I sort of did this." Here Olivia waved her hands over her head like a snake charmer. "I don't know why, but it was very effective."

"But no Amanda?"

"No," said Olivia. She sighed.

"I don't know why she's acting so bizarrely," I said. "Blame it on me all you want, but I didn't do anything to her, and I don't find this pseudo-coyness very funny anymore."

180 SABINA MURRAY

"I don't blame you," said Nathan.

"Did it ever occur to either of you that she might be embarrassed? That she might be avoiding us?" Olivia was sincere.

I saw Nathan process this for a moment of polite concern, and then he said, "No."

I laughed. But it was time to head for the ferry to go get Nikos. Clive had fought me for the privilege, but I reminded him that he was recently invalided and, along with gaining all the extra attention, he had lost his autonomy.

I drove the Vespa dangerously fast to the port town, inordinately pleased to be seeing Nikos again. I had a lot to tell him, both gossip and real news, and this gave me a sense of purpose, which, for me, was rare. In an unlikely turn of events, the ferry had arrived early, and when I rode up to the pier, Nikos was already walking along with his bag. I parked and ran up to him; I grabbed his shoulders and shook him.

"Nikos, Nikos, Nikos," I said.

"Hello, Rupert," he said. He smiled a big smile, then stepped back to light a cigarette. "You have sun on your face. What have you been doing without me?"

"I have a lot to tell you. I don't know where to start," I said. "I'm so glad you're back."

I refused to let Nikos leave the port town before sharing a private drink with me. There was so much he didn't know. There was the head. There was the cave and Jack and Thanasi. There was strategizing over how to get the head—which certainly looked authentic—to New York. And I had to break it to him that Amanda had gone off with Tomas. I was honest with the particulars of the night she'd disappeared, and Nikos took it all with a few fatalistic shrugs in some of the more sensational places. When I was done with all my telling, he nodded to himself.

"This thing with Amanda had to end, but this with Tomas—it isn't good."

"Are you surprised?"

"I want to say no, because then I am cool." He raised his eyebrows to assess whether he was using the correct word, and I nodded. "I know she sleeps with many people. But Tomas . . . I am surprised."

"Why?" I said.

"Because Amanda is always thinking about her place in society." Nikos seemed to feel bad about divulging that. "She thought marrying Jack would make her rich," he said. "She said he works and works all the time but never has much to show for it. They are always short on cash."

"Why was she telling you this?" I asked.

"What is that word in English I can never remember? It means making excuses."

"Justification," I said.

"Yes. Because she felt bad."

"Well, she did take good care of him. I mean, running off to Hydra because he was on a drunken tear."

Nikos nodded. "And there was the art."

"What do you mean?" I asked.

"The pieces for the gallery in New York. Amanda had found a new agent for Jack, and he was supposed to pack up whatever he had in his studio and ship it all to the States. That's why Jack went back to Hydra."

"I thought he went back because the muse had whispered in his ear."

"Well, maybe." Nikos shrugged.

"But it was money that made him leave," I said, as though I'd suspected as much all along.

"Amanda," said Nikos, "was not calling Jack all the time. Sometimes it was to this person in New York." Nikos stubbed out his cigarette thoughtfully. He looked at me, smiling with his eyes.

"What are you thinking?" I said.

"Amanda has an obsession with the rich, but her family doesn't have any money."

"She went to Smith."

"Scholarship."

"So what about it?" I said.

"If she was poor, she would fuck Tomas because she was poor. If she was rich, she would fuck Tomas because she wouldn't care. But there, in the middle, clinging to all of us by her teeth . . .it's hard for me to believe."

It wasn't hard to talk Nikos into having another drink, and another. Then we climbed onto the Vespa and made our way back to Stavri. The garden was filled with music, a Louis Armstrong song, loud and happy. I remembered the first time I'd walked to the house like this, side by side with Nikos, and had heard the bellowing Victrola. I pushed the gate open and we went in. Nikos was instantly mobbed, but I saw Amanda standing alone, shadowed by a tree. I wondered where Olivia was. Amanda caught me looking at her and I went over because I had no choice.

"Hello, Amanda," I said.

"Hello, Rupert," she said.

"What have you been up to?"

"Don't start," she said. "Does Nikos hate me?"

"No," I said, "but I think it's safe to say it's over between the two of you."

"You know," Amanda said, looking at me, "I wouldn't think that honesty was your strong suit, but you always tell me the truth."

"I would think that was an admirable trait."

Amanda laughed. "You hate me," she said. "I bet you hated your wife."

"That's really none of your business."

"Do you know why Olivia is your ideal woman?"

"You have an opinion?"

"Because she's going to die. You can make peace with a memory, but an actual living, breathing, smelling woman scares you to death."

"You know," I said, "you are beginning to remind me of my ex-wife." Amanda was swaying a little and I knew she'd had quite a bit to drink. I thought I'd earned the right to leave, but she grabbed my arm and clung to me.

"Don't be so hard on me," she said. "I only want a few things from life. How can you begrudge me that?"

I wanted to ask her what she was talking about and, regardless of what it was, why she needed my approval. But I didn't have a chance. Clive came over, his hand dramatically bandaged, and asked if I was interested in going into Stavri for some food. I went upstairs to wash my face and comb my hair. I also managed to sneak up on Olivia and give her a scare as she put on her lipstick. I was surprised to see Amanda still with us as we began to walk down the path into town. Olivia held my elbow and I was feeling rather proud—proud because we were a fairly dysfunctional group and my particular pairing was actually one of the more successful. Nathan and Clive were together up ahead, Clive was singing, and Nathan was enjoying it. Neftali and Nikos followed them, involved in a rapid-paced Greek explication, which, from Neftali's frequent glances back over her shoulder, must have been about Amanda. Amanda, bringing up the rear alone, seemed lost—more lost than drunk—and I thought I saw her push a tear away with the back of her hand.

I leaned down to Olivia. "Maybe you should walk with Amanda."

"That's very kind of you," she said.

"Find out what happened to Tomas," I added. Olivia shook her head in indulgent disapproval and then dropped back.

I decided to walk with Neftali and Nikos, who politely switched languages and subjects to include me. But I begged them not to bother. I liked hearing their Greek. What could be better than having such fine company and not having to converse? I had other things on my mind anyway. I had yet to show Nikos the head. Though I was convinced it was a fake, I was also convinced that Uncle William would love it. The provenance would hold up under scrutiny—at least his—and since the thing had been planted in the field, we hadn't had to pay extra. Serendipity. Maybe it was not the kind of serendipity that put the Venus de Milo into a farmer's field, but Tomas's desperation paired with Jack's extracurricular activities created a serendipity all its own. I would have to clear this with Nikos, but I knew he would accept my judgment. He was a pragmatic person from a pragmatic nation. Nothing romantic, nothing flowery. This was why Greece had been capable of such art: art that held up under scrutiny. Art one could look at and enjoy with the intellect, not the heart, not the surge and surge of boiling blood but rather the sublime process of reason.

"What's the word?" said Nikos. Neftali looked over her shoulder expectantly.

"Justification," I said. "The word is justification."

Neftali ordered a fish for dinner and the thing was a leviathan. As the cook set it down, we all cheered. There were a couple of guys with bazoukis singing away, and the wine was light as spring water yet strong enough to numb the tongue. And this is one of my most often visited memories. The candles are flickering, throwing shadows up on everyone's faces. Olivia, across from me, looks dazzling and young. In this light, you can't see the dark circles, the graying of her skin. Her eyes are brilliant and her face full of expression. Someone's telling a joke, not her, but she's listening actively; she smiles waiting for the punch line, small smile, big smile, eyebrows up, a moment of disbelief; then she bursts out laughing. She says, "I'm cutting you off, Clive. That was disgusting." Then she takes a sip from her glass and says, "Wait a minute. Give the boy some more wine." She fixes me with an admonishing gaze, the I'm-not-dead-yet look. And I raise my glass, because where we are is just a moment moving over our lives, something to hold in the mind, and the present is just a point of reference. It doesn't exist, and thank God for that, because if I believed in the present—actual experience tied to a moving instant—as I believe in the past and future, I would never survive.

Everyone kept saying that Olivia was very sick, Olivia was not supposed to make it through the next twelve months, but I had never really understood it. I had accepted it as part of my identity: I was a man in love with a dying woman. This was, strangely enough, a place where I felt comfortable. But a part of me always believed that no one is dead until they are dead, and although Olivia had no appetite, had lost some weight, and perhaps was not as lively as she might have been, it was hard to look at her—sitting in bed, reading the back of a pill bottle—and think about death except in the most abstract of ways. When I tried to remind myself that she was very ill—which I did, because, along with Nikos and Neftali, I doubted my capacity to make decisions—I kept seeing her tombstone superimposed over her face. Or even more ridiculous, partner to Alastair Sim, flying over London, introducing him to his past. This was recalled from a film version of A Christmas Carol, which had made about ten years of childhood bedtimes a torture of darkness tinged with the promise of spectral visitation.

I had gotten out of bed to pour myself another glass of whiskey, and she was lying there with the covers pulled up to her neck.

"You drink too much," she said.

"Yes, I do," I replied. "Are you going to try to stop me?" I made it sound like an invitation.

"I have my own battles, thank you," she said.

"I think we should get married in the Highlands," I said. "Get some crazy minister in a kilt, some pipers, a person banging a drum, and a yak."

"Why a yak?"

"Don't they have yaks in Scotland?" I seemed to remember having seen a picture of a particularly small one that was indigenous to the Scottish Highlands.

"You're out of your mind," said Olivia, laughing. "We're not getting married. I really don't know you."

"Marriage, Livvy," I said, "it's the best way to know people. Trust me."

"Just stop," she said. She managed a brave and unattractive smile. "I came here to escape feeling sick, but you are a constant reminder."

"Me?"

"I've stopped the radiotherapy and the chemicals. It wasn't working. And they've removed just about everything south of my rib cage."

She smiled again in a challenging way. "I thought you'd want to hear it from me, because marriage is out of the question and I'm tired of arguing with you. It's depressing."

I realized I was holding my breath. "I'm sorry. I'll stop."

"Thank you."

"I do love you," I said. I came to sit on the side of the bed. I knew she was feeling sorry for me, and I felt sorry for myself.

"Rupert," said Olivia, "are you all right?"

"No," I said, "of course not." I sighed. I suppose the general mood was intimate and Olivia, clever girl, was wondering what undiscussable thing she should try on me.

"Why do you call your father Uncle William?" she said finally.

"I'll tell you if you want," I said, "but to be honest it doesn't bother me much. In fact, I actually see the wisdom in it."

"You do surprise me," she said.

"Oh, yes. Handsome, damaged, and surprising." I took a sip of the whiskey. "My mother wanted to put me up for adoption, but Uncle William wouldn't hear of it. But he wasn't ready to be a father. Anyone who knew him knew I was his child. He doesn't have any siblings." Here I laughed. It had taken me years to find this funny, but I now found it hilarious. "He took my rather maudlin circumstances and cast them in a romantic light. People wanted to know who my mother was, and of course Uncle William always traveled a lot. Maybe I was royalty. Maybe my mother couldn't marry a commoner, but he loved her. He could not claim paternity so as not to expose their relationship. He would have to say I was adopted."

"People really believed that?"

"Yes. Some still do," I said. "I did until I was eleven." I reached for the cigarettes off the nightstand and lit one. "And then there was the possibility that he really was my uncle. Did he have a mystery sister living abroad? Some people even claimed to have known this sister when she was young." I shook my head.

"But didn't the news of who your mother really was get around?"

"Of course it did," I said. "But the circumstances aren't that interesting, and who wants to believe that? And of course Uncle

William denied everything, and he'd had a lot of affairs, and my mother was shipped off to relatives somewhere when her situation became obvious."

"Well, that's quite a story," said Olivia.

"I made up my own stories too," I said. "I always wanted to believe that the relationship Uncle William had with my mother was special. True love. The one that mattered. But it wasn't." I was momentarily thoughtful; I blew a series of smoke rings up at the ceiling. "My Uncle William is a terrible father but he is an exceptional uncle. The best. And not only that, he loves me very much."

"Happy ending," said Olivia.

I nodded, because I was still open to the possibility, but both of us knew that it wasn't over yet.

I was just getting ready to head back to the front room, to my little twin bed, when I heard someone banging on the door downstairs. My first thought was that Jack had shown up. I stayed at the railing, and the knocking continued, and someone yelled something in Greek. Amanda was nowhere to be seen. I felt Olivia's small hands grasp my elbow. Clive had clearly been sound asleep, but Nathan was holding a book, keeping his place with his index finger. And Neftali was there, masked in green face goo. Then Nikos came out.

"Why don't you open it?" he said, addressing us all.

Nikos walked right down the stairs. He opened the door, and there was a moment of suspense. Then he stepped back, swinging the door open so we could see our visitor, a bemused look on his face. Of course I recognized who it was immediately, but what was he doing on Aspros? What was he doing here in the dim light of the hallway, his cigarette hanging out of his mouth, his fingers raking through his hair, which even in the darkness gave off a burnished glow?

It was all very strange, because our visitor was Steve Kelly.

12

No one really saw the bad news coming. They all assumed that Steve was visiting me. But I knew he wouldn't be on Aspros unless there was a story to cover, and my mind began racing as soon as I recognized him.

"Rupert, nice to see you," he said. "I knew you were on Aspros. I didn't realize you were staying at this house."

"Nice to see you too," I said. I went down the stairs and shook his hand. "Who are you looking for?"

"I'm looking for Amanda Weldon. I've been told she's staying here."

"Amanda's not here," said Clive with some authority. "Are you a friend of hers?" He grabbed Nathan's wrist and looked at the time. It had to be closing in on 2 A.M.

"I'm sorry," I said, "this is Steve Kelly. He's a journalist."

There was silence, then Olivia said, "Pleased to meet you."

"Pleasure's mine," said Steve hastily. "So Amanda Weldon isn't here?"

"Is it important? I know where she is," said Clive. "I can go get her."

"It *is* important," said Steve. He rubbed the two-day stubble on his chin and regarded first Clive and then me. He had some bad news, that much was obvious. "Jack Weldon's been murdered."

We had all poured ourselves a drink, except for Clive, who was off to Tomas's to fetch Amanda. The light in the living room seemed too bright and, with the exception of me who was not dressed for bed, we all looked rather silly. Neftali and her face mask, her hair up in curlers and netted, was slumped over her glass of whiskey. She was tearing up and I knew, from spending time with her, that she felt personally responsible for Jack's death; somehow his murder had been a direct result of bad hospitality. Nathan's pajamas looked as if they'd been ironed and Olivia was wearing her bed turban, an item I'd never really understood but which she thought was essential.

"How did Jack die?" I asked.

"He fell from a cliff," said Steve.

"What was he doing on a cliff?" asked Nathan.

"You've never been to Hydra, have you?" said Steve.

I wanted to laugh because Nathan sounded annoyed and seemed to think it was just like Jack to stand on a cliff and get murdered.

Nikos said, "Where is the police?"

Steve was sitting on the edge of his chair and looking from Nikos to me to Nikos, with an eager, greasy demeanor. "I got here first. Weldon was found this morning and no one knows where Amanda is except for me, and a few others."

"How'd you get here?" I asked.

"*Kaïka* from Páros," he said.

I had a hundred questions flying through my mind. I looked over at Nikos and he raised an eyebrow, quick, meant for me. I stood up, and addressing Steve, said, "Why don't we go out and get some fresh air?" I picked up my drink so that Steve knew to bring his.

It was a quiet night but breezy, and the trees were rattling the wind in their leaves. I gave Steve a cigarette.

"Are you up for some questions, my friend?" I said.

"Oh, I'm prepared for that, believe me." Steve was exhausted, but he managed a smile.

"How did you know Amanda was here?" I asked.

"Custard was tipped off by some of his American friends who were tailing one of her acquaintances."

I thought for a moment. "They were following me," I said.

"Are you one of her acquaintances?" Steve knew he had to come up with some sort of pretense but was having a hard time finding the energy for it.

"Why me?"

"I don't know." Steve gave me an honest look. "I thought you would."

"Well, I don't." I thought for a moment. "You were following me too. I saw your car in Delphi after you'd supposedly left."

Steve shrugged. "You were suspicious."

"Suspicious?"

"How's the hiking on Aspros?" he asked. There was a play of exhausted humor in his eyes. "Or is it better suited to numisiatic activities?"

"The word is numismatic," I said. "And I don't know what you're getting at. Are you forgetting that you know me? I'm Rupert. I'm not capable of all this." I gestured with my cigarette, because I didn't know what *all this* was. "I'm not averse to helping you. Just ask me something I might know the answer to."

Steve processed this and then inclined his head in a way that implied both an inquiring mind and the onset of a headache. "What can you tell me about Jack Weldon?"

"Nothing, really," I said. I'd forgotten that Steve had an interest in Jack. "He was a jerk. He hit his wife. He drank too much." Would anyone care that he was dead? "How can you be so sure he didn't kill himself or fall by accident?"

"Well," said Steve. He winced. "Someone clubbed him on the back of his head, and he landed on his face. And there were signs of a struggle, trampled greenery, two sets of footprints, that sort of thing."

"Some villager might have had it in for him. Pushed him."

"That is one theory. One old lady says she saw him arguing with a man."

"No description?"

"The man was wearing a straw hat."

"Not much to go on," I said. I took a long thoughtful drag on my cigarette. "Thanasi," I said. "Jack had a friend, this Thanasi, a local potter."

"Do you know where he lives?"

"On the coast north of Faros, a fishing village. He lives down a dirt path. There's a sign for his studio, I suppose for tourists. Maybe some even go."

"Could you find it?"

"Now?"

I needed Clive to find Thanasi's place because I'd never been there. Clive wasn't sure either, but he had dropped Jack off once before. Clive and I hopped on the Vespa, and Steve followed on a scooter he'd managed to rent from one of the restaurant owners in the port town. Amanda was sobbing and frightened when we left. Probably embarrassed, too, since she'd been in bed with Tomas when the news of Jack's death reached her.

The headlight on the Vespa was out, but I had a flashlight and that, coupled with the nearly full moon, was enough to light our way. I was having a hard time with what Steve had said. Why was I involved? Who would want to kill Jack? What on earth was my connection? Who was investigating Jack, and why? I hadn't come to any conclusions, but by the time we reached the path that led to Thanasi's house, I decided I knew more than Steve and probably knew more than any of them—Custard and his British Intelligence or CIA, or whoever—had picked up. I knew more; I just had to put it together.

Clive pulled over by a wooden sign. It said, REAL LOCAL POT-TERY. I took the flashlight and shined a path through the scrubby brush and debris. In the low plants were bottles, misfired pots, and donkey dung, and then, giving me a right heart attack, a donkey, who nuzzled my cheek as I passed.

"Jesus Christ!" I said.

Clive was frightened at first, but then he started laughing. I swung the flashlight around, laughing too, but then I saw Steve, and he had pulled a gun.

"What?" said Steve.

"It's just a donkey," I said. "Why do you have a gun?"

"Custard gave it to me, just in case."

I turned off the flashlight. We were huddled there: me, Clive, Steve, and somewhere—not visible but I could smell it—Thanasi's friendly donkey. "Steve," I asked, "am I in danger?"

"I really don't know," he said.

"Why would you think Thanasi is armed?"

Steve seemed relieved I'd asked him that. "He might be," he said. He put the safety on his gun. "The thing is," he said, "Weldon's been buying weapons for Greek Communists."

"What?" I said.

"It's true."

I looked over at Clive, who shrugged, apparently willing to entertain this possibility.

"Why would the Communists have anything to do with Jack?" I asked.

"Well, it was kind of his own splinter group," said Steve. "His own guerrilla army."

"No," I said. "That's impossible. He doesn't have that kind of money."

Clive snorted derisively, but I knew he was having trouble following the conversation.

"Wait," I said. "Does this have something to do with that band of twenty rebels in Delphi?"

"Not Delphi," said Steve. "Farther north, up by the Albanian border."

"Seems like a very small guerrilla army," said Clive.

"And contained," said Steve. "Not of much interest to anyone except the local officials and the far right, and therefore Custard. Until Jack's murder."

"Jack did have a lot of political convictions," I said. "But they seemed so—"

"Fake," said Clive. "Just another way of condescending."

There was a moment of quiet where we heard the donkey, still close by, tearing at the grass.

"So what's going on?" I asked.

"No one really knows," said Steve. "Jack was producing some-thing that raised a significant amount of cash and then he was turn-ing around and buying guns that were funneled through Albania."

"Maybe he was selling drugs," I suggested.

Steve shrugged. "Opium production in Turkey is at an all-time high, but we've been watching the borders, and there's nothing to connect it to Jack. Whatever it was, Jack was producing it locally."

I pondered for a moment. "Doesn't Custard know who killed him? Maybe one of Custard's American friends?"

Steve shook his head. "This was not organized. Don't get me wrong. Weldon is potentially embarrassing, and his death might be convenient. But Custard was trying to figure out what he was doing. He wanted to know who else was involved, who the Greeks were, the Albanians."

"Well, Thanasi might know something." I found it hard to be-lieve that he was a key figure. This situation gave Thanasi an im-plausible sophistication.

"What do you know about him?"

I shrugged. I didn't know anything. But I thought of the crate Jack had taken on the ferry, of the comrade-style embrace that he and Thanasi had shared. "Put the gun away. Thanasi is just a crazy potter with a head full of dreams," I said. "Let me go first. He's prob-ably asleep."

"No, no," said Steve. He put the gun in his satchel. "I should go. I speak Greek."

Steve went ahead, but Clive and I followed close behind. I could hear the waves hitting the rocks, but where Thanasi lived there was no beach. Just a cliff, sheer, imposing, beautiful. I wondered if Thanasi knew what a premium this sort of location had in other places, or if he just felt he was stranded at the end of the earth. I thought of the saying, *The sea is a road that leads anywhere*, but Thanasi wasn't going far. I had a hard time picturing him anywhere but Aspros.

I waited outside with Clive while Steve went inside the cottage. I would have been happy to stay in the fresh air, with the view of the ocean, the moon, a shred of cloud drifting over it, but the mosquitoes were vicious. I wondered if there was some stagnating pool, a frenzy of mosquito sex and exotic fevers. I edged my way inside the door and Clive followed me.

I assumed that Steve must have broken the news of Jack's death to Thanasi because of the dejected way he was sitting on the edge of his bed, a small one with a flat mattress and dirty sheets, that he must have just risen from. I felt bad for him. What light had Jack shone on his ordinary life? What dreams had now died?

I was trying to think of what Asprian things could be worth something on the black market, and all I could come up with was *myzithra*, the local cheese—one did need a license to sell it. Cheese. Chickpea croquettes. Caper salad. That's all Aspros had to offer. Thanasi's house was barely the size of my room at Neftali's, and it was difficult to find a polite place to look. Half the cottage was given over to Thanasi's work, and a pyramid of sunbaked terracotta bowls dominated the space. A sheet was thrown over half of this, and I could see that some of the work—plates, maybe, but the light was dim— had been glazed and fired.

And then I thought, *pots*, and then I thought, *local pottery*. On a plank set on two squares of yellowed marble, probably pilfered from an ancient wall, was a book in English. Of course this was suspicious because that Thanasi read—even in his own language—seemed improbable. I picked up the book and opened it. On the front page it had been stamped INSTRUCTOR COPY. It was left over from Jack's teaching days. I flipped a couple of pages and saw an amphora, black figures on red, much like the bell krater the dealer in Athens had described to me, and then a *lekythos*, almost deco in appearance, with a young woman in profile holding a water jug—the work of the Achilles painter—and this appealed to me, as it should.

I had purchased it, although on a plate, that night in Athens all those weeks ago. My plate hadn't been dug up in the Peloponnesus. It had been made right here, and by having Kostas purchase it I had funded Jack's army. Of course Thanasi, and therefore Jack, would know that Kostas, as my agent, was looking for classical pieces. Everyone on Aspros did, just as everyone knew I had the money to pay for them. All Jack had needed was a middleman, some rebel to take the bus down from the Albanian border in his too-short pants and show up on Kostas's doorstep in the middle of the night, a blanket of goodies bundled on his back.

I put the book down. Clive looked over. I picked up a knife, left on a cutting board next to some very dry-looking cheese. Clive looked at me questioningly, but I raised my finger to my lips so he knew not to follow. I slipped out the door. I was lucky that the Vespa was far from Thanasi's house. By the time Steve heard the engine, even if he ran out, I would have a good head start. Would he even follow me?

How long would it take for Steve to figure out that he was leading a sting on forged artwork? Would Thanasi let Steve believe that pottery was the full extent of their business, or would he go on to talk about the heads? I wondered if Thanasi even knew I was in possession of one of Jack's exquisite replicas. I guessed that he didn't. Clive and I had created a disturbance over the last twenty-four hours that made his recent return to the cave improbable. And I was sure that Tomas had stolen the head before passing it on to me, thinking, correctly, that I would keep it hidden from the others and he would be not be exposed as a thief.

I knew the head was inauthentic but was not prepared to sacrifice it as such. I thought of all its sisters resting beneath the waves in Faros. If I could just get rid of them, my head would stand alone, an important find. Disputing the authenticity of a single head would be much more difficult than relating it to a known group of forgeries.

The Vespa didn't throw off any light, but it was very loud. Still, the road was deserted and there didn't seem to be anyone around to hear me. I had started driving with the knife in my teeth, but the handle tasted very bad. I thought of Thanasi's dirty hands and took the knife in my right hand as I drove awkwardly in the mild moonlight. I thought of Olivia sleeping in her turban and wondered what could happen to me. Who was this man who had killed Jack? Did he want me dead too? I couldn't see why, but I also couldn't figure out how offing Jack would benefit anyone.

I made it to Faros without skidding in the gravel and losing my skin, nor did I stab myself or drive over a cliff. I cut the engine, and when I did I heard Steve's Vespa sputtering on the same road, although he was still across the valley. I hid the bike in the same alley where Clive and I had left it the last time we'd gone to the caves. I ran, ignoring the tearing sensation in my lungs, along the path that led up the hill and then down the path to the beach. I slipped once and lost the knife, and in the time it took me to find it, the blood pounding in my ears, wasted a few precious minutes. If Clive and Steve were heading for the cave, which seemed likely, I had to beat them.

I reached the water's edge and began to undress. There was such a silence and peace here it was hard to believe that I had anything to do, that there was anything at stake. I remembered a tale from the Arabian Nights where a prince had to cross a body of water without making a sound. The breathing of the waves, the moon, the path of light to the moon, the cool pebbles beneath my feet—all were more of a story than the reality of the actual moment. My sudden transformation to action adventurer also seemed implausible, more the stuff of fantasy—although not my fantasy—than anything else.

I waded into the cold water and began swimming, the knife in my teeth again. I was already worn out, but I began to freestyle my way out to the cave. I saw the entrance finally, and swam inside and quickly to the ledge. My foot hit something—a fish?—on the way over. I lit the candle and held it over the water. There was a monster in there with me, a moray eel. I saw it flicker into view and for a second was mesmerized by its thick undulating muscle of it, then it disappeared into the darker shadows of the cave. But there was the net hanging from its hook, the net filled with marble heads, the heads of Theseus and Hadrian and some lovely woman who would be known as Aphrodite or Artemis or Hera, and I had to drown them all.

I swam through the water, circling my arms gently, barely moving my legs. Somewhere down there, peering from its aqueous cave, was that eel, all spiked teeth and appetite. I reached the net and stood ankle deep in water on the submerged rock. The breeze entered the cave, bringing with it Thanasi's and Steve's voices. Faros was not far from Thanasi's house by water; and perhaps it had been Clive driving the other Vespa. By taking the road, I had made a wild detour. I wondered if Steve and Thanasi knew I was there. The candle would be throwing out light, but maybe the bright moon and reflecting waters would confuse it into something natural.

I started to saw at the ropes, but the knife was dull. I began to wonder just how dry Thanasi's cheese was, and whether or not it was possible to cut such unappealing cheese with this ineffective knife, when a breeze blew into the cave and extinguished the candle. My eyes took a second to adjust. I would have to finish slicing the ropes by pawing them like a blind person.

The first rope finally snapped, and then, just as I was hearing the dip of oars and the voices of Steve and Thanasi, close now, a second rope snapped. I had two more to go, but as I tugged and sawed and sliced, I realized that the net had grown slack. The heads must have been sinking into the deep. I thought, in an opportunistic way, that maybe I could come back in twenty years and discover them. Maybe they would be waiting for me, eyes angled to the surface, their features worn away by salt and years, as history rattled by on its rusty tracks above, uncaring, unaware.

I unhooked the net and threw it and the knife into the center of the cave. I hoped the eel would find this distracting. Then I heard voices outside, and before I could gauge the intelligence of my action, I was swimming out, holding my breath underwater. When I finally had to come up for air, I was about fifteen feet from the boat. Steve and Thanasi were shining a flashlight into the cave and didn't see me. I swam back to shore slowly, so as not to create much noise, but also because I was exhausted. Suddenly I wanted to sleep. I couldn't really see where the shore was. It seemed to be moving farther and farther away, but then I saw a little red glow in the darkness. Clive had followed me and I had a beacon to steer me home. When my feet could finally reach the bottom, I started walking to shore. I collapsed, next to Clive, where he sat smoking beside the heap of my clothes. We were quiet for a couple of minutes.

Then I said, "How'd you figure it out?"

And Clive said, "Figure what out?"

Clive had no idea why I'd left Thanasi's or what the urgency was. He had a certain faith that I knew what I was doing, but when he found my clothes on the beach—he had been instructed by Steve to meet him with the scooter since Steve was accompanying Thanasi to the caves in the boat—he wasn't sure what my late-night swim was supposed to accomplish. Clive was waiting for Steve.

"Well, then," I said, pulling on my pants, "it would be better if Steve didn't know I'd been here." I'm sure he'd found my disappearance odd, but, hopefully, was too busy to dwell on it.

When I finally reached my bed, it was four in the morning. I must have been asleep, but it was one of those dormancies where you close your eyes for one second to the darkness and then open them to the light of the next day. I sat up in bed, gasping, and looked for my watch. It was 7 A.M. The house was still. I got out of my bed and looked under it. The head was still there. Nikos was sound asleep, breathing peacefully. He was hugging a second pillow.

"Nikos," I whispered, "Nikos. Wake up."

Nikos opened one eye and shut it. "Rupert, you must go away."

I shook him again. "You have to wake up."

"It is not important," Nikos said. He rolled away from me.

"It *is* important," I said. "Nikos. Nikos."

He opened his eyes and looked at me with skepticism. "What?"

"It's seven now. I think you should be on the eight o'clock to Mílos."

"Why?"

"Because that's the next ferry to leave."

"There's nothing on Mílos," he said.

"Please, Nikos," I said. "Please."

Nikos groaned, and I knew he was getting up.

Nikos dressed while I packed for him. I drove to the ferry because Nikos looked drugged and didn't seem capable. I was terrified that he was going to drop the head, that it would go rolling off a cliff or get smashed into rubble. Nikos was of the opinion that he could sit on the Vespa, hold the head, have a cigarette, and all the rest. But I hadn't let him smoke. I hadn't let him bring his suitcase. I'd only let him pack what would fit into his knapsack, and although I knew he didn't care about it right then, it was certainly going to bother him later. When we reached the port town, there were a few people milling around the dock, all foreigners. The ferry was supposed to arrive in ten minutes.

Nikos surveyed the scene. "No Greeks," he said.

Sure enough, the ferry was an hour late. I was glad for this, because I needed to speak seriously, and Nikos was useless without his morning coffee and cigarette.

Nikos downed his shot of coffee then waved at the waiter to bring him another. He shook his head. "So Jack was making fakes to pay for guns for the Communists?" Nikos seemed completely disgusted. He rubbed his unshaved face.

"He was an idealist," I said.

"He was an idiot. What is this thing he said about Byron?"

I thought for a minute. I quoted, *"That old fag? He was carried off by his own shit."*

"To Jack," said Nikos, raising his empty coffee cup.

There was a moment of silence. Somewhere, in the kitchen, someone knocked over a stack of plates and I heard an *Opa!* and some laughter, and then some angry shouting. The waiter came over with the second coffee. I ordered some toast. I suppose all the swimming the night before had made me hungry. There was still salt in my hair.

"And that plate we got from the Peloponnesus," Nikos said, stirring in sugar. "It was from here?"

"Made by Thanasi. At least I think so. He had a picture of it, and we know he's making fakes."

Nikos rubbed his eyes. "So why am I going to Mílos?"

"I want to get our head off the island as soon as possible. I'm sure Thanasi has told Steve Kelly that he was making them. I don't want our head to become part of his story, and I don't want to get mixed up in the investigation."

"Does Steve know you are buying art?" Nikos asked.

"He's suspicious of me, which is why I want you to take the head."

"And you will stay here and pretend nothing is happening?"

"Yes."

Nikos thought for a minute. He lit another cigarette and gave me a lopsided smile. "Does this make sense to you?"

"Sort of," I said.

"What does Steve know about you?"

"I don't know," I said. "He saw my art books. He saw me lurking on Pandróssou Street. Clearly I was looking for art."

"Or he thinks you are CIA," said Nikos mysteriously. "Maybe you were here to follow Jack."

"Why not?" I said. "Stranger things have happened."

"Or maybe he thinks you are a Communist sympathizer."

Here we both laughed. "He couldn't think that for long," I said.

"There is only one thing that really bothers me," said Nikos.

"What's that?"

"Who killed Jack?"

I pondered this. I had no idea. Could he have been killed by one of Amanda's lovers? Did the Greeks have their own intelligence and take care of Jack themselves? Jack's was a useless death and I felt an involuntary sympathy. "A guerrilla army." I said, marveling. "What was Jack trying to accomplish?"

"Who knows?" said Nikos. "People like that are always trying to change things."

"I suppose that's admirable."

Nikos winced at my sentimentality. "What if there's nothing wrong?"

The next week passed in a blur. I had come home to find Olivia packing her things. It was time for her to leave Aspros. She and Neftali were going first to Hydra to help Amanda with the funeral arrangements. I was good at folding and helped Olivia put her clothes together.

"Amanda's holding together quite well," said Olivia. She's decided to cremate Jack and scatter his ashes over the bluff by their house."

"He'll have the rare privilege of being thrown off a cliff twice," I said.

"You are rotten," said Olivia, but she found it funny.

I waved Neftali and Olivia off the next day, just as I'd waved off Nikos, and I realized I was going to have to leave, and soon, so as not to be left.

Clive, Nathan, and I spent the last few days hiking in the morning, swimming in the afternoon, and drinking at night. Even Nathan was drinking more than usual. One night we ate dinner in the old town, which is something we'd meant to do all summer but had never found time for. Nathan managed to convince a farmer to lend him a donkey and Clive took him on a mad pony ride all over Stavri while I took pictures. And then I found someone to take our picture, and I still have it: Nathan on the donkey, cradling a loaf of bread wrapped in a dishcloth, a towel on his head, while Clive and I fall on our knees in adoration.

When the day of our departure finally came, it was sunny and warm. I could feel the weight of it on all of us, and as Clive packed up the Victrola, carefully wrapping the horn, stacking the records neatly, and draping the whole thing in a pristine white sheet, I heard him say, "Goodbye, old friend."

We took our things down the steps of the house and out the gate. The caretaker and his wife waved at us. The old woman was wiping tears, which I found touching, because we were loud, unruly, messy, pathologically irreligious, and had never learned enough Greek to say anything more than *thank you*. We walked around to the dirt road where the taxi was to pick us up.

"Do you really think it's coming?" asked Clive.

"Neftali set it up," Nathan said.

"But that was days ago," said Clive.

"But the caretaker was instructed to follow up this morning," said Nathan.

"I don't know why I care," said Clive. "I don't want to leave. I hate the United States."

I noticed Tomas, who was standing behind a tree, watching us in complete stillness. It occurred to me that maybe Nikos would forget about him. He wasn't my favorite person, but seeing him standing there brought out a philanthropic desire. I made a mental note to remind Nikos of his offer to find him work. Clive hopped up and went over to him. Clive and Tomas talked for a minute and then embraced. Then Clive shook his hand and let go. Clive came back and patted me on the shoulder.

"He wants to talk to you," he said.

I saw the taxi at the foot of the drive. I thought it might be nice if I gave Tomas some money.

"I'll be right back," I said.

At closer look, Tomas seemed upset. I wondered if it was just the prospect of our leaving: leaving with all his prospects. I gave him a few bills, and he tried to refuse them. But I wouldn't take it back.

"I must to tell you something," he said, very serious.

"Yes," I said.

"It's not good," Tomas said. "It's all lies."

I figured he had to be talking about the head. I nodded, amazed at how upset this had made him, and actually felt guilty at having misjudged him. "Don't worry, Tomas. I already figured it out," I said. "I know everything."

"Yes?" Tomas seemed surprised.

"It's taken care of. Just don't tell anyone, and everything will be all right."

13

When I reached New York all the talk was of Jack Weldon, what a genius he had been, and the suspicious circumstances surrounding his death. Since I had known Jack in his final weeks, I found myself invited to every cocktail hour, dinner, and event. I had a capacity for parties, but this deluge of invitations, combined with a week of uninterrupted rain, was beginning to test the limits of my sanity.

At some retrospective at the Guggenheim, I saw Amanda across the room. She was swarmed by a phalanx of admirers, or maybe they were detractors, but they were all drawn to her. There was no longer any evidence of "Amandirt" at all. She had cropped her hair quite short and, in her sheet of black cashmere, looked surprisingly elegant. She had stunning black pearl earrings and an Etruscan-revival necklace, all hand-hammered, high-quality gold, a bit like a string of candy corn. Against all the black, the necklace looked contemporary. I had never known her to wear makeup, but now she had on bright red lipstick. Her eyebrows, once bushy and blond, were now plucked and penciled into two black slits, and her eyes, in contrast, seemed enormous.

My companion on this particular jaunt was Uncle William, who had taken to going to all the openings. I wondered at his sudden interest. He'd always found these galas insufferable, talked about the new money trying to get tips on how to look like old money. No one was looking at the art. The men were looking at the women, and the women were looking at the women to see what everyone was wearing. I knew it had something to do with the head, which Uncle William loved. The head—artist unknown—was now mounted on a ghastly Corinthian column, all serrated leaves and mannerism, something Uncle William had had an Italian mausoleum fitter carve up for him in New Jersey. I had suggested black granite, plain but highly polished, which would reflect the classical architectural features—well, Georgian, but who cared?—of the vestibule in an abstract, referential, yet current way.

I would have stayed longer, Uncle William wanted me to, but I'd seen Hester appear at the far end of the room. The rain had already edged me towards a depression, and Hester—who would have thought it was possible for her to lose weight?—had the appearance of an opium addict. She was again reminding me that once my life had been very centered, that it wasn't normal for thirty-year-old men to spend their time divided between attending parties and choosing shirts. I had to get out of there before Uncle William made me talk to her.

"I have to go," I whispered. "I'm meeting someone for a drink."

Uncle William put his hand on my shoulder. "We were having such fun." I was leaving for Scotland at the end of the week, and Uncle William was getting proprietary about my time.

"Stay up," I said, "I'll be home by one." Although I knew he'd fall asleep by midnight.

I went to the restroom and made a phone call. Clive. He was staying on a friend's couch and hating it. I wasn't really sure if I was up for Clive. He liked to complain about Nathan all the time, Nathan whom he'd hardly seen since the return from Greece, and it was tiresome because Nathan was my friend. But there wasn't anyone else in New York I really wanted to talk to. I could have asked a woman out. That was usually the easy thing to do, but that seemed disloyal to Olivia. The fact that she had no expectations of me made me want to behave. Clive and I set a time and place, and I returned to the atrium.

"I thought you were going to Scotland."

I turned around, and there was Amanda.

"Don't suppose you'd want to step outside and get some air, have a cigarette," she said.

"Sure, why not?"

We walked outside, and I gave Amanda a cigarette. She hadn't smoked much in Greece but now, newly re-created, seemed to need it. "Nice necklace," I said. "Is it Boucheron?"

"You tell me," she said. "It was a gift."

"Something to take the sting off of Jack's death?"

Amanda judged me coolly and laughed. "Why do I always talk to you when you are, without fail, so insulting?"

"Because you trust me," I said. I might have added that she, in her constant morphing, needed someone to remind her of who she really was, but I didn't.

"Rupert," she said, and laughed again, "I don't need your approval." She smiled a very wide, very nice smile, all those teeth, those handsome cheekbones. She tossed her cigarette into the street and turned to leave. I watched her disappear through the glass doors, and then it was just me, and me reflected back. She hadn't needed to finish what she was saying because I understood. She didn't need my approval. She had everyone else's, and she was now a very wealthy woman.

Clive and I sat side by side at a bar mostly inhabited by Columbia students, which is why I knew it. I had been frequenting it for nearly fifteen years. I was still in my tux, and Clive was wearing a black turtleneck and some boots. He looked like a beatnik, which made me want to laugh.

"So how wealthy is old Amandirt?"

"Well," I said, "she's got a lot of Jack's works. She's only sold two of them, but they fetched close to twenty thousand apiece."

"How is that possible?" said Clive. "How much does a real piece of art sell for, one of those little Degas ballerinas?"

"It's not my forte, Clive. But you and I both know there's no such thing as *real art*. People don't care. Something is worth whatever someone is willing to pay for it, and people like stories. Anything of Jack's now has this amazing story. I read a piece in the *Times* last week about his idealism. His guerrilla army. He's as hip as Che Guevara, only Jack made art."

"Well, when the art runs out, what will Amanda do?"

"Don't worry about Amanda," I said. "She was wearing a neck-lace. I'm pretty sure it was a Boucheron, probably from the 1850s. The gold alone had to be worth quite a bit."

"What's your point?" asked Clive.

"She didn't know anything about it. A gift, she said. She has at least one wealthy suitor, so even if she's not that cash rich, her stock has gone way up."

Clive drank some beer. There was something wholesome about sitting around drinking beer in the dark while the rain pounded on the pavement. I noticed a young college student eyeing Clive, and I whispered to him. "You have an admirer."

Clive looked over at him, bored, then looked back at me. "I'm tired of America."

"You've only been back for two weeks."

"I can't stand people like that. He only wants me to educate him, and then he'll feel all full of experience, and then he'll marry his girlfriend."

I wanted to say Clive didn't know that, but it occurred to me that he might.

"I want to go back to Europe," he said.

"You want to go back to Aspros."

Clive nodded. He raised his beer, and we clinked glasses and drank some more. "You must wonder what we were all doing there at the same time. You, me, Thanasi, Jack . . ."

"I have," I said, "and have come to the conclusion that there was less coincidence than on first appearance."

"Really?"

"You never met Kostas, so you wouldn't understand. Nikos's fa-ther wanted my Uncle William to get the best possible piece of classical art, preferably statuary. He knew the only place to get that was Aspros."

"But it's a fake," whispered Clive.

"It is still classical. It is still statuary. Uncle William loves it. What would be achieved by my telling him?" I undid my tie because it was choking me.

"So Kostas knew it was a fake?"

"He knew it was an opportunity."

"I thought he was your uncle's friend."

"He is." I looked at Clive, who was feeling naïve. "My uncle is deliriously happy. Kostas made a little money. Neftali hosted a fabulous six-week party. I spent the summer in Greece."

"Do you think Nikos knew?"

"Knew what? Remember, it was my responsibility to authenticate. And there *is* real stuff on Aspros. That pot I dug up with the nautical figures is real. Besides, it doesn't make any difference to Nikos. Real. Fake. It's all ugly to him. He doesn't like anything before Brancusi. Not even Rodin."

"I absolutely agree," said Clive. "Of course I don't know what you're talking about."

"Besides," I continued, "we've had a couple of people come by the house, including one of Uncle William's old college buddies who teaches art at Yale, and no one knows it's a fake."

"That's amazing," said Clive. "Does it bother you, Rupert, that it's a fake?"

And I shook my head. Because it didn't, not at all. "What isn't?" I said.

I spent the next four months in Scotland, and there, I am sorry to say, nothing exceptional happened, good or bad, except that Olivia was much the same for the first three and a half months, and then she declined. How to say this in a way that makes sense? I am not good at grief, which is strange, given the fact that I am constantly attracting it. Uncle William had told me that this was my own fault, marrying a terminally ill woman. What was I thinking? Was I thinking?

Olivia and I were happy for a while. She seemed to have a lot of property all over the place, an apartment in Edinburgh, a cottage in the Highlands, a sleek modern flat in London. She had me weed the garden at the cottage and pointed out that I'd pulled out all the flowers too. They weren't blooming. How was I supposed to know?

Nathan got Clive a job as errand boy in the London branch of his publishing firm. Clive didn't make much money, and his apartment was rat-infested, but he seemed very happy. I asked Olivia if he could stay in the London flat, but she said her in-laws also used it. Olivia encouraged me to visit Clive and I did, every two weeks or so. Clive had a stylish haircut, and at his suggestion I began growing mine out.

The cottage was four miles from the nearest town. There was nothing to do, which is why I'd attempted gardening. I began taking long hikes, walking around with a stick like an extra from a Robin Hood movie. I would walk for hours. I found this behavior remarkable, but Olivia just laughed and said, "Everyone does that around here. That's what the Highlands are for." After one such hike—it was a windy day and I was beginning to question the wisdom of growing my hair—I returned to see a strange car pulled up in front of the house. When I reached the house I heard Olivia yelling, and then a hushed man's voice volleying back, and then Olivia, all outrage, yelling again. I swung the door open and was surprised to a see a man built like a fireplug, with receding black hair and sideburns. I was a bit surprised, because the man appeared to be Olivia's deceased husband.

I said, "Is everything all right?"

To which the man responded, "Are you that Rupert Brigg, then?"

And I said, "Most likely."

And he looked at me and then at Olivia and laughed so loudly in my face that it stirred my hair. He then left in his car with a great crunching and spitting of gravel.

After he was gone, I turned to Olivia and asked, "Was that your deceased husband?"

Olivia was sitting in the red armchair. "Don't be funny, Rupert. I'm not in the mood."

I decided that protesting my sincerity was not the right tack, so I went over to her, sat on the arm of the chair, and took her hand.

"That was my brother-in-law," she said.

"He finds me very amusing," I said.

Olivia smiled a little and then one eyebrow shot up intelligently. "Do you still want to get married?"

"Are you asking me?" I said. "Because you could be more romantic."

The next day we drove down to the town hall and after calling in the gardener, who was trimming the hedge in front, and flagging down an old woman who was walking her dog, we got our witnesses, got married, then went over to the pub, and bought a couple of rounds for whoever was interested in drinking at two o'clock in the afternoon. And, not surprisingly, there were quite a few takers.

I had never driven a car, so Olivia taught me in the field out behind the cottage. She didn't think it was a good idea to bring a bottle of whiskey, but I did, and we had great fun driving around. I drove into a tree once, but we were only going ten miles an hour: I was trying to figure out how to get in second gear and was looking at the shift. I mastered second and then, having finally made it into third, tried to steer around a sheep, couldn't, tried to stop, but hit it. There was a moment of remorse. Olivia and I got out of the car and walked around to inspect the fallen. The sheep was lying quite still, peacefully, and I felt very bad for it, but suddenly the sheep leaped up, looked me straight in the eye, gave an angry bleat, and trotted off.

I began driving Olivia to Edinburgh for her appointments. There was morphine, to make her more comfortable, but she didn't like to take it unless she felt really bad. I met Clive in London for his birthday, at Olivia's insistence, and when I came back she was in the hospital. I packed up my stuff from the cottage. I realized I probably wouldn't be hiking around the Highlands anymore and ceremoniously threw my walking stick off the side of a mountain. My lonely drive to Edinburgh was miserable, a thin sheeting rain, and my thoughts were as black as they get. And she was fine for a week, and then one day she asked me, "What was the name of your son again?"

And I said, "I never told you."

And she said, "I'd like to know."

And I said, "Michael."

It was about three in the afternoon. I told her I was slipping out to have a cigarette and took the elevator down, my mind tired and blank. I went outside the hospital; I needed the fresh air. I was about to light the cigarette when I was overwhelmed by a feeling of panic. *Michael. Michael. Michael.* I ran inside. There was a crowd of people in front of the elevator. I took the stairs. Olivia was on the fifth floor. She was due for some medicine. That's why the nurse had gone in there, but when I arrived there were four nurses and a doctor and I was once more reminded of how Olivia never wasted her words. How to the very end she was thinking of me.

At maybe 8 P.M. I came conscious weeping in the bar across the street. The bartender was looking at me, concerned but kindly.

I said, "My wife just died."

"You told me," he said.

"I'm sorry," I said.

"I'm used to it," he responded. "It's the location."

I pushed the half glass of whiskey across the bar.

"You shouldn't be alone," the bartender said. "Is there someone I can call?"

"My closest friend is in London."

"Do you have the number?"

The bartender called Clive. Not only that, he had the bellhop from up the street check me into a hotel. He didn't think I should be going back to the apartment. He was more than a bartender, he was an official manager of grief. I called Uncle William, who listened for an entire hour on the phone, until I felt the need to throw up and had to let him go. Then I called Clive over and over, wondering where the hell he could be. And then at midnight, there was a knock on the door and there he was, in Edinburgh, having taken the first train out of London.

Clive stayed for the funeral. I was pretty much drunk, right up until the night before, but then Clive and I thought it best to dry out. I knew Olivia wouldn't want me and Clive snonkered and staggering at her funeral, even if it were the result of genuine grief. We went to see *Waiting for Godot*, and Clive fell asleep.

Olivia was to be buried in the Macintyre family vault. Apparently, she'd promised her deceased husband. There were quite a few people gathered at that funeral, then at the side of the grave, and honestly, most of them seemed interested in me. Apparently, there had been quite a set of rumors circulated about me, the young opportunistic Yank. The fact that I had spent the last week in the company of an even younger, obviously gay man had done nothing to subdue the gossip. I took heart in the fact that somewhere Olivia was witnessing this and when she wasn't laughing, she felt bad for me.

After the funeral, Olivia's brother-in-law came up to me and said, "I don't think we've been properly introduced."

And I said, "I'm that Rupert Brigg."

And he said, "I'm Guy Macintyre." And we shook hands. "I don't like to bring up business at funerals, but rumor has it you're returning to America tomorrow."

"That one's actually true," I said. I caught Macintyre eyeing Clive and hoped to God that Clive wouldn't wink back.

"I'm going to pack," said Clive. "I'll see you back at the hotel."

I turned to Macintyre and said, "Do you want me to sign something?"

"Maybe we could have a little chat," he suggested. I nodded and we made our way to his car, that same sleek car I had seen in front of the cottage. First I got into the driver's seat, thinking it was the passenger seat, and then I got out. Macintyre gave me a funny look, but I didn't care. When we were driving he said, "My brother loved Olivia very much."

And I said, "Of course he did."

This both surprised Macintyre and shut him up. He drove us to a street of small restaurants. When we were out of the car, he said, "You look like you could use a drink."

"Do I?" I said.

"I could too," he said. "I know it's Olivia's funeral, but it was like burying my brother all over again."

Then he fixed me with a look I didn't care for, and who cared? I only wanted my drink, to sign whatever it was he had in the oxblood briefcase, and to get as far away from him as I possibly could.

We got our drinks. He ordered a Scotch, and I got an Irish whiskey, which I hoped would bother him. He said, "How long did you know Olivia?"

"Not long enough," I said.

"You met in Greece?"

"Is that a question? Because it sounds like an accusation. I'm really not in the mood for this. What's in the briefcase?"

"The will, for one thing."

"I haven't read it."

Macintyre clicked open the briefcase and studied me. "She left you everything. Of course, we're going to have to contest some of it."

"You can have the cottage. I don't care."

"There's also the castle."

"She had a castle?"

"Not a big one."

"You can have it."

"And there's the apartment in Edinburgh."

"I don't want it."

"And the flat in London."

"I hate London. It's full of English people."

Macintyre stopped rifling through his files. He looked at me with some sympathy. "Mr. Brigg, I think I've misjudged you."

"Yes, you have," I said. "I loved Olivia." I took some whiskey. "And I'm not gay."

Even after signing off on all the Macintyre property, I was still left with a sizable sum. I didn't really want it, but then I realized that with it, I could do something different. I didn't want to go back to New

York. I could go live in Greece. I could buy a house on Aspros. But then I remembered that in the winter it would be just me and the caretaker and Thanasi. And Tomas, if Nikos hadn't rescued him. At least Tomas spoke some English. I thought of Andreas, the teenager who had worked on the dig, and pictured the two of us sitting in a café, if any were open in the winter, having a conversation something like, "Do you like to eat oranges?" "Yes, I like to eat oranges. Do you like to eat oranges?"

No. There was no returning to Aspros. Aspros was a magical kingdom built on a cloud. Aspros was more of memory than of place.

I had a final drink with Clive at Heathrow.

"I know you won't write, " he said, "but try to keep feeling like my friend, because I don't know what I'm doing after London and when I try to move in with you I don't want it to be awkward."

"You're always welcome." I felt indebted to Clive. "But I'm not sure I'm going back to New York. I don't think I can face it. All those people feeling sorry for me—or, worse, not caring at all."

"Where else would you go? Los Angeles?"

"Why Los Angeles?"

"The sunshine. I think you could use it."

I exhaled in a defeated way.

Clive watched me. "I think you should keep busy."

"Busy?" I considered this. "I don't know if you've noticed, Clive, but I don't do anything. That makes keeping busy difficult."

"That's where you're wrong, Rupert." Clive seemed convinced of this, which showed an anomalistic faith in himself. "You're an antiques dealer. It's not fancy, but it is a profession. You should open a shop."

"Open a shop?" I sounded as disparaging as I could, but Clive was not easily discouraged.

"What are your options? I know you miss Olivia, and you probably have this wonderful image of you drinking yourself to death. But you won't do it. You might try, but you won't succeed."

"And how do you know that?"

"Because you're a survivor, like me. We have that in common."

And of course I couldn't argue with Clive, because I'd tried that variety of grief before and had failed.

"You didn't think you were going to miss her this much, did you?" said Clive.

"No." I closed my eyes. "How much do I miss her?"

"A lot," he said. "What's your plan?"

"I think I'll buy a car."

"In New York?"

"Not in New York."

"Where then?"

"Vermont," I said. I'd been at camp there as a child, swum in its frigid lakes, breathed in the air. Vermont signified escape for me. And possibly regression. And—although I avoided this truth at the time— was baldly romantic, which was likely to soothe my damaged spirits. Clive waited for an explanation, but I didn't have one good enough to share. I just lit a new cigarette off his and blew rings at the ceiling.

14

Uncle William came to meet me at the airport. On the phone from London, I'd tried to convince him that taking a cab was fine. But he'd insisted and it was good to have him there, hands clasped in front and feet a shoulder's width apart. I knew I looked awful and felt somewhat safe as a result. I told Uncle William that I intended to buy a house in Vermont, some place with a barn—a vision had articulated itself on the plane trip—to run as an antiques business.

He said, "I'm glad you're thinking of your future."

This terrified me, of course, because I'd expected an argument. A panic set in as we left the terminal and got in the car. Now my beautiful farmhouse and converted barn seemed bleak and lonely. I imagined myself blundering from one structure to the other, mad and disheveled, with a relentless Brontëan wind as my only companion. Why would I want to grow old there?

"Of course, it's just for a few years," I said.

We were quiet for some time, and when the driver coughed it seemed very loud.

I said, "You would have liked Olivia. She had a good sense of humor."

Uncle William said, "I wish I had met her."

And we rode silently into the city.

Uncle William went with me to buy the car. I, of course, wanted something sporty, but he didn't think that was appropriate. Wasn't

I going to Vermont? At this point it was December, already bru-
tally cold and windy, dry, but I could imagine snow. The racing
green Jaguar I had been dreaming of would do me little good in Vermont. We looked at a couple of things. I realized, with some surprise, that I really didn't care what I drove. I kept having a sense of
déjà vu and finally attributed it to the time Uncle William and I
had gone shopping as I headed off to prep school. He'd been keen
on buying the right shirts and shoes, and of course knew exactly
what they were, and I hadn't cared then either. At the Oldsmobile
dealership, it was he who argued with the salesman. I overheard him
say, "I really don't want him driving anything that makes him look
like he's in the Mafia."

Which, actually, sounded rather appealing.

"So the car is not for you?" asked the salesman.

"No," said Uncle William. "It's for him."

The salesman glanced at me surreptitiously.

"What do you think, Rupert?" asked Uncle William.

I looked at him and shrugged.

Finally, we decided on a navy blue tanker that looked like it
would do well in the snow. I liked the radio, and Uncle William liked
the velvety seats. I thought I should pay for it because it was my car,
but Uncle William wanted to treat me. We argued back and forth.
The salesman stood very still, waiting for us to be done. Finally, Uncle
William insisted that he would get the car because I needed to save
my money to buy myself the house.

Uncle William had driven as a young man. He had a photograph of himself in a convertible. He said the car was yellow, but
the picture was black-and-white. He had not driven since. I now
had a British driver's license and had never driven a car on the right
side of the road. I think it was Uncle William's faith and ignorance—
that unmatchable pairing—that fueled my ability to get out of the
dealership, which was far west on 48th Street. I took a deep breath
and pulled into traffic. In a way, I was glad for all the cars because I
had a desire to drive on the left side of the road, and all the traffic
made that fairly impossible. And then I just wanted to stop as soon

as I could, but Uncle William thought we should see what the car could do. Uncle William didn't seem to understand just how challenging this was. I was a very poor driver. He was enjoying himself, drumming on the dashboard. When he thought I should slow down he tapped the air with his fingers, his hand relaxed and open—a conductor's gesture for calming the woodwinds. When he thought I should increase my speed, he pushed his fist forward. We drove for an hour, got lost on Long Island, asked many people for directions, and reached home after dark.

Christmas came and went. I managed to avoid the parties because of my recent loss. Nathan called, and we went for lunch. We talked a lot about Olivia, and it felt good and bad at the same time. Then we talked about Amanda. She had sold another piece of Jack's sculpture. Nathan wanted me to pull strings to find out how much it had fetched, because it was rumored to be a lot.

"Who's she sleeping with?" I asked.

"You're not really interested, are you?"

"Interested in Amanda, no. Interested in who she's sleeping with, very."

"Why?"

"He has good taste in jewelry."

Nathan didn't want to tell me because he'd heard it from Amanda, who had asked him to be quiet about it.

"That's complete bullshit," I said. "You knew before she confided in you, didn't you?"

"I'd heard something," said Nathan.

"Then it's not a matter of confidence. It's preexisting knowledge."

"This is not a legal matter," said Nathan. He was refolding his napkin and smiling at me with his eyes.

"Your not passing on the information is complete hypocrisy."

"Yes," said Nathan. "And what's wrong with that?" He'd let someone else tell me. "Rupert, do you know what the opposite of hypocrisy is?"

"Honesty?" I ventured.

"No," said Nathan. "It's anarchy."

I found my farmhouse three miles outside of Brattleboro. The house was a great brick building on a bald hill. There was one tree beside the house, an oak, which when the weather warmed up would be black with crows. In the fall the oak would drop acorns on the roof. I wanted to put a swing there, but who would swing there? It was just me, after all.

The barn had needed some shoring up but was nice and dry. I ordered a number of pallets and replaced some of the planking in the loft. The farmer next door had used it for a while and one cow, a sweet brown thing with eyes like a dog, would show up every now and then, forgetting it was no longer home. We would eye each other shyly, suspiciously; after all, who really belonged?

News circulated that I was interested in buying old things, and people began to bring them in. I ventured farther north to some junk stores, found a good furniture restorer, went to estate sales, and began to build inventory. I had a vague notion of hooking up with someone in New York, someone who could place the quality pieces. The obvious choice for this was Hester, but I didn't want to work with her. I also didn't want to work with one of her competitors, because she'd hear about it. I felt constantly presented with creative ways to complete her destruction, but I didn't follow through. Instead, I did nothing. I found an exceptional Hepplewhite dresser with all the original brass and locks and sent it to Uncle William as a present.

One morning I came in from the barn to find the phone ringing. It was Nathan.

"I'm passing through Brattleboro on my way to a friend's cabin. If you have time, I'd love to stop by and see how you're doing."

"I have time," I said.

I was inordinately thrilled by Nathan's impending visit. I went into town to see if I could find some cheese that wasn't cheddar and a good bottle of wine. I found both. I got some logs from the woodshed and made a nice pile by the fireplace in the kitchen.

I hurried across the windblown hill, what I referred to in my head as the "the steppes," to the barn. The smell in there was of dust and oldness. I had gained quite a collection of crystal and silver, shaving mirrors, and family Bibles. There were all sorts of prints and a few nice French hutches and English sideboards. I had tried to maintain some order, but this was not easy. The figurines were crowding the china cabinets. I loathed figurines—all those cloying shepherds and small-footed ladies—but I had a hard time saying no to people. Frankly, if you showed up at my house with something to sell, I was probably going to buy it.

I rooted around through a couple of bins, through the cluttered shelves. I was looking for candlesticks. I had a number of them. For some reason, candlesticks survived, and I thought a mess of them, crystal and silver, in the front windows might be festive. I found a good pair of sterling sabbath candlesticks, which I'd purchased from a woman a month earlier. I'd been careful to hang on to these because I was nursing a hope that she might want them back.

One cold Saturday morning I had answered the door to find the woman standing there, pulling her coat around her. She had her two children in tow, a boy and a girl. There was an elegance about her that didn't match her clothes or her vehicle, a battered pickup with Jersey plates.

"Can I help you?" I asked. I'd just made coffee but hadn't yet had a chance to drink any.

"Someone at the gas station said you bought antiques."

"Yes, I do." I invited them in and gave her a cup of coffee and the children some doughnuts, which were stale, but they wolfed them down. Although I wasn't usually that friendly, living on my bald hill in my empty house had made anything at the door possibly entertaining. "Tell me what you have."

The woman eyed me nervously. "Do you know about Bonaparte?"

"Napoleon?" I ventured.

"No. His brother."

"Joseph, the king of Spain?"

"That's the one." She smiled nervously. "I have a couple of things that have come to me, and I'd like to sell them."

"We'll take a look, when you're done with your coffee. I'm in no hurry." Her children had sat down on the floor next to the kitchen fireplace, a large old-fashioned one big enough for me to stand in. They were drawing in the soot on the brick. The little girl had loopy yellow hair and fat cheeks. The boy, older, looked much like his mother. He had a precocious weariness about him, and I had a feeling that somewhere in New Jersey his father was waking up and wondering where they'd gone. "Have you had a long drive today?" I asked.

"Yes," said the woman.

"Do you have relatives in the area?"

"Yes," she said. She drank down her coffee and set the cup almost silently on the table. "Thank you for the coffee. Do you want to see the pieces?"

I said I did. She called to the children, but they looked warm and happy so I told her to let them stay. Out of earshot, I told the boy that there was milk and cheese and some cold chicken in the refrigerator; if he and his sister were hungry they could help themselves.

It was a freezing cold day, in the teens, with a wind. The woman had a tarp over the things in the back of the truck, which had been packed in a hurry. There were dolls flung in there, along with clothing. On the top was a garment bag printed with an old Saks logo, probably from the forties. The zipper had come open a little, and I could make out black fur, probably a mink, inside. Somewhere someone had come down in the world, married down, I thought. Married for love, maybe her mother.

She caught me looking and said, "Do the contents of my truck interest you?"

And I said, "Isn't that why you're here?"

She had a dresser that took up half the truck, and it was this she wanted to unload. I helped her into the truck bed. She had the dresser protected by a sheet and she revealed it with a certain amount of ceremony.

"This dresser belonged to Joseph Bonaparte," she said.

I knew all about Joseph Bonaparte.

In 1816, Napoleon's brother Joseph, once king of Naples, once king of Spain, finding himself without a kingdom and banned from living in France, made the unusual choice of relocating to New Jersey. He created an estate called Point Breeze just over the river from Pennsylvania and began calling himself the Count de Survilliers. The house he built was enormous and he filled it with stuff, including works by Titian, Velázquez, Rubens, Rembrandt, and da Vinci. I'd read somewhere that he had a mirror hanging over his bed and that the walls in his bedchamber were covered with paintings of nude ladies and famous conquest scenes along the lines of *The Rape of Europa*. The paintings were all auctioned off in 1847, along with the other stuff—the tables and chairs, bookcases, dressers, and candlesticks, the fine china and sterling flatware.

The Count de Survilliers had owned many things, but if one third of the Joseph Bonaparte antiques were actually genuine, there would have been enough objects to clutter fifty Point Breezes. And that's only counting the pieces people had tried to sell me.

And here is the woman standing in her truck, and she's shaking because the wind is blowing hard. Some miracle of strength is holding her together and she has just unveiled the dresser. The sheet is whipping in the wind and tears are streaking out the sides of her eyes, and it might just be the cold but it probably isn't.

"Are you sure you want to sell it?" I asked.

She inhaled and thought for a moment and then said, "Well, sir, are you in the habit of doing only what you want?"

Even from where I was standing, feet solidly on the ground, I knew the dresser was American. True, there had been quite a few fine cabinetmakers in Philadelphia, possibly influenced by the trendsetting count's presence in the area, who made wonderful furniture. I thought of Charles Honoré Lannuier and Michael Bouvier. But I knew this woman was under the impression that the dresser was European, part of the Bonaparte hoard, and this certainly would have helped its value. I hopped up on the back of the truck. It was a nice dresser, but it didn't set my heart pounding. I opened the drawer and, just as I had suspected, the secondary wood was white pine. This was no European piece and frankly even New Jersey seemed too far south for its provenience. I dated the piece somewhere in the 1880s. Our friend Joseph Bonaparte had left for Europe, never to return, in 1839.

I bought the dresser and the candlesticks, which were worth more than I paid—German 1880s, sterling—but I had lost a lot of money on the first transaction and needed something to remind myself that I was a businessman. I was transfixed by the little boy. He was pinched and thin, and the way he wrapped his sister up in her scarf and carefully put on her mittens, feeling for her thumb, the way he shook my hand and thanked me for the food, affected me. As they were walking off to the car, I had a fleeting desire to try my charm on the mother, just to have the children stay. But she was a destroyed woman and I let her go, back to her parents or wherever it was she was seeking refuge. The little boy gave me a quick wave as they pulled off, I suppose to assure me that everything was going to be all right. I hoped it would be, but as they drove off, I felt a terrible renewed loneliness.

Nathan showed up around four in the afternoon. He was three hours late and the snow was beginning to collect in drifts. I had already called the police to see if they'd run into him in the course of investigating the day's accidents, but no one matched his description and I wasn't sure what he was driving. The car belonged to his friend, and delivering it was apparently the occasion for Nathan's visit. Finally, I saw lights at the foot of the hill. I ran out with a flashlight, and sure enough there was Nathan.

"Rupert, hello," he said. He was just out of the car and was adjusting the cuffs of his gloves. He looked at me with concern. "Is it all right if I leave it here?"

There was an uninterrupted sea of nothing upon which the blue car sat. "A little to the left would have been better," I said, and Nathan knew I was joking.

For dinner, I was warming up some beef stew that had been left for me, and there were potatoes roasting in the fireplace. Nathan held his glass of wine. He was drinking very slowly, although he had assured me that the wine was good. I wondered if it was too sweet. The best wine I'd seen for sale had been this white, a Gewürztraminer, and a French claret that I was saving for dinner. I caught Nathan eyeing me in a concerned way. He seemed rather disturbed by my transformation.

"What are you wearing?" he said.

"It's a sweater," I said.

"Looks more like a colossal tea cosy. Did someone make that for you?"

"Yes," I said. The sweater was somewhat remarkable, all coarse cables and knots. It weighed about seven pounds.

"The Bavarian milkmaid?" Nathan inquired.

"You've been talking to Clive," I said. "Her father owns the dairy next door. And where did this Bavarian bullshit come into play? Are we in Bavaria?"

Nathan waved me off. "Don't be so defensive," he said.

"She passes the time," I said. "She stops me from thinking."

"Then it's not serious?"

"Of course not," I said, and added, "I might starve to death without her. That's kind of serious." And Nathan smiled, although with limited sympathy.

Later, he said, "We all miss Olivia, Rupert. We don't all live in Vermont."

Nathan's room was across the hall from mine and had its own fireplace. I'd stacked up enough wood to last through the night. With the wind fairly shrieking around the house and the crackle of wood, it was all quite romantic and appealed to Nathan's finely honed aesthetic sense. I gave him an extra pair of wool socks, just in case his feet got cold. The Bavarian milkmaid had tidied the room up that afternoon and put a wreath of bittersweet over the head of the bed. She had also rescued and laundered some lace doilies that apparently I had purchased along with a rolltop desk, and these were strategically placed on wood surfaces around the room. I didn't know how to decorate in Vermont. I thought all the lace would look cloying, but it more underscored the severity of country life, and I rather liked it. As I drifted off I was happy that Nathan was there, across the hall, where he should be.

The temperature warmed up the next day and by noon the roads were open. I was disappointed because I'd hoped that Nathan would have to stay another night.

"I really have to go, Rupert. I'm expected."

"You could call," I said.

"He doesn't have a phone."

"Must be a very important friend to have you driving through a snowstorm."

Nathan smiled and nodded. "Yes, Rupert, a very important friend."

He got into his car. I was wearing the sweater again, I think in defiance, because I—unfairly, no doubt—felt Nathan was abandoning me.

He started the engine and backed the car around, then shouted out the window, "I almost forgot. Neftali is visiting in a month. She wants to see you."

A few days after Nathan's visit, I was surprised by the appearance of the Bavarian milkmaid's father on my doorstep. It was a Saturday morning and I was still in my pajama pants, with the sweater because the house was cold.

"Good morning, Mr. Wetzel," I said.

"Rupert," He sniffed. His cheeks were chapped and he seemed upset. "I'm looking for Veronica."

"Maybe she's out with the cows," I said.

"You know she's not."

Out of the corner of my eye I saw his daughter scuttle out of sight behind the barn. She must have gone out the back door. "Coffee?" I offered.

"No, thank you." He looked me in the eye. "What kind of man are you, Rupert Brigg?"

I had an idea, but it was too early to face this.

"I want to like you. In a way, you've helped people out. You've bought their junk, and don't argue with me, Veronica's told me. It's not always art and antiques. But what's Veronica ever done to you?"

I stayed quiet.

"How many times have you been married?"

I knew that one. "Twice."

"And how old are you?"

I knew that too. "Thirty-one."

"Veronica's nineteen."

I might have shuddered, although I was aware of her age.

"She's going to make someone a good wife. You're not that man and she doesn't know it."

After Wetzel left, I poured myself a drink and lay down on the couch. The phone rang later. I knew it was Veronica, because it rang at one of the times of Wetzel's regular cow-related activities. But I didn't answer it. I was under the impression that I should leave Vermont. I felt like a poison on the landscape, but the thought of returning to New York scared me. The thought of moving anywhere—motion itself— seemed impossible.

I had been happy in Scotland with Olivia and I believed that I had made her life better, helped her out, kept her final months more like living and less like rehearsal for whatever was to follow. But I'd been carrying around a lot of guilt ever since she died and hadn't been able to talk about it with anyone. Because it was a horrible truth and I felt somehow responsible. Olivia, in the end, had killed herself. Her final moments hadn't been a benevolent fog of last-life confusion but rather an anxiety of figuring out how to administer a lethal dose of morphine. The doctors had questioned me about it, but I hadn't known what she'd been thinking. And wasn't it selfish to think it was all about me anyway? She'd lived in pain for two years. The chances of her leaving the hospital with anyone but the undertaker were very slim. She'd been enjoying a few of life's pleasures but was losing that ability. Why wouldn't she kill herself?

Vermont was a complete failure. I felt as if the last four months had been some sort of out-of-body experience, a story that someone was telling me over drinks, definitely not my life. What I had wanted was to fall apart in an amazing way, like Hester—all bones and gloom and scratchy suits—whose grieving I admired. I'd wanted to destroy myself so all would be forgiven and I could live a quiet life with some dignity. But no. Here I was, fucking the juicy Veronica from next door, who cooked for me and did my laundry, giggled in bed, and only occasionally smelled like cheese. I remembered Olivia sitting in her favorite chair, her nose wrinkled, the paper collapsing in front of her, disbelief—I must have said something stupid, but I can't re-member what it was. I thought of my little son waiting for me, waiting—red sweater, ball, runny nose, smile—and I began to crave pain. The thought of that kind of obvious physical grieving made sense, seemed almost capable of comfort. I knew why, in the Bible, grief-stricken people flogged themselves and tore their clothes and shaved their heads, but I also knew that I would do none of these things. Vermont had not healed me but had laid me bare. And here I was left with myself, which amplified my own presence to a dis-heartening degree.

Later, when the bottle was done and I came to in the dark house, I could hear Veronica tapping on the windows, calling "Rupert, Rupert," in a projected whisper, but I just pulled the couch cushion over my head and prayed that she would go home.

I spent the next few days cataloging the various things I'd accumu-lated in the barn, doing the things I had avoided, liking checking all the hallmarks on the figurines to see if they were worth anything.

There was a truly ghastly ceramic lion the size of a terrier, tongue sticking out, in good condition. The lion was a Sheffield, 1860s, some coronation piece. I decided to send it to Hester. She liked the big pieces. I put a card inside that said, *I'm sorry*. Then I took that card out and wrote another, *Because you collect these*, which also seemed stupid. I thought of *Greetings from Vermont*, but that seemed to encourage optimism, although I doubted she had any left. Something about *greetings* had always sounded sexual to me. Finally, on my good stationery, I wrote her a letter saying that I had been finding pieces of good quality and, although I had acted badly, perhaps she would not mind entering into some sort of business arrangement. At least now, if she rebuffed me, I could approach someone else with the items.

I drove up past Manchester to attend an estate sale and bought a couple of good paintings that I would take with me next time I went to New York. These had a few condition issues—some flaking and, on one, a sooty grime that had to be cigar smoke—but I felt that once cleaned up the paintings would fetch a good price. I bought an armoire, French, and a wooden plate that was unassuming but, if it was really a frontier piece, would be valuable. I made arrangements to have the armoire delivered and left. On the drive home I thought it might be fun to have Neftali and Nathan visit me. After all, there was room. And if I was inviting them, I might try Clive. Maybe Nikos had some available time. And if I was doing all that, I really should call Amanda, because I didn't have a good reason to exclude her. I pictured some sort of memorial for Olivia and a woman from the village hired to cook.

After some difficulty, I placed a call to Clive in London. I'd only spoken to him once, when I first moved to Vermont. Clive had written a few times but, as predicted, I hadn't answered the letters. One was fourteen pages long and seemed to have been written when Clive was very drunk. The last eight or so pages were all about someone named Barry, a titled Irishman—were there titled Irishmen?—who had broken his heart or something else, but I couldn't make it out and after trying a few times wasn't sure I wanted to. The phone rang, a vague yoo-hooing into another dimension, but no one picked up. I tried again. This time a woman answered, which was disconcerting. I was inordinately pleased that she spoke English, in London, but I still had trouble understanding.

"He's gone back," she said. She said this several times before I got it, and then, to her delight, I rang off.

I went back to Clive's last letter. After all the Barry-centric drunken scrawl, there were a couple of lines in Clive's easy handwriting: *I'm transferring to the American office. I hate London. Hate it. I hope you've cheered up. Clear your couch.*

But I'd heard nothing from him. I suppose a couch in Vermont just wasn't that appealing.

I tried Nathan next, but there was no answer. I wasn't sure if I really wanted Amanda there, but with her social life she'd probably have other plans anyway. I found her number tucked into the pages of my address book. She had scrawled it on the back of a ferry ticket while we were still on Aspros, and I hadn't entered the number because I wasn't sure how long I'd need it. I made the call. The phone rang a couple of times, and then a man answered.

"Hello?"

It was Clive.

"Clive," I said.

"Rupert!"

"How long have you been back?"

"Just a few days. How did you know I was here?"

"I didn't."

"You were calling Amanda?" Clive was surprised. "Why?"

We talked for an hour. Amanda's apartment was in Chelsea in a dilapidated building that she and Jack had lived in together, which they had sublet while in Hydra. She was looking to move. She had draped sheets over many of Jack's sculptures, and this Clive attributed to grief. Amanda had been drinking a lot and Clive, in a whisper even

though he was alone, predicted that at this rate she would not age
well. "And she doesn't seem that happy. Maybe it's the guy she's
dating."

"Who is it?"

"It's kind of hush-hush. He's engaged to someone else."

"You know what?" I said. "I really don't care."

"But you know him, from college."

"I do?"

"His name is Kiplinger, Kiplinger Sand."

Later that week, at around 4 A.M., the phone rang. I had lost people,
so I never let the phone ring at night. Although Uncle William was
in good health, I still worried about his heart, that fantastic Brigg
ticker, which unfortunately had a history of blowing up without
warning. But it wasn't anything connected to Uncle William.

"Rupert," said the voice, "I am waking you up. But you have also
woken me up a few times, yes?"

It was Nikos. "My God," I said. "How are you?"

"I have been late to tell you that I am sorry because of Olivia,"
he said. His English had stiffened up over the last few months.

"Don't feel bad, Nikos," I said. "She's still dead."

"Yes," said Nikos. We were quiet for a moment. "I have to tell
you that I am getting married."

"Really? Really? Well, congratulations," I said. "That's amazing."

"Why is it amazing? You know I have a fiancée."

We talked for a while about Kostas, Neftali's visit, the date of
the wedding, and Amanda, whom he hadn't forgotten. I asked him
if he'd given Tomas any kind of help, and that's where the rot about
Amanda was evident. "There are words for him in Greek," said
Nikos, laughing softly, "and I'm sure in English, but I don't know
them."

I had an idea. "Nikos, why don't I come for a last hurrah, before
you get married? We can travel a bit. Do a few islands."

There was silence, and I was worried I'd offended him.

"I'm not trying to avoid your wedding. I just thought—"

"Shut up, Rupert," he said. He'd been planning in his head. "That will be fantastic."

I wanted Nikos to join us in Vermont, but a visit was out of the question. He was hard at work. Nikos was quite an adult over the phone. He was calling from the office, and when he interrupted our conversation to yell at someone who had clearly angered him, he sounded exactly like Kostas.

"End of May," said Nikos. "We go for a week, then you can be in Athens for a week, meet my fiancée, see your friend Steve Kelly."

We hung up. I gazed out the window, where the first gray light of morning was coldly projected across the fields. No one stirred there, nothing, but then I saw a fox, trotting at a quick pace. He stopped, turned, and I think he might have looked straight at me. He continued on with a great sense of purpose, but I doubted he knew where he was going.

Nathan called me at about 9 A.M. to say that he and Neftali were going to hit the road, which meant, if they stopped for lunch, they would arrive sometime in the late afternoon. Clive was riding with Amanda, and who knew when they would show up? The woman from the village arrived at around ten and began cleaning. There were four bedrooms upstairs, and I wasn't quite sure who should stay where. Two rooms had double beds, and two rooms had twins. I had the woman make up all the beds and was in the process of raiding the barn for some large serving dishes when I saw Veronica walking purposefully up the hill.

We hadn't spoken since her father's visit, but she had made her presence known. Once, in the middle of the night, I'd woken up to hear a car revving and guttering on my lawn and some drunken laughter. I'd looked out the window to see Veronica and some towheaded thug standing at a distance. The thug had his arm around her and they were drinking from a bottle. I felt a bit responsible. I had a sneaking suspicion that before her involvement with me, Veronica might not have been cruising around with drunken thugs, that my "liberating" of Veronica might have left her with no sense of right and wrong. Not that I believed in right and wrong. But seeing Veronica there, sticky-faced in her poorly fitting pencil skirt, I felt that having removed her bourgeois prudishness, I should have at least left her with a sense of the advantageous and the appalling, a knowledge of *bella figura*. The boy she was with was wearing a leather jacket, poorly fitting, that was probably purchased at a pawnshop. I was just about to return to bed when he turned his back and dropped his pants, his white buttocks glowing in the moonlight.

After this episode, there was a cow-time ringing of the phone, but I now felt completely vindicated. Veronica owed me an apology. If I didn't let her deliver it, she would continue to owe it, and that seemed advantageous.

But here she was walking up the hill and, even though I wanted to run into the barn and lock the door, I knew I was going to have to speak to her.

"Hello, Veronica," I said, when she was closer. "Does your father know you're here?"

"I may not be as old as you," she said, "but I sure as hell don't have to listen to him anymore."

We stared at each other. "I have to get some things out of the barn," I said.

She followed me in. Veronica usually talked and talked, but now she had adopted an almost predatory silence. I found a platter and flipped it over to see if it was worth anything. Veronica's eyes narrowed and she threw up her chin.

"I saw you watching us the other night," she said.

"I had to look," I said. "I thought someone might be lynching me. Your boyfriend is quite a free spirit."

"He's not my boyfriend," she said. "He's really young. I like my men older." She came over and wrapped her arms around me, pinning

my arms to my sides. I was holding a platter, heavy and valuable pro-
vided I didn't drop it. I looked down at Veronica's yellow hair. Her
head came up to my breastbone. "Come on, Rupert. It's not like we
haven't done it before."

I was not prepared for this. Something in her voice frightened
me.

"What we had was good," I said. "Now it's over."

She let go of me and stepped back. "Why?" she asked. She pondered this and then smiled. "Is it for my own good?" Her voice was
childish and thick with accent, which had the surprising effect of
making her sound witty.

"Maybe."

"Or maybe it's for your own good, because who knows what my
redneck father is capable of?"

"It just doesn't seem like a good idea anymore," I said.

"You liked me when I didn't know anything," she said.

"That's not true," I said.

For a moment I thought she might cry.

"You're a beautiful girl, Veronica," I said. "You're going to make
someone a wonderful wife."

Veronica was by the doors. She held my gaze in a way she never
had and said, "Who wants to be someone's wife?"

Nathan and Neftali arrived at five. We went for a walk, avoiding the
neighboring dairy, even though Neftali wanted to see it. I showed
them my barn. Nathan volunteered to take my new canvases back
to New York and drop them off at the restorers, and I was carrying
them up the hill when Amanda and Clive arrived. It was about 60
degrees, but they were riding in a convertible with the top down. The
car was baby blue, very flashy, and I knew it had to be Kiplinger's.
There was a lot of ooing and ahing about my house, about how thin
I had become—I only knew how to cook steak, so I'd been living on
steak and cheese—about how wonderful it was to get together. Neftali
started to cry about Olivia at one point, and everyone joined in, and

then I decided that we needed to start drinking vigorously as soon as possible.

We had roast lamb for dinner, plain but very fresh. I wondered if the lamb had come from close by, then thought about lambs, then forced the thought from my mind. I was supposed to drive the woman back to the village after she did the dinner dishes, but I was too drunk so Nathan took her. I was thinking clearly, but I couldn't walk straight; it was all the red wine. There was a piano in the living room and Clive, to my surprise, started playing it. We sang some show tunes, but Clive didn't know that many. He did, however, know every Christmas carol, religious and secular, so we sang our way through those. The fire was merry in the grate and the wine would not run out. After the Christmas carols, we sang "Onward, Christian Soldiers," and "Jerusalem." I was the only one who knew all the words to "Jerusalem." I finished loudly, and punctuated this by draining my glass and slamming it on the piano. The others were respectfully awed.

Later that evening, I found myself holding Amanda's hand.

Nathan asked, "Are you still seeing the Bavarian milkmaid?"

And I told him that I wasn't.

Amanda was wearing knee-high boots and a short skirt. I found myself studying her legs and then pulling to consciousness. I looked over at Clive, thinking he would be passing some sort of judgment, but he had a drunken, sloppy look to him. I also realized that Nathan and Neftali were no longer there. Amanda and Clive were gossiping about some New York person I didn't know, and she was laughing with those big clean teeth. I had decided that I had to sleep with her because I had to sleep with someone and she was the obvious choice. The wine must have lost its hold a little. It was now 2 A.M. and I had been drinking steadily since six, but it was possible that I had forgotten to keep drinking or had lost the energy to refill my glass. I was going to get more wine, but those words from Macbeth flashed across my mind, "It provokes the desire but weakens the performance," so I remained in my seat. Clive saw my hand on Amanda's thigh and wisely chose to go to bed.

Later, when Amanda was straddled across me, leaning on my wrists, with her breasts hanging near my face, I asked her, "Why are you with Kiplinger?"

And she said, "Because you won't have me."

A part of me wanted to believe her, but I knew it was bullshit.

The light woke me up first, flaring and flashing on the far wall. My eyes were barely open when I heard Neftali screaming in Greek. I threw Amanda's arm off and got out of bed. I had just pulled my shorts up when Neftali ran into the room in her bathrobe.

"Rupert!" she said. "Your barn!"

I ran downstairs in my underwear, wrapped in a blanket. I got my boots on in the hall and slammed the door open. The sky was heated and glowing. Flames quivered and flared out of the roof, and the hot breath of the barn's burning warmed the night. There was a tense creaking, an agony of wood, and then a loud crash as the roof collapsed. On the hill, a few neighbors had gathered to watch, to listen to the groaning timbers and shattering glass, occasionally a splintered explosion as something blew. I held my breath. Neftali came beside me and squeezed my arm.

"Quite a spectacle, isn't it?" I said.

"Oh, Rupert, all your beautiful things."

My barn, courtesy of Veronica, was going up in flames.

Of course, I never pressed charges. A man from the insurance company came to call. I'd only gotten around to insuring some things —not all—in the weeks before the fire, and I suppose this looked suspicious. I asked Uncle William to call one of the higher-ups in the insurance company. I thought he might know someone, and he did. Then the police found a gas can, but they must have known it wasn't mine. I wasn't sure what to do with the house. As I packed up

my things, I wondered if I'd ever live in it again. The house already
had a deserted feel.

I stood by the window taking a last look around my bedroom.
There were no real memories here, and the view of the stark horizon
depressed me. I wondered why I'd ever found it comforting. The cur-
tains had been taken off the windows by the cleaning woman, to be
stored until a tenant could be found. And that was why I saw the
earrings—Amanda's—that she had left on the windowsill a week
earlier. They were large emerald-cut solitaire diamonds. They made
an extravagant present, one I immediately attributed to Kiplinger. I
wondered if Amanda remembered where she'd left them and she must
have, but she was probably waiting for me to straighten it out.

I suppose I could have met up with Amanda in New York and returned the earrings over dinner. That would have been polite, but
then I remembered—with a measure of relief—that she was still seeing Kiplinger. Our having dinner was not exactly proper. Mailing the
earrings would be not only easy but discreet. I looked through my
address book, found the ferry ticket with Amanda's number, and di-
aled. The phone rang a couple of times. I flipped the ticket over and
began reading it. I would not have done this, but I wanted to read
the Greek letters as practice for my impending visit to Nikos. This
ticket was from Piraeus—I could see that much—but the destination
was not Aspros but rather Hydra. The date was the fourth of August.
There was something significant about it; maybe it was a birthday.
What was the fourth of August? And then I remembered. I hung up
the phone.

The fourth of August was the day Jack had been murdered.

15

Nikos and I spent the first week of my trip in Athens. There weren't that many tourists yet, and whoever had made the journey was serious, middle-aged, or unattractive, and usually a combination. Knee socks were popular. So were maps. I made a call to Steve Kelly and was told by someone at his office that he was out of town. When I asked them where he was, they wouldn't tell me. I left my number. He never called. I thought of dropping by the hotel to look for him—I was staying with Nikos at his house—but somehow never did.

By myself, I walked up to the Acropolis. I had a sketch pad with me and I saw a little boy pointing at it. Maybe he thought it was funny that a grown man would want to draw. Maybe he was jealous. He had his finger raised and held it, and I looked into his wide face, his blue eyes.

"Stop pointing," said his mother, or something close in French, and hurried him off.

I continued up the slippery marble walkway, up the steps, trying to imagine someone from the deep past making this same trip in leather sandals, someone whom the heat did not bother: Socrates, pre-hemlock. I felt I was being followed and looked quickly over my shoulder, but the stairs descended in emptiness, until a dog crossed on its way to somewhere else. The shadow of a dove flying, a brief darkness on the yellow stone, crossed after. There was no one in sight. On my right was the Agora, a peaceful dusty meadow, a few pieces from monuments strewn around, but they didn't suggest greatness, only monumental decay. An Asian man with a camera snapped a

picture. He sensed me watching him and turned around. He was
wearing sunglasses and I couldn't see his eyes. If I had been closer,
I'd have seen myself reflected and staring back.

It wasn't that hot, but I was dizzy. I remembered the café where
I had sat with Steve. I pictured his red hair and the bougainvillea
falling over him, and the ice in the glasses and his beautiful friend. I
took an alley to the left which, in my invented map, led to this same
place. I wandered on, but here it was deserted and dirty. I stopped to
think. An ancient wall was marred by a rotting wooden door. Graf-
fiti in wavering Greek coursed over the rock in a perversion of hi-
eroglyphics. Twitching on the doorstep, a needle still in his vein, a
young man groaned in a combination of pleasure and grief. He didn't
notice me, and I walked past quickly.

I was not going to find my café. I headed upward, upward. The
path curved to the right. At a distance I saw a man walking with a
cane. He was wearing a hat. He was old and walked slowly, but I
couldn't catch up with him. I walked faster, but the distance remained
between us. I wondered why I was chasing him, and then I realized I
thought he was Michaud, the French archaeologist I had encountered
in Delphi. But Michaud was dead. And this man, with his cane, disappeared around a bend in the road, and when I finally rounded it
he was gone.

I bought a bottle of water at a shop that sold cigarettes and lot-
tery tickets and drank half.

The Acropolis had many people wandering it, climbing on the
rocks, looking up at its curving pillars as if somewhere there, contained in the language of the metopes, was an explanation of the
nature of man. Why, despite what we knew of the battle, savagery
versus reason, our Centaurs always triumphed over our Lapiths.

I felt very lonely as I walked back down the mountain. Everyone seemed to be a couple or a part of some other gathering of souls.
A little boy stood screaming, mouth wide, his hands fisted at his sides
as his mother, a beautiful anachronism in black, heeled oxfords, and
hat, did her best to wipe the tears. Two priests in front of me, like
chess pieces in their matching black, glided down the path. The whole

walk down seemed strange as if I'd wandered into a hall of mirrors, able to see yet not be seen—not seen by the couple embracing on the ancient wall, or by the two little boys chasing each other, or by the old man talking to his cat. Ahead there was a young man with his wife, and they had a little boy, and I wondered if that's what I would look like walking with Olivia and Michael. But we had never walked together.

Suddenly I had to sit down. I didn't want to be here. I didn't want to be anywhere. And I remembered why Uncle William had sent me to Greece, nearly a year ago. He thought it would heal me. He couldn't bear to see his "golden sunshine" so extinguished. He'd told me years ago that I had saved him. He had been lost. He had destroyed a string of lovers and felt so alone that he traveled and traveled and traveled, always two steps ahead of that one who was stalking him: himself. This was when I was in college, just accepting that I could love this man and learning to enjoy him. The whiskey had him but his words were sublime and pounded on my eardrums, unlike anything he'd said before.

I stood up from the wall. I was sweating. I had to get something to drink. I took a few cautious steps, conscious of the blood humming in my brain and there were dark purple splotches dancing in my peripheral vision. I placed my feet on the ground in front of me, one after the other. I had a moment of consciousness, where I remembered wondering why people didn't just sit down when they felt this way. Why they pretended that they could stand and walk and function. But I couldn't bring myself to sit down. I just wanted to get away from the ancient buildings, the churning eternity of people. I thought of all the bones beneath my feet, all those dead philosophers and ordinary Greeks. I thought of my house on its bald hill with its one tree and wondered if this hill had once looked like that. Once a hill, but now choked with buildings, some falling in disrepair, all rotting window grilles and splintered wood held whole by glossy paint. I stopped to rest and then I saw someone, reflected in a dirty window, looking over my shoulder. I turned quickly, but there was no one there.

It was just a reflection, ungenerous, altered by mood.

Something in the shading of this blackened glass aged me. I looked heavier. My hair was pushed off my forehead with sweat and looked as if it had thinned. It was me, older, less handsome, in a wrinkled suit.

Back at the Nikolaides house, I fell into a deep sleep, and when I woke up it was ten-thirty. Nikos was waiting for me, waiting to eat. We sat on the terrace on the roof. The food smelled of olives and dill. I realized that I was starving. Nikos had spent the day trying to get a form through some ministry, which seemed to be a ministry set up to stymie the progression of forms of its invention.

"I need a break," said Nikos. "I'm glad we are getting out of Athens."

A light breeze scattered the paper napkins. On the street, unseen but loud, two young girls gossiped back and forth.

"You're wrong about the Acropolis," I said.

"Why? What did I say?"

"You said there was nothing to see there."

"When did I say that?"

"It was the first time I met you. You said, 'Every Greek has the Acropolis at his back.' And then you said something about wanting to know the future."

"I don't remember saying that," said Nikos. He gave me an incredulous look. "How can you walk around with all those things in your head? Memories are for old people."

After dinner, Nikos asked to see my sketches. At first I resisted, but then I remembered Olivia with her poem, who had read it just to avoid appearing too serious about it, and this seemed a wise course of action. I went upstairs and got the sketchbook.

"Very nice," he said. "But this is just your hand." He flipped up the pages, over and over, and there were maybe fifty studies of my left hand at all different angles. I had stayed sketching at the Acropolis for hours.

"It's the only thing I can draw," I said. I flipped a few pages later

and there was an attempt at one of the caryatids of the Erechtheion.
I had imposed some sort of sensibility on her because I hadn't trusted
a nose that big to be beautiful. The eyes were round and bulged out
over her other features, and I had flattened the whole. Nikos flipped
to the earlier pages, to a sketch of the octopus bowl that we'd excavated from Aspros. I had put all the fragments together on the page
in a way that I thought made sense.

"Maybe there's a part of you that is an artist," said Nikos.

"No, Nikos," I said. "There's a part of me that wants to record.
I like to hold on to things. I never think of something and want to
draw it. Or want to make something."

"No imagining of things?" asked Nikos.

"No creative urge. No obsession. No glorious dementia." I took
back my book. "No gift."

Nikos nodded at me thoughtfully. We had had a few drunken,
carousing nights, but both of us were a bit subdued, Nikos because of
his impending wedding and me because being in Greece reminded
me of the previous summer and Olivia. And Jack, whose death was
bothering me.

I asked, "Are the police still investigating Jack's death?"

Nikos shrugged. "They can investigate all they want, but if they
were going to find the killer, they would have already done it."

"So the killer gets away with it."

Nikos was surprised at my concern. "Does this upset you?"

"I'm not sure," I said. Because I wasn't.

Nikos thought my depression would pass. He had decided to get
married and was of the opinion that I should get married. What was
good for him was good for me. Number three is the charm. He thought
I should go back to work. He didn't seem to think my business in
Vermont qualified and, much as I protested, I rather agreed. He kept
looking at my sketch of the bowl and saying how very good it was,
how I'd impressed him in Aspros, sitting in the violent heat with my
basins and bowls, patiently looking at all the fragments. He sounded
vaguely parental on this point. I really didn't need that kind of attention, not from Nikos, but I had a suspicion that later in life I would

revisit this annoying episode in our friendship with a certain amount of affection.

After I'd left Vermont, I'd been nagged by a desire to learn more about Jack. I met Neftali for coffee the day before she was to return to Greece. Neftali and Jack had been close once, long ago. I wondered how she tied in with Jack's fascination with Greece. They might have been lovers when Neftali was in her twenties, although she said nothing to confirm this. Their involvement, although it had never previously entered my mind, now seemed certain. Despite—or perhaps because—of what they'd been to each other, they remained friends. That's why she'd had him at the house in Aspros, and it was Neftali who'd helped Jack and Amanda move to Hydra. Yes, his drinking had bothered her, and the young wife sleeping with everyone, but artists were like children. Sometimes you had to look the other way.

Jack was born in 1916, somewhere in Missouri. A sister and a brother had died during the Depression, the sister from pneumonia, the brother from a tractor accident that had left him with one arm for the last two days of his life. Jack had nursed the brother through this, and apparently, although I'd never seen it, Jack's breakthrough exhibit was a series of male figures all with one arm. Jack's coming to art was something of a mystery, but he'd had some formal training at the Art Institute in Chicago. He painted for a while and some of the canvases survived.

"But he loved sculpting things," Neftali told me. "He liked to put something into the space, and see it move out all the air."

I hadn't seen anything of his, other than his replicas, but from the way Neftali was shaking her head, it was clear that she'd been impressed.

"You know, Jack was in the war, in France. There was a grenade that landed somewhere close. It killed everyone but him. He stayed in a ditch with his leg broken up, the bone sticking through, for four days, waiting for death. Waiting. And someone came and saved him.

And then one day he is killed by a man with a hat." She was angry. "That's all we know. But this great artist is dead, dead, and he was only forty-seven."

Of course I wanted to tell Neftali this "man with a hat" had actually been Amanda, that the hat was Olivia's missing donkey-driver straw. If I'd shown Neftali Amanda's ferry ticket to Hydra, she would have come to the same conclusion as I had. After all, Amanda's only alibi had been Tomas. But I didn't want to torture Neftali with this information. She was better off without it.

"I don't hate Jack anymore," I said. "I don't know what he meant to accomplish with his little army, but there's something sincere about it."

Neftali put her hand on mine and squeezed. "Rupert, you think you're worse than you are."

I wondered why Jack had chosen Hydra as his home. Why not be closer to his rebels up in Macedonia or Thrace—or anywhere, for that matter, on the mainland? I sipped my coffee and looked at the harbor. The sunlight hit the surface of the water and was shattered into a million brilliant pieces. Boats came back and forth. Workers leaped onto the hard brick of solid land. Convoys of horses, standing patiently, all strung together, waited for their loads. There were no cars and no bicycles on Hydra. People walked everywhere or rode horses. The place was too quiet, which made it seem as if everyone were shouting. A few elegant yachts were at anchor in the harbor, and I could hear a volley of accents: English, Danish, and American.

Nikos came out of the café and sat down. He fixed his eyes on me in that overly patient way that let me know he was prepared for an argument.

"Tell me we're not here to see Amanda," I said.

"We are not here to see Amanda," he said.

"Why are you even in contact with her?"

"She's selling the house. She needed someone to help her."

"And you agreed?"

"She has an agent," said Nikos. "She just wanted to check with someone she trusted."

"And why am I here?" I asked.

Nikos shook his head in a patronizing way. "Look," he said, pointing at some sort of old fort. "Look," he said, gesturing up the hill at a bank of mansions. "Look," he said. He grabbed my head and turned it toward an old clock tower that looked vaguely German. "Water," he said. "Boats." He looked around. "Horses! Lots of horses."

"I'm looking," I said.

"This is Hydra," said Nikos. "Even the Greeks come to look."

"Very pretty," I said.

Nikos put the paper down. "It's not far away, just up there. Five-minute walk."

"You go ahead," I said. "I'll follow in about an hour."

"You are angry," he said. "She's all alone here. She's helpless. Her husband is dead. Why don't you like her?"

I thought. "She's self-serving."

"And you are Florence Nightingale in Turkey?"

Which, of course, was both valid and funny.

I looked at my watch. Nikos had been gone half an hour. The waitress asked me if I wanted another coffee, and I ordered whiskey. I sipped it slowly, watching the boats come in, expertly lining themselves up. What kind of life had Jack and Amanda shared here in all this quiet? How had they passed the time? When I was done, the waitress came by again. She pointed the way up to Amanda's house. Apparently, lots of people visited. They left flowers on the path or found the spot where Jack had fallen.

"Did you know him?" I asked.

The woman nodded. "I didn't like him very much. He was always drunk, and his wife, sleeping with everyone. I don't know why he stayed with her."

"Maybe he loved her."

The woman gave me a concerned look and took my empty glass.

"Can you take me there?" I said.

"The house is just up there. See? Follow the path."

"Not the house," I said. "The place where he fell."

"You are an admirer?" she asked.

I pondered this. "I think I am," I said.

She walked a way with me up the main path that, if I had continued along it, would take me to the house. But she turned after a restaurant and we started to the right. A cat and her kittens were living beside an overflowing garbage can, and they yowled when they saw me, as if I were likely to feed them. I offered the woman a cigarette and she let me light it. She smoked holding it between her forefinger and thumb.

"Does it take long to get there?" I asked.

"That depends on where you're coming from," she said.

I thought and said, "That's a joke."

She looked at me suspiciously. "You are too serious."

She gestured for me to go ahead and I pushed my way under an olive tree. I could see that the grass was trampled here. Someone had put a few bricks together to make a low altar, and on this were some dew-stained cigarettes. The grass beside these bricks was tinged with a red residue.

"Is that. . . ?"

"Wine," said the woman. She looked at me again. She thought I was out of my mind, and I was beginning to share her opinion. "They pour it into the ground there. Maybe they think he's going to grow up, like a vine."

I crouched down and looked at the altar, then up at the dizzying rise of the cliff. The mountain pitched upward like a jagged tooth, but at the top I saw a low wall. Jack must have fallen from there.

"Can we go?" asked the woman.

"I'll stay here, if it's all right."

She nodded, unimpressed. "Should I save you a fish for your dinner?" she asked.

"I hope to join you," I said politely, "but I have to catch up with my friend."

She shrugged again and left.

I don't know how long I stood there. This spot was unremark-
able, but I felt the same involuntary awe that found me in cathedrals.
There was a sense of God. Maybe it was the quiet; I could hear a horse
some distance away, the flick and flick of its tail. A cloud passed over,
creating an instant of shadow. For a moment it was as if all time had
stopped. But then I heard a woman laughing. Amanda laughing. She
was sitting on the wall, that same wall Jack had fallen from. She wasn't
scared. She was laughing and laughing; Nikos was delighting her in
some way. Then she looked over. I couldn't see her features because
she was backlit by the sun. All I saw was her fuzzy golden halo of hair
and her strong arms.

"Rupert," she called, "is that you?"

"Yes," I said.

"You should come up and have a drink," she said. "I'm just putting together some *mezes*."

Almost a year passed before I saw Amanda again. Of course, she was
never convicted of killing Jack. She was never even a suspect. I had
no real evidence and was still piecing it all together. But on seeing
Amanda at the Metropolitan Museum of Art, in her red silk sheath,
a narrow cape extending down to the floor—the stunning Amanda,
a woman I had never known, except carnally, the murderer of her
husband—I felt a cold and unforgiving condescension.

The occasion was Uncle William's donation of the head. We
had fought over this for months. I wanted to protect the head and
Uncle William, who believed in it, from too much scrutiny. He thought
I was being ungenerous. I sat through many lectures on the need
for patronage in public art. All those little Negro children from the
Bronx who would never see a head like this if he didn't provide it.
Had I no feelings of responsibility to those less fortunate? Had he
failed to teach me the sanctimonious serenity that is noblesse oblige?
The only good to come of this, as far as I was concerned, was that I
met Dr. Schultz from the University of Pennsylvania. Dr. Schultz

had come to authenticate the head before its acceptance by the museum. He was a pleasant man with an almost religious quietness and humility. His hair was gray and cropped in a neat cube over his ears. His suit must have been nice once but now had shiny worn patches. When he asked the particulars of finding the head, he turned his ear to me in such a way that I was reminded of something, that I only later attributed to recollections of the Victrola. He had large ears and, when he listened, was absolutely still.

Dr. Schultz was heading to northern Iraq, where he'd started an excavation in conjunction with some French archaeologists. I was startled when he invited me to join him. I was moved by this generosity and immediately accepted. I was to join him in a couple of days. I had my bags packed. There were little brushes and a small pick and some other stuff. Uncle William had had my initials burned into the wooden handles.

I supposed there was to be some sort of address by the director of the museum, and then Uncle William would be honored. I couldn't see him anywhere. I knew he was taking a few moments to pull himself together because he had a tendency to get emotional at things like this. There was a waiter gliding around with a tray of champagne flutes, and I took one. I decided to look for Clive, who was lurking somewhere, listening in on other people's conversations. I found him standing by the head with a rather handsome-looking man, maybe ten years his senior. I stood at a safe distance with my drink, pretending to be interested in a grave stella that was displayed close by.

I heard Clive say, "Do you really think it's Antinoüs? Aren't the eyebrows a bit wonky?"

"I have no doubt in my mind that it is he. Do you know his story?"

"No," said Clive.

"He was the favorite of Hadrian. He drowned in the Nile under suspicious circumstances. Hadrian was distraught. He made Antinoüs a deity. Gave him his own constellation. He was the last god added to the pantheon."

This man seemed genuinely saddened by this. Clive said, "But isn't it funny that we know who it was, but we don't know the artist. Today it's different. Everyone knows the artist, but they don't always know the subject."

"That's very true," said the man.

I, of course, wondered if Clive was being ironic, but he'd probably just gotten carried away and forgotten that he did know the artist. But Clive was right. The subject was no longer the divinity, the artist was. Old Jack. Jack, wherever he was.

And then I saw Amanda walking toward me.

"How are you, Rupert?" she said. "I thought you were going to call me when you got back from Greece."

"I still might," I said.

"That was ten months ago," she said. She had an enormous canary diamond on her left ring finger. She had once worn an unfaceted topaz set in bronze, something Jack had made. I picked up Amanda's hand and admired the ring.

"Kiplinger," she said.

"I was going to say Cartier." I let the hand drop. "Nineteen twenties. Very nice."

"Aren't you going to congratulate me?" she said.

I took a moment to think. "I'd rather wait till Kiplinger's dead for that."

There was a silence.

"I don't know what you're talking about," she said.

"Of course you don't." I raised my glass and Amanda left me.

I wandered into the next gallery. I was surprised to see Uncle William standing there, completely alone. He seemed to be hiding.

"Uncle William," I said. I handed him the champagne.

"I hate champagne," he said.

"I know," I replied, "but I think you need it."

Uncle William was looking at a modern piece, some wooden female figure rising upward like a flame, with her hands above her head and the whole thing swirling at an angle. The eyes of the figure were closed and the mouth open, just a little. The breasts were full and the stomach kind of flattened, not rounded as women's stomachs usually were. The musculature was exceptional for a woman: pronounced, lean, and strong. I looked at the face for a moment and recognized her. I wasn't surprised at the artist: John Weldon. The title of the piece was *The Lovers*. Amanda floated out in a whirlwind and I thought I saw an influence, one of churning figures—was it Paulo and Francesca?—from Blake's illustrations of the *Inferno*. I looked at the base of the sculpture and it seemed to be rising out of a molten heap of dark bronze, but there were holes in the bronze, and showing through this were goat hair, fragments of bone, a twist of rusted wire, and a piece of marble rubble that under scrutiny revealed the flattened oval of an eye, Jack's eye.

I must have been quiet for some time, because Uncle William patted my arm.

"It's amazing what goes for art," he said.

I laughed. "I'm actually an admirer," I said. "Weldon had a great capacity for life."

Uncle William looked at the dates, 1916–1963. "Well, he's dead now."

I looked at the writhing figures. Jack was trapped in there, with Amanda. They were caught in marble and the wood, everything, even their pulse. "Take a closer look," I said.

He did. "Rupert, it's atrocious."

"I don't agree," I said, placing my hand on his shoulder, "it's divine."

FORGERY

Sabina Murray

A GROVE PRESS READING GROUP GUIDE
BY MARIANNE LARCA

ABOUT THIS GUIDE

We hope that these discussion questions
will enhance your reading group's exploration
of Sabina Murray's *Forgery*. They are
meant to stimulate discussion, offer new viewpoints,
and enrich your enjoyment of the book.

More reading group guides and additional information,
including summaries, author tours, and author sites for
other fine Grove Press titles, may be found on
our Web site, www.groveatlantic.com.

QUESTIONS FOR DISCUSSION

1. The artifacts that Rupert finds may be forgeries or frauds but many of the characters in this novel are also not what they appear to be. Discuss some of the characters and their secrets including Uncle William, Kostas, Steve Kelly, and Jack Weldon.

2. Kostas's son Nikos is a free spirit interested in modern things. "He doesn't like anything before Brancusi" (p. 207). Rupert is unhappy, weighed down by grief at the loss of his son Michael. Rupert wants "to know how old the things are" (p. 131). Compare and contrast Rupert and Nikos.

3. Why did Uncle William send Rupert to Greece? What arrangements had Kostas made for Rupert? Why was he supposed to keep his reason for being there secret?

4. What reason did Kostas use for rejecting the concept of forgery in the world of Greek art? Who was Pheidias?

5. Rupert seems to have conflicting or unresolved feelings about Uncle William at various times in the novel. Discuss some examples of why you think Rupert did or did not forgive Uncle William for hiding the truth about his birth.

6. Rupert studied art history. He wanted to know how old things were. Why was he so interested in the past?

7. Rupert seemed to enjoy the time on Aspros. Why didn't Rupert care that the head was not authentic?

8. When Hester came to Aspros with her father's ashes Rupert "thought of Grolsz who had loved me and whom I had loved" (p. 146). What role did Max Grolsz play in Rupert's life? Why was Rupert so sad at the death of his father-in-law?

9. Rupert didn't treat Hester kindly. What reason had he previously given for the divorce? What were the real reasons that they were finally able to speak about?

10. Rupert was drawn to Olivia because he felt they had something in common. How did he explain their bond? Why did he go to Scotland with Olivia? He questioned himself later. "What was I thinking? Was I thinking?" (p. 207). Rupert was aware of her condition from the beginning of their relationship, but what happened that made his grief more difficult to bear?

11. Olivia's in-laws misjudged Rupert. He refused to accept the properties that Olivia left to him in her will. Should he have accepted the money from her estate?

12. After Olivia's death Rupert chose to move to Vermont and set up a business. Explain why the move to Vermont was "a complete failure" (p. 226).

13. Rupert often makes questionable choices or choices for the wrong reasons. Many of his choices seem driven by circumstance, to which he responds passively. Why did he marry Hester? Why didn't he speak to his mother when he was at the café?

14. Clive asked Rupert if he wondered "what we were all doing there (Aspros) at the same time" (p. 206). Rupert answered that he did and that he came "to the conclusion that there was less coincidence than on first appearance" (p. 206). Explain what Rupert means by this statement.

15. What was an unintended consequence of Rupert's attempt to make his uncle happy?

16. What did Rupert mean when he said that Jack's sculpture of *The Lovers* was "divine" (p. 248).

17. Rupert's former job and main interest was searching for provenance. Why does he give the forgery to Uncle William? Why does he take the risk of being found out?

18. "I had never seen such adoration of anyone for anyone" (p. 51). Was Rupert envious of the relationship between Kostas and Nikos? Why?

19. At times Rupert was overwhelmed by his grief. Why couldn't he help Monsieur Michaud, the archaeologist?

20. Discuss these statements about art: "Art is what gives man his soul"(p. 1). "There's no such thing as *real art*. People don't care. Something is worth whatever someone is willing to pay for it, and people like stories" (p. 205).

21. Why did Uncle William travel? Is Rupert following in his footsteps?

22. Discuss how Rupert's life would be different if Michael had lived?

23. "Every Greek has the Acropolis at his back. What I want to know is what is at the front" (p. 10). Nikos embraced the modern world but did he totally reject tradition? Explain.

24. Rupert didn't like Amanda. He felt she was "a great manipulator" (p. 121). Yet he slept with her in Vermont because once again it was convenient, "she was the obvious choice" (p. 233). When he saw her in New York knowing what he did about the death of her husband, he felt "a cold and unforgiving condescension." (p. 245). Why didn't he reveal her secret?

25. Rupert's relationships with women were either meaningless or filled with grief. Discuss some of Rupert's relationships with women. Why did he have such difficulty in these relationships?

26. By the end of the novel does it appear that Rupert has accepted Uncle William? Explain.